Praise for *Natalie Tan's Book*

"Sprinkled with real recipes and hints of . . . . , this tale of homecoming makes for a light bite to satiate yourself with." —*Vogue* (HK)

"Lim serves up love, loss, heritage, and hints of the supernatural on a silver platter in this magical and mouthwatering debut. . . . This eminently filmable tale of finding one's own path while honoring one's history is delicious and spellbinding."

—*Publishers Weekly* (starred review)

"Vivid and lyrical with a touch of magic. *Natalie Tan's Book of Luck & Fortune* explores culture, community, and the complex love between mothers and daughters, leaving your heart full . . . and your belly hungry. I absolutely loved it."

—Helen Hoang, author of *The Kiss Quotient*

"*Natalie Tan's Book of Luck & Fortune* is for every reader who likes a side of magic with their foodie fiction. You'll want to move into the Chinatown neighborhood for the mouthwatering dumplings and the charming, eclectic neighbors. Exquisitely written, [this book by] Roselle Lim sifts through the complicated relationships between mothers and daughters, the freedom in unraveling family secrets, and the power of resilience."

—Amy E. Reichert, author of *The Coincidence of Coconut Cake* and *The Optimist's Guide to Letting Go*

"Roselle Lim serves up a feast for the senses and the heart with this magical tale of love, loss, and redemption in San Francisco's Chinatown. Filled with luscious, mouthwatering recipes, *Natalie Tan's Book of Luck & Fortune* explores the hidden ties of family, mental illness, and desires lost and found, through the delectably transformative power of food."

—Yangsze Choo, *New York Times* bestselling author of *The Ghost Bride* and *The Night Tiger*

"Filled with lush, lyrical writing, *Natalie Tan's Book of Luck & Fortune* is the kind of book that'll fill you with warmth, and make you extremely hungry." —Book Riot

Praise for *Vanessa Yu's Magical Paris Tea Shop*

"If you're searching for a summer dose of whimsy, look no further." —Shondaland

"Lim follows *Natalie Tan's Book of Luck & Fortune* with another picturesque fabulist rom-com.... Lim flexes her descriptive powers.... The eccentric and lovably meddlesome Yu family are a constant delight. . . . The characters sparkle, the magic successfully enchants, and Lim skewers the anti-Asian racism the Yus face in France with pointed and timely commentary. This feast for the senses will especially appeal to hopeless romantics." —*Publishers Weekly*

". . . similar to the sweet fabulist-rom-com style of Lim's debut, this new book follows a young woman's culinary and magical adventures." —Book Riot

"A fun story, a light read. . . . I really enjoyed this book." —The Lily Cafe

"Lim has proven herself to be quite the gustatory provocateur.... Everything sounds delightful and oh so delicious." —Cultured Vultures

"Brimming with family, food, and fun, *Vanessa Yu's Magical Paris Tea Shop* is a sweet story that celebrates Paris, paintings, pastries, and the joy of discovering your own unique path through life." —All About Romance

"The author's lush descriptions made the story come to life. . . . It was so delightful to travel through Roselle Lim's writing and wander the streets of Paris with Vanessa." —Read by Tiffany

Sophie Go's
Lonely Hearts Club

ROSELLE LIM

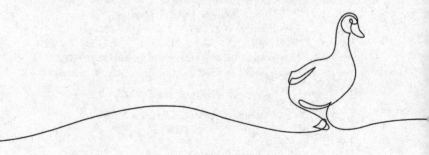

BERKLEY · NEW YORK

BERKLEY
An imprint of Penguin Random House LLC
penguinrandomhouse.com

Copyright © 2022 by Roselle Lim
Readers Guide copyright © 2022 by Roselle Lim
Penguin Random House supports copyright. Copyright fuels creativity,
encourages diverse voices, promotes free speech, and creates a vibrant culture.
Thank you for buying an authorized edition of this book and for complying with
copyright laws by not reproducing, scanning, or distributing any part of it in
any form without permission. You are supporting writers and allowing
Penguin Random House to continue to publish books for every reader.

BERKLEY and the BERKLEY & B colophon
are registered trademarks of Penguin Random House LLC.

Library of Congress Cataloging-in-Publication Data
Names: Lim, Roselle, author.
Title: Sophie Go's lonely hearts club / Roselle Lim.
Description: First edition. | New York: Berkley, 2022.
Identifiers: LCCN 2021059082 (print) | LCCN 2021059083 (ebook) |
ISBN 9780593335611 (trade paperback) | ISBN 9780593335635 (ebook)
Subjects: LCGFT: Novels.
Classification: LCC PR9199.4.L5545 S66 2022 (print) |
LCC PR9199.4.L5545 (ebook) | DDC 813/.6—dc23/eng/20211206
LC record available at https://lccn.loc.gov/2021059082
LC ebook record available at https://lccn.loc.gov/2021059083

First Edition: August 2022

Printed in the United States of America
1st Printing

Title page art: Duck © Tetiana Garkusha/Shutterstock
Book design by Elke Sigal

To Tan Se Eng and Purificacion Tiu;
Lim Son Yee and Juanita Cong

And to Jim

Sophie Go's
Lonely Hearts Club

Chapter One

I wanted a parade: a procession of acrobatic chipmunks, dancing squirrels, and a bagpipe band of red pandas and ferrets, complete with oversize balloon animals hovering overhead and intermittent bursts of edible sour string confetti.

Instead, I settled for my pen's succinct scratch across the contract of my first apartment lease, accompanied by the firm handshake of the property manager.

After exiting her office, I withdrew the translucent bag of sour gummy worms from my pocket and popped a yellow-and-green one in my mouth.

Loneliness was a disease. A matchmaker was its cure, salvation, and babysitter. I, a newly minted matchmaker, had returned home. My calling—my responsibility—was to tend to the romantic needs of this large city.

Toronto's previous matchmaker, Madam Chieng, had presided for six decades. I'd had the pleasure of meeting with her a few times, and she came across as the perfect balance of force and finesse—depending on what the situation or match called for. She had encouraged me to go to Shanghai for schooling and anointed me as her eventual successor. With her passing three years ago, and my return, I claimed Toronto as my territory and filled the vacancy.

Large glass windows illuminated the small, round lobby of the Strawberry Fields condominium complex and the swirling blue mosaic marble floor. I was under the impression we were goldfish in a fishbowl left in the sunlight: jackets and coats swishing like fantails as our bulging eyes spied on fellow neighbors.

A Chinese woman with white permed hair styled in a rounded pyramid-shaped bob crisped at the edges approached me. This, paired with her large dark brown eyes, gave her the air of an inquisitive bichon frise. "Hello, are you the matchmaker who arrived from Shanghai?"

"Yes, I'm Sophie Go. Pleased to meet you."

"I'm Mabel." She called to another woman wearing a faux fur coat and an even puffier perm, hers dyed chocolate brown. "And this is my friend Flora."

Flora smiled. "Are you taking on clients yet?"

Immaterial spindly red threads, visible to a matchmaker, dangled unconnected from their hearts to their waists. The gauntness of their threads contrasted against a passing couple's plump linked one. These women were starving for love. The thinness reflected the extent of one's longing for romance, though not everyone wanted romantic love. So many full threads were left unmatched.

The first time I saw the red threads, I'd thought they were the most beautiful, ethereal sight. Now I overlooked their beauty for their information. The threads joining several couples together glowed in varying red shades with knots of differing size. Each knot indicated the kinds of turmoil or hardship the relationship had undergone. Every tone, every place in the color spectrum, expressed the relationship's duration to the day. My fingers itched to unravel every tangle—from a tiny snag to a Gordian knot.

Ever since I was young, I wanted to connect people together. The instinct to solve puzzles came naturally, and matchmaking, by extension, was a giant game with rewards—love and happiness, and the power to affect lives for the better. My favorite fairy tale had always been *Cinderella*, as the Fairy Godmother was the most powerful figure. She was a matchmaker, and I wanted to be like her.

My reasons, however, weren't wholly altruistic. Matchmaking was my permanent ticket away from my mother and into a life where loneliness wasn't a constant companion. It meant freedom—physical, financial, and in every sense of the word. I'd waited for this moment since my gift emerged when I was six years old.

Loneliness was only a problem if you acknowledged it.

If I had a thread, I imagined it to be full and unattached; as thick as a herringbone braid. But that choice wasn't mine to make. Madam Chieng told me during our first conversation that romance couldn't be a part of our lives because we guided its course.

"Not yet, but soon." I reached into my pocket to fish out two business cards. "Please feel free to contact me."

"Oh, we will. This is so exciting!" Mabel held my card with the care of a child clutching her new favorite toy. "Are you visiting here for a consultation?"

"No. I've just signed my lease. I'm living here now."

The two women giggled and whispered to each other. Unlike unwanted amateur efforts from busybody relatives, a successful professional matchmaker commanded a seat of honor at any gathering with a client list spanning generations.

It was the joy and privilege for new matchmakers to establish their own individual client list by forging bonds in the community.

"Please feel free to tell your friends." I handed them two more cards.

"Oh, we shall. Have a wonderful day." Flora accepted the additional cards while Mabel waved goodbye. The pair walked away with brisk steps punctuated by excited chatter.

And so it began. Word of mouth always worked in a matchmaker's favor. The integrity of my reputation relied on the tongues of others: testimonials, referrals, and even juicy gossip. I wanted to make lasting connections, exude reliability, and transcend my position: matching the unmatchable and even going as far as to fix the pesky knots of marriages. Madam Chieng was the best—I aspired to be even better. She had been so kind, and even though I had met with her fewer than a dozen times, I missed her. The last time was her funeral two weeks before I kept my word and left for Shanghai. Saying goodbye then was difficult, but I'd made a promise to her that I'd be a master matchmaker one day.

I pulled out my apartment keys. My new place was on the second floor, and most days I'd prefer the stairs, but no grandeur lay in taking that route today—not for my first entrance to my own place.

While waiting for the elevator, I noticed my presence had skewed the age range of the building down. Most of my fellow residents were past their prime—they moved like a snowy- or silver-haired human forest dotted with the occasional bald pates. Every once in a while, puffy, cloudlike perms hovering over smooth scalps arrived in clusters in the lobby.

I'd had an Audrey Hepburn–inspired pixie-cut and color done in Shanghai; a drastic change from the blunt shoulder-length bob I'd worn all my life. The Korean stylist assured me that it highlighted my high cheekbones and overall bone structure. She also insisted that short hair was conducive to my low-maintenance preference, that it would grow out beautifully, and that—if all else failed—a little bit of gel and a collection of headbands would be a great help.

The sharp ding of the elevator's bell echoed in the lobby. I stepped inside and stabbed the Close Door button with my index finger. Fishing another sour gummy worm from my pocket, I slurped it as if it were a spaghetti noodle. Being the single occupant of the lift afforded me the privacy for a brief celebratory shimmy before the doors opened to the second floor.

When I had returned to Toronto a week ago, I came back to my old bedroom at my family home, but I no longer belonged there. I had lived on my own in Shanghai; it was possible to live without interference, judgment, or unwanted demands from my mother. Independence was the headiest drug, and I was hooked, but I was afraid that if I squeezed too tight that it would burst and disintegrate.

Having my own apartment had been a dream come true in Shanghai, but the true test was setting up shop here in the city and holding on to the independence I craved. This was the culmination of years of crying myself to sleep. I was free and I had my own space.

Freedom came in the form of playing the Beatles aloud instead of resorting to earphones, eating when and what I wanted instead of waiting for approval or permission, locking my own door instead of facing accusations of secrecy, and the luxury to answer only to myself for any decisions no matter how minute.

Apartment 2E was a short stroll away from the elevators.

I turned the key and opened the door to my place: twelve hundred square feet of heaven with two bedrooms, one bath, and a kitchenette. Three thousand dollars a month for rent, a bargain for the Greater Toronto Area. I had saved around twenty thousand from my three-year stint in Shanghai, which covered only six months of rent on this "bargain." One hundred and eighty-three days. I would cherish each one.

The common area and the kitchenette's hardwood floors gleamed from the afternoon sun shining through the large windows overlooking a busy intersection. It was an empty space brimming with possibilities. I had ordered my furniture ahead of time with the delivery for late afternoon and early evening: a microwave, a small fridge, a daybed, and a desk with a chair. Frugality was my interior design aesthetic.

A small basket of clementines sat on the counter with a red balloon tied to its handle. The card was from my property manager. I loosened the balloon from the basket and wrapped its string around my wrist. I walked to the windows with the red bubble trailing behind me on its ribbon leash.

This was all I needed.

Freedom.

My coat pocket, the one without the baggie of gummy worms, buzzed. I pulled my phone out and checked the screen.

My red balloon popped.

It was my mother.

Chapter Two

✣

Calls from my mother always brought belly cramps. Even now as my finger hovered to press the button to accept, churning acids sloshed against the delicate lining of my stomach. Yanmei, my roommate and classmate in Shanghai, once equated my mother's check-ins to a nonconsensual enema.

I steadied myself by leaning against the counter. The clamminess of my hands left smudges on the dark glass.

With my voice pitched higher and coated with manufactured cheeriness developed over years of practice, I answered the call. "Hi, Mom! I've been meaning to call you back."

"No, you haven't. If you had, you would have called already. Don't lie. You know how much I hate lies." My stomach clenched at the accusatory tone in her voice.

"I'm sorry."

"How is the job hunting going?"

"I have two leads." Flora and Mabel from the lobby.

"You wouldn't have such trouble if you had returned to work at the bank. They would have taken you back."

The data entry department, where blank-eyed zombies crouched in rows of lidless boxes in the dark, windowless basement, was where I'd worked for the last five years leading up to matchmaking school. The steady money was a bit more than retail and paid for my trip to Shanghai. I had no desire to return to the odious chorus of finger tapping. I was grateful for what it provided at the time, but it had never held any joy for me.

Matchmaking was my career.

Nothing else in the world made me feel as special. This was a rare gift, an honored calling. My soon-to-be lucrative salary and longevity rivaled prized professionals like doctors and lawyers. Walking into a room elicited reverence, respect, and recognition. In most households, the discovery of a matchmaker was met with rejoicing. But not in mine.

I would bring people together, create happiness where none existed before. Because of its scarcity, the gift of joy accompanied by romantic love exceeded any monetary or material equivalent.

I'd never thought about doing anything else. I had no backup plans. My mother couldn't take this away from me.

Any parent would be happy to have a child with this profession, yet Mom had been dead set against it from the beginning. She reasoned that it was an impractical vocation with no guarantees of stability. She feared that I'd waste my time and hers, only to fail. Mother always thought she knew best, but she didn't—not when it came to me and my life . . . or abilities.

"What I'm looking at is better than the data entry job. More money."

"Oh." I noted the audible click of my mother's mood change. "Be home for dinner tonight. Your father missed you last night. I'm cooking your favorite: salted duck egg congee. Don't be late."

My furniture delivery would need to be rescheduled to tomorrow. I snuffed the groan that was building in my throat. "I won't."

"Love you."

"Love you," I echoed.

An aborted sigh escaped my lips until my lungs were drained of air. I released my grip on my phone and lowered myself to the floor, gathering the scattered pieces of tattered latex: the remnants of the exploded balloon. As soon as I was done, my stomach finished its revolt and I headed for the bathroom.

They didn't know I was moving out. All of my possessions were still at my childhood home.

You couldn't choose your parents.

You had to cherish the ones you had.

They loved you and you loved them.

WITHOUT DELAYS ON THE MAJOR highways, my parent's house was a thirty-five minute drive south to Scarborough. The snarls of Toronto traffic turned lanes into amusement park waiting lines regardless of the time of day. I came equipped with *Abbey Road*, *Revolver*, and *Rubber Soul*.

Where some people escaped into books or television, I drowned myself in music: the strings of George's guitar, the steadiness of Ringo's drum line, and the complementary vocals of Paul and John. Ringo and George were my favorites, but if I had to choose, I'd pick Ringo. His quiet personality called to me. I'd always been drawn to those whose talents dwarfed their egos.

Driving through the neighborhoods with their old shade trees, cozy parks, and dated plazas, I marveled at how much had changed, and yet how much remained as I remembered from childhood—the multigenerational families crammed inside two-bedroom homes stacked like bento boxes.

I arrived at my parents' two-story semidetached house ten minutes early for the seven o'clock deadline, but five minutes too late according to my mother's timer. The measure of time differed per person. A minute might mean sixty long, languid seconds for one, but for another, a heartbeat. The passage of time brought elation (when you were having fun) to some and misery (when you weren't) to others.

After emptying my pockets of candy, I assessed my reflection in the rearview mirror. In my house, tardiness was mistaken for laziness, and both were considered cardinal sins—ones I was condemned for.

I slammed shut the door of my ten-year-old Honda Civic and hustled inside. My mother and father were already waiting in the living room. After hanging up my jacket in the hall closet, removing my boots, and putting on house slippers, I greeted them with hugs and kisses on the cheek, sprinkled with profuse apologies.

My mother sat on the left side of the salmon-pink pleather love seat, my father on the right. Stacked by her elbow on the side table were her prized reading materials: *National Geographic Traveler*, *Travel + Leisure*, and *Condé Nast Traveler*. Her dark hair, dyed to a specific shade of bronze brown, fell to her chin in a blunt silken bob. Years ago, she'd purchased silver shears to trim any stray hairs before they marred her jawline. My mother's vanity was her hair, which she gardened religiously; she was so zealous, I'd often joke to myself that her overeagerness to prune resulted in my father's baldness.

Dad, bald as a perfectly peeled quail egg. Everything about him was round: his spectacles, his dark brown eyes, his face, and his belly. The latter due to Mom's cooking and his love of Tsingtao beer. Even now, his left hand cradled the green bottle tighter than the TV remote. Dad worried about premature baldness—he checked the thickness of my hair just in case.

Irene and Raymond Go were the children of immigrants, the product of their parents' maximized opportunity, living the life of middle-class luxury facilitated by consumer debt. My parents took lavish trips as soon I was old enough to be left at the house on my own. Photographs peppered the living room depicting their time all over the globe. Mom's four-by-six diplomas of culture and worldliness cost as much, if not more, than a real degree.

She and Dad were determined to have the liveliest conversations in their social circles. She kept her full, expired passport by her nightstand and often admired the colorful stamps inside. One of Dad's funniest stories was of Mom bossing the customs officer around in Bulgaria so that the stamp would be leveled and positioned perfectly on the page. Dad was scared they'd end up in a European detention cell. I pulled out this story when I was sad and revised it so that only Dad came back to Canada.

Most of Mom's time outside of work was spent vacation planning. A pile of journals teetered in her craft room, each detailing dining options, designer shops, tourist attractions, and local neighborhood maps of walking paths around the hotels. Every page was color-coded, assigned its own sticky flag, and decorated with Washi tape. Asking Mom about her travel plans tended to diffuse any situation.

"Where's the next vacation?" I asked, sitting down.

Mom's pinched expression loosened as she broke into a smile and travelogue. "Amalfi Coast. Italy will be wonderful to return to. The last time your father and I were there we were in Sicily, remember?"

I nodded and kept doing so at the appropriate breaks in her soliloquy. I made sure to ask the occasional question, to perpetuate the ruse that I was interested in anything she had to say.

Trips and vacations were her obsession, not mine. I hadn't wanted to live in Shanghai full-time, but it was required for school.

It was only my second time traveling on a plane outside the country. The first had been eighteen years ago with my parents to Paris when they realized that traveling by themselves was more fun than bringing their child with them. I was so miserable during that trip that I hadn't minded being left out of future ones.

Dad gestured for us to move our conversation to the kitchen. He placed his hand on my shoulder as we sat in our usual seats around the round table: Mom to my left, Dad to my right, me in front of the fridge (the designated position for beverage refills).

Mom placed the large tureen of salted duck egg congee on the squeaky, wooden lazy Susan with its small tray of condiments: soy sauce, white pepper, chili sauce, fish sauce, and red vinegar. I pulled the three serving bowls from the cupboard with corresponding spoons. The last item was the ladle; I served my parents before filling my bowl.

Dad poured iced tea into our glasses and set the cold aluminum pitcher on the rotating wooden platform, before turning it to get to the condiments. He handed the chili sauce to Mom and helped himself to the vial of white pepper. His liberal snowfall of the spice contrasted with the three delicate dots of red in Mom's bowl.

Dad talked about the office while Mom chimed in with her work woes. It was the same conversation over and over, a classic TV sitcom rerun without a corny laugh track. Instead I, as a child in the presence of elders, provided the expected silence.

There was one spoonful left in my bowl when I decided to tell them the truth.

"I'm moving out."

Chapter Three

Dad dropped his spoon, rattling the bowls and condiments. "Where? Why?"

"I found a place and I think it's time. Ever since I came home, I've been looking for one, and it's perfect."

"We assumed you were job hunting." He clucked his tongue before picking up his utensil. "We didn't know you were looking for an apartment. Why didn't you tell us?"

The disappointment in his voice cut me. I didn't want to hurt my father, though I knew it would be collateral damage in my pursuit of freedom.

"Because I thought you'd be happy to have me out of the house. You're both used to me being gone after all these years. Besides, I'm ready to start my practice. A wonderful new career! I mean, it's not a surprise, is it? I don't think you expected me to stay here after I finished matchmaking school."

He creased his brows and frowned. "I suppose, but still. How can you afford to be out on your own? You're only starting out; do you even have clients? Your mother and I don't have extra income to support you. We have fixed expenses. There's no room in the budget. We love you, of course, but we worry."

"Dad, I'll be fine. I have savings from Shanghai."

My mother continued to eat without saying a word. She kept her focus on her congee, pushing her wide, ceramic spoon around until it hit the edge of the melamine bowl. The clinking sound stopped the conversation.

"Your room will be here when you need it," she said, her voice flat. "It's good for you to be out in the world on your own."

My hand shook as I waited for the ashes from the fallout. The silence stretched across the table so thick that even my father knew not to break it. There was always more. She commanded the table as if it were a chessboard, and the final move was always hers. To say something now would be foolish.

I met my father's eyes, and he shook his head. This unspoken language between us had begun when I was a toddler. He had imparted the value of knowing when to speak and when not to; a strategic lesson of survival in this household.

Mom lowered her spoon into her empty bowl. "I'm thinking our second trip should be to Singapore," she said to my father. "We can schedule a few days at the zoo. It's so large and lovely. Nisha told me that the orangutans roam free. So do the birds. It's a gem of a place."

She detailed every single animal interaction: listing the variety of cute creatures and how close she would get to them. My father chimed in with his enthusiasm. The itinerary she presented was laid out in micro detail. "Capybaras roam free. I might be able to pet one. You love that animal, don't you, Sophie?"

Fear of incurring her wrath fueled a forced smile. "I do. They're adorable."

"Oh, then I will make an extra effort to find one. Nisha mentioned they're highly intelligent and social. I'll send you the video when I do. It will be an amazing experience."

My mother hated animals.

There was nothing thoughtful or kind behind her declared intention. When most parents were away from their children, if they came across something that reminded them of their offspring, they would take a picture or, if possible, bring the item home. In all of her trips, my mother had never brought home a souvenir for me. If she offered to take a picture now, it wouldn't be for my benefit, but hers.

This was my punishment.

Mom's go-to method of discipline had historically involved taking away something I loved and enjoying it in front of me. It began with candy, but she stopped after it triggered her sugar addiction. Mom graduated to items or experiences. The only way to appease her was to show my feigned resentment or jealousy. I often felt neither and had to fabricate said emotions to prove my contrition. This form of admonishment wasn't effective on me, yet I'd allow her to believe because it was easier.

My father gave me a half smile of support. Her ensuing glare caused him to visibly shiver as if she'd shoved snow down the back of his shirt. Any gesture or word dried up in his throat.

Dad had tried to commute my sentence for a minor transgression once eight years ago, and the scorch marks from that confrontation were still healing. If he were to say something now, I feared there'd be nothing left but a greasy, round stain on the kitchen floor.

"When dinner is done, go upstairs, and pack only your clothes. You don't need anything else. Raymond, I'll help with the dishes." Mom's soft voice made it sound like I was going to an extended sleepover and wasn't "allowed" to take anything with me but my

clothing. I had no doubt in my mind that she expected me to return home soon.

All the bedrooms were on the second floor, mine the first
door on the left. It was the smallest in the house. The largest was
my parents' master bedroom with their en suite powder room.
The last was the guest room slash Mom's craft room. The closet
was crammed full of scrapbooking papers, stickers, containers of
Washi tape, and knickknacks from hobbies she dabbled in and
discarded once they became difficult: paper cutting, embroidery,
watercolor painting, macrame, and wood burning. Mom was in
love with the idea of being an artistic savant, excelling in everything. Dad and I joked how Mom hoarded supplies and possibilities but never made a single thing. One of her favorite icebreakers
was to show her Pinterest board of planned artsy projects. He
called her out on it once and ended up sleeping on the couch for
two weeks.

With the exception of my bedroom, the entire house had been
renovated on credit—from cosmetic to a huge kitchen redesign.
At my request, my room was spared from Mom's makeover madness. It had been a nursery once. My window overlooked a field
of power lines across the street and, below, the rusted porch roof
over our postage-stamp backyard where Dad had installed tiny
wooden planters full of tiger lilies and Double Delight roses. The
aged white wallpaper bore thin lavender stripes and clusters of
pastel stars. It was here when we moved in, and though it peeled
at the edges, I never took it down because I believed in the memory of the child who might have loved these walls as much as I
did. Wherever they were, I hoped they were happy; that they'd
found a new place to pitch their stars.

My sparse closet would delight any minimalist. Less than half
full, the top shelf held a box of photographs I'd intended to mount
in an album one day. It took five minutes to pack everything into

a small suitcase—the same one I'd taken to Shanghai. I hummed my favorite Beatles tune of a girl belonging to the starry sky. After I yanked the zipper closed, I patted the rough poppy-red fabric with its occasional snags as if it were a trusty steed.

My entire world was once no bigger than this room.

I touched the wallpaper and whispered my goodbye.

Downstairs, Mom and Dad stood by the front door, waiting for me to leave.

"Just because you're no longer sleeping in the house doesn't mean that you'll be missing a weekly dinner." She placed her hand on my arm. "You can't neglect family."

I swallowed the wrong answer of "I know."

It took a while to put on my boots and my jacket; long enough for my mother to head back into the living room and turn on her favorite Wuxia drama. The instrumental, string-heavy soundtrack threatened to drown out any conversation between myself and my father.

Dad patted my shoulder. "I'll miss you."

He returned to the kitchen and came back with a packed container of leftovers along with a random jug of soy milk. "Make sure you take care of yourself. Call us if you need anything."

I thanked Dad and squeezed him tight without dislodging what he'd been carrying. He emitted a surprised yelp in reaction to the show of affection before opening the front door. I juggled the heavy bag with one arm and the suitcase with the other as I made my way out.

"Watch your step. I salted the pathway, but you can't be too careful." He stepped past the doorway in his slippers, reached into a nearby bag of ice melts, and scattered a handful of the candy-like teal pellets onto the shoveled narrow pathway.

"Dad, I'm going to miss yo—"

Mom called him from the living room. Might as well have

been an invisible hand tugging Dad's arm to pull him back inside. He raised his palm and retreated, shutting the front door behind him.

WITH THE APPLIANCES RESCHEDULED TO the next afternoon for delivery, I stored the jug in a makeshift snowbank on my tiny balcony. Refrigeration in the subzero Canadian winter included the option of throwing beverages outside in a pinch. Soy milk wasn't as sexy as a case of beer or bottles of wine, but at least you could put it into coffee after it thawed.

The first items I'd bought for my kitchen were to house my candy addiction. Rows of glass jars lined the white subway tile backsplash, grouped by color: Kasugai strawberry gummy, dried mango slices, Nobel Super Lemon, green apple Hi-Chews, Horlicks Malties, Kasugai ramune gummy, and pastillas de ube. A rainbow of delight. My candy choices tended to be Asian while my snack options bore no locality restriction.

The perks of living on my own included the freedom to eat as much candy as I wanted. The previous prohibition on sweets had been enforced by my mother. She cared about her waistline. The extra sugar intake—and her lack of willpower—wasn't ideal. I once found her crying in the bathroom because she'd eaten an entire Black Forest cake. My sweet tooth was inherited—she and I shared the same sugar addiction.

In between glass jars holding Meiji Chelsea butterscotch and Haribo Happy-Cola, I pulled out a White Rabbit candy. I peeled off the white-and-blue wrapper, wadded it up into a tiny ball, and tossed it in the trash. The rice paper–covered pliant candy melted in my mouth. I never chewed these. There was more satisfaction in sucking something out of existence; the beauty was in the breakdown.

My phone buzzed from an incoming text. Yanmei asked if I had officially moved out of my parents' house.

I responded with two confetti emojis.

Yanmei and I met in matchmaking school in Shanghai. We were roommates who hit it off. She was my first true friend after a lifetime of acquaintances. I made her laugh; she returned the favor threefold.

My best friend rationalized her confidence in me as an investment. Yanmei believed in people, but only a handful, because she was the most judgmental person I had ever met. Somehow and some way, I'd managed to pass her rigid standards. One day, I caught her writing in a tiny black notebook labelled "家族" (family) and inquired about it. Yanmei had grouped each of her family members into types of animals: prey, predator, size, natural enemies, and habitat. For instance, her auntie Joan was an eastern chipmunk: resourceful, quick, solitary, and only emerging for booty calls. Judging by the provided snapshot, her prominent cheek implants reaffirmed the assessment. The profile also listed net worth, assets, and affiliations.

Her matchmaking database had the same classification scheme. It was standard practice to preserve our clients' privacy by providing code names. I hoped to build an esoteric taxonomy system of my own. At the moment, my database was nonexistent, but that would change soon.

Yanmei gave me a list of leads three months before I left Shanghai. Her connections to relatives and business-related acquaintances extended to this continent. Yanmei's family owned a successful investment firm with foreign branches in major cities, including Toronto. I followed up on every one of them before I returned home: sending strings of emails, tiny forays of polite introductions, cultivating, watering, hoping for encouraging sprouts of interest.

This vocation thrived on connections between people: through red threads, the joining of families, and the discovery of new links. I was duty-bound, as a matchmaker, to explore the potential of what my territory had to offer. According to matchmaking rules, Yanmei's help wouldn't be a conflict of interest—she was based in Singapore. I agreed to return the favor by sending any leads her way.

Her friendship and support had come as a surprise.

Growing up, I was never allowed to go to birthday parties, let alone sleepovers. After that became common knowledge, my friends stopped inviting me. Even if I had been the type to ask, I doubted I would have been granted permission to go. Companionship instead came in the form of books, nature documentaries, and music. A true friend like Yanmei was a novelty.

My phone dinged from an incoming email.

An invitation to a wealthy entrepreneur's golden anniversary banquet set for Friday night.

After an impromptu victory wiggle, I sprinted to the bedroom to assess my wardrobe options. This city would soon know that I had arrived and taken my place as their matchmaker.

Chapter Four

I emptied my coat pockets of candy and filled them with business cards. Having crammed my tiny, fashionable clutch full with two hundred, I needed more. A waiting hand—left empty—was a sign of lost opportunities.

Matchmaking solved the modern-day dilemma of dating. On their own, clients often drowned in hundreds of swipe-able profiles, puked from dizzying rounds of speed dating, or staggered away from botched setups by well-meaning friends and family. To add to all of this, the search for romantic love almost always had a self-imposed time constraint, even when biological clocks weren't ticking.

I checked the time and returned to adding the final touches of my coral lipstick. The reflection staring back was that of a bright-eyed matchmaker. The lights over the vanity mirror glowed pink with approval before returning to their natural blue-white hue.

My phone dinged.

Yanmei: Good luck at the banquet tonight! Make sure to mingle and not just stuff your face.

Me: Ha ha. I have my eye out for the Su-Winstons. They are the hosts. 3 eligible daughters and 1 son in that family alone. At least 8 if I count the cousins.

Yanmei: You've got this! Take on the easy ones first for quick victories. Once you've built a good rep, you can be more choosy. No one wants to be stuck with a difficult unmatchable. Btw, I heard from Tom yesterday. He's still stuck with a sixty-four-year-old picky auntie. The old lady has him by the balls. He'll never match her.

Me: Thanks for the tips. I gotta go. I promise to avoid the geriatrics.

Yanmei: Did you apply for your accreditation yet? You need to get that done.

Me: I know.

I had four months. I failed to graduate with the rest of my cohort, so I had to be recertified by the Society to practice as a sanctioned matchmaker; otherwise, I'd lose my ability to see red threads, and once that was gone, it was permanent. Doom and gloom aside, I had plenty of time, and without clients, I couldn't build a great case for my application anyway.

Yanmei: Make sure that you do. I'll continue to nag you. I know you won't do it until it's the absolute last minute. This is important and not something you should be taking lightly.

Me: When I have a good client base, I'll do it. I promise! Talk to you soon.

I hurried to grab my keys. I didn't want to be late.

THE ANNIVERSARY BANQUET OF MAXWELL and Jeannette Su-Winston was held at a posh two-story Chinese banquet hall three blocks from my condominium complex. Classical music playing from hidden speakers drifted in and out among the buzz of conversation. Glittering chandeliers, brocade-trimmed tall windows, giant arrangements of fresh-cut slipper orchids and tea roses, coat service, and a concierge desk promised a galaxy of wealthy prospective clients.

These were the types of people Mom salivated over. She often bragged of Dr. Acosta, a cardiologist friend of hers, yet here were three hospitals' worth of specialists and surgeons. In my mother's mind, when you didn't attend medical school to be a doctor, the next best option was befriending one, or as many as manageable. It wasn't the free medical treatment she was after; the social connections proved more precious in her eyes, as if a cubic zirconia within a case of diamonds raised its value.

I shoved the ghost of my mother's presence away. Allowing her real estate in my brain would compromise my ability to focus on tonight's networking opportunities.

The handsome young clerk manning the coat check desk handed me a ticket with a shy smile. "Have a wonderful evening. Leave room for the dessert. I mean, the rest of the banquet is excellent, but it'll be a shame if you miss the egg tarts."

I yanked my ticket back, flashed an awkward smile that showcased more gums than teeth, and then slammed my right shoulder into the corner of a wall. I fled into the crowd. My shoulder throbbed, and the skin on my face was aflame.

My best friend would have been mortified yet unsurprised. I imagined her covering her forehead with her palm. The dysfunction around prospective men was purely me, not because I didn't have a red thread. It never stopped Yanmei from dating or having short-term hookups. She blamed my romantic affliction on Mom. Yanmei blamed her for everything from climate change to juvenile diabetes. They had never met, and I wasn't sure I wanted them to.

The soreness of my shoulder didn't dampen my buoyant hope that tonight would be a professional triumph. There were potential clients in this venue waiting for my introduction. I played with my cards.

The Su-Winstons commandeered two large ballrooms upstairs. The official dinner wouldn't start for half an hour. This time was peak social circulation: long enough to check in with acquaintances and pay your respects to those you chose to ignore in private, and short enough to wiggle out of any unwanted conversations or interactions without offending. I needed to make a quick impression and hand out as many cards as possible before everyone sat down to eat. News of a fresh matchmaker in town should be on everyone's lips. Food and gossip paired better than wine and cheese.

I rushed up the staircase, taking care not to bump into anyone or anything else. Clumsiness wasn't part of my matchmaking pitch.

"Hello, Sophie." I knew who she was before I turned around. Dr. Zeny Acosta's deep gravel voice could strip five layers of paint. A cardiologist, she was the most intelligent woman in my family's sphere, with an uncanny ability to see through people that rivaled even Yanmei's acuity. Dr. Acosta always had kind words for me, yet her friendship with my mother remained a puzzle. A thick red thread dangled from her chest, unconnected.

"Good evening, Dr. Acosta."

"You look well. How was Shanghai?" She gestured for me to walk with her toward the ballrooms. Her wavy black bob softened her sharp features under the venue's many chandeliers.

I did my best to keep up with her brisk, efficient steps. "Great. I learned so much and made a wonderful friend."

"Being on your own must have been freeing." She lifted a dark brow and wore a hint of a smile.

"It was . . . nice." I chose my words with care. As my mother's friend, there was a looming threat that I was participating in a game of broken telephone I didn't want to play. Instead, I handed Dr. Acosta a card.

She read it and laughed, a hollow, dry sound traveling up her throat, crackling in the air before dissipating into nothingness. "This won't be for me, but I'll pass it on to someone I'm sure will be in need of your services. Have you started making your rounds?"

"I'm about to."

"Allow me to introduce you to some people you will want to meet." She linked her arm with mine and guided me into the wide entrance of the ballrooms.

The dividing wall between the two massive spaces accommodated the fifty tables of twelve seats. Gold dripped from the silk tablecloths, the elaborate sconces, chandeliers, and vases holding red roses. Every table had a clear view of the head table and the ten-by-ten-foot red rose wall display. A square dance floor separated the celebrants from their guests. This was a wedding disguised as an anniversary, but without the pesky caveat of buying presents.

Dr. Acosta introduced me to a group of fellow specialists and some members of the hospital board. After several minutes of polite conversation, I handed out a dozen cards and moved on to a nearby group of investment bankers. In clinical fashion, I swept through every cluster on the way to the sweets table.

The spread of European cakes and pastries was my finish line: cream puffs, fluffy cakes, mousses, sugary eclairs, macarons, and an assortment of fruit tarts with buttery golden shells. I didn't care about spoiling my appetite. A fluffy pavlova loaded with seasonal berries trounced expensive lobster Thermidor any day. One person stood between me and the rainbow selection of various mousse cakes.

He examined each of the round pastries by lifting up the tiny plate and wobbling it. After he repeated the gesture five times, I determined that the subtle movement was calculated. My stomach growled with impatience.

I grabbed a strawberry pink mousse cake.

"What do you think you're doing?" he asked.

Chapter Five

✠

My back stiffened. I froze, the plate cradled to my chest.

From the large-faced watch to the tailored dark crimson suit, he reeked of the same affluence circulating in the air. It wasn't the window dressing that gave it away; it was the meticulous way he monopolized the sweets table and how no one challenged his claim. Mr. Particular.

His dark eyes assessed me as if I was one of the mousse cakes on the table.

I refused to wobble. "I'm going to eat it."

"Please put that one back. I haven't examined it yet."

"Why test them?" I asked before handing him my cake.

Mr. Particular raised the plate to eye level. "It's the gelatin. It has to be set the right way or the texture will be compromised. It's all in the jiggle. If I want to eat the best cake, it has to dance."

He demonstrated by replicating the same controlled movement. He grinned. Apparently, the pink cake undulated with a frequency to his liking. "This is the perfect specimen, and," he said, handing me back my plate, "it's yours."

I waved him off. "Well, I can't take it now. You invested all that time testing."

He sighed with relief and accepted the cake.

I selected a random plate, opting for matcha at the last moment. "How do you know the happy couple?"

"I don't. I mean, not yet. I have to introduce myself. I'm hoping they'll be interested in my matchmaking services."

His eyes lit up. "You're a matchmaker?"

I pulled out a card from my pocket and gave it to him.

"Perfect. I'm in need of your services."

Mr. Particular was in his early thirties, tall, attractive, and wealthy. Clean shaven with high cheekbones, a square jaw, and a full mouth—the kind of beautiful Asian man Yanmei fell for. His thick, expressive brows piqued my interest. They seemed fluid, like the ink trail of an active calligraphy brush. His gaunt red thread sagged as the end floated upward, searching for its match.

"Am I the first matchmaker you've hired?"

"No. I've tried three already. They've been disappointing." He tapped his watch. "We can discuss this later. I have your contact information. Dinner is starting in two minutes."

I hadn't even met the guests of honor yet! Not knowing which table I belonged to, I darted toward the exit to check the seat arrangements list.

AFTER A LAVISH TEN-COURSE BANQUET and the ensuing food coma, the live band's cover of "Can't Buy Me Love" floated in the air, motivating a migration to the dance floor. I was more interested in waltzing in social circles. Maxwell and Jeannette Su-Winston held court near the head table. The receiving line stretched along the length of one ballroom.

I queued in line behind a familiar dark red jacket. Unable to resist, I tapped him on the shoulder. Mr. Particular invited me to stand beside him.

"How do you know the Su-Winstons?" I asked.

"Uncle Maxwell was my father's schoolmate and Auntie Jeannette is in my mother's book club." His focus was ahead, watching the progression of the line. "Is this your first event as a matchmaker?"

I swayed to the beat. "Yes. I came back from Shanghai a week ago."

"Hard then to ask for references or testimonials. The previous matchmakers had different levels of experience. Their methodologies also varied. Is there a cardinal set of conduct?"

Yanmei worked with intuition while using traditional astrology charts. Our instructor, Madam Yeung, advocated for numerology. We were always encouraged to find whatever method worked for us.

"No, there isn't a formal code of practice. I rely on pure intuition. However, we do have a strict code of ethics."

"Intuition. Interesting. No one else did that. They preferred established, traditional methods. The oldest one used haruspex."

I gasped. Out of all the available avenues we were given, that approach was the worst. No one in my class practiced it. Even Madam Yeung called it barbaric! "What was she? Ninety?"

"Approximately. Although, to be honest, I never asked."

We moved up a few feet in line. By the rate we were advancing, it would be another ten minutes. I didn't mind. It gave me time to get to know my first potential client. Mr. Particular would be a challenge, having chewed up three other matchmakers.

"Did they all come to the same conclusion?"

"Yes."

I didn't want to know what it was. The best approach was for me to discover it myself. He wasn't the ideal first candidate. Yanmei had advised me to choose easy clients to build up my database, but I never resisted a daunting task.

"You're aware of the interview process then?"

"I'm interested to see what kinds of questions you'll ask."

We stepped forward as the line advanced. The dance floor had dwindled to a handful of swaying couples as the swish of gowns and clicks of heels echoed off the polished floor. A quarter of the crowd had left after having gone through the receiving line, while the rest lingered at their tables, in a lengthened version of speed gossip. Every so often, a member of one table would get up and sit at a new one, toting with them tidbits of scandal.

"Does this mean you're officially signing up as my client?"

"Yes. I imagine that getting on your list right now is ideal before you start filling up." He tipped his head toward the front of the line. "You already know about their four unmarried children?"

"The lone eligible son is Wilfred, age forty-one, investment banker. Then there's the three daughters: Helena, Susanna, and Annabelle. Helena is thirty-five, pediatric surgeon on three charity foundations. Susanna, thirty-two, an event planner and chronic traveler with 100K Instagram followers. Annabelle, twenty-nine, dabbles in failed start-ups and is addicted to partying."

"That is an accurate assessment, but have you met any of them yet?"

"No. All I have is reconnaissance. Firsthand research is the next step."

Mr. Particular bobbed his head to the band's rendition of Bobby Darin's "Beyond the Sea." His short ink-black hair was fuller in the front and spiky at the tips. The way his hair gel caught the light reminded me of a school of slick sea otters frolicking in the waves. His attractiveness would aid in future matches. By default, humans were shallow creatures seeking to mate with another who matched or exceeded the same level of beauty.

If he were not a potential client, I'd be tripping over my feet or hiding behind some plant. My natural clumsiness flared up in the vicinity of attractive men, but my sense of professionalism and need for clients overrode those usual tendencies.

"Your profession fascinates me. It's nothing like mine. I have to be smarter than the next guy. It's a cat and mouse game: constantly solving puzzles." He adjusted the hem of his silk suit jacket. "Speaking of puzzles, there's a strong belief in many cultures and religions that people have multiple soul mates. What do you think?"

The compatibility of several soul mates existed—as divorce and affairs had proven. As matchmakers, we matched widows, widowers, divorcés, and divorcées. The bottomless capacity of romantic love ensured the continuation of our profession.

"I've been taught that it doesn't conflict with what we practice. The thought of one and done is fatalistic and tragic."

"Of course! It's better for business that people have more options."

"Why? Do you find the idea of only having one person restricting?"

He opened his mouth but paused. "I believe you only have one soul mate at a time. It's all about focus. I'm not one of those types of people who can love more than one person romantically."

"That's good. Polyamory, as good for business as it might be, isn't really sanctioned by matchmakers. It makes everything complicated."

The line shifted again. We had finally reached our destination.

In their late seventies, the Su-Winstons stood side by side, bright-eyed and animated, their energy radiating around them in tiny golden sparks. Maxwell wore a fitted onyx tuxedo while Jeannette glittered in a sleeveless, high-necked silver gown. A diamond choker paired with a matching lariat necklace highlighted her elegant, swanlike neck. Maxwell held his wife's hand in his, fingers intertwined.

The couple's gaze focused on us as we stepped forward.

"Hello, I'm Sophie Go. I'm a matchma—"

"Don't lie, Sophie." My mother emerged to my left. A jade pendant hovered above her throat, accentuating her poppy-red sheath dress. Her mauve lips formed a thin line.

Why was she here?

She placed her hand over mine. "You know better than to lie, daughter."

Chapter Six

⟫⟪

My heartbeat thundered in my chest. It sped, galloping, crashing against my ribs.

The lovely introduction I had planned evaporated. The imaginary paper it had been written on, set aflame by the presence of my mother. When I'd checked the seating chart earlier, it had been organized by table. I hadn't seen her name.

"I'm sorry. Who are you?" Maxwell asked her.

"Irene Go. Ruth Chen insisted I come in her place as she's unwell." Mom held out her hand to the startled host. "I'm also Sophie's mother."

It took all of my will to stay standing. I was mute, yet I didn't want her to talk. What came next had all the carnage of a high-speed car crash, but I was the sole casualty.

"She was in Shanghai to attend matchmaking school, but she was expelled. I found out this morning. She never graduated and isn't accredited. To say she is a matchmaker is deceitful and opportunistic. If I had known she would do this, I would have, of course, forbidden her to come."

I escaped the ballroom in tears.

IT TOOK TEN MINUTES FOR the hiccups to subside and for the blotchiness of my complexion to lessen. I still wore the humiliation of what happened on my skin, but I couldn't hide in the bathroom forever.

No one came after me. Mr. Particular, Dr. Acosta, and those I'd met stayed in the ballroom. As did my mother. I wouldn't have known what to say anyway. After collecting my coat, I walked to my car.

"Sophie!"

I flinched, squeezing my eyelids shut.

Mom called out again. "Sophie, we need to talk."

"There's nothing to say." My ragged breath formed into clouds in the cold air. The puffs shifted, coalescing into a thick stack to conceal me. The privacy was short-lived—my mother stepped in front of me.

She pointed her finger at my chest, pressing until she hit my collarbone. "What were you trying to accomplish with this lie?"

The urge to cringe, to go into my shell and hide was overwhelming. It threatened to drown me. "I know what I'm doing. I may not be 'officially' accredited, but I'm still a matchmaker. I don't need a certificate to practice. I'm not breaking any rules, Mom."

"You humiliated me in front of important, influential people. What will Jeannette Su-Winston think of me at the next hospital fundraiser?" Mom drove her finger harder into my chest. "You never think about how your actions affect our family, how they affect me. Presenting yourself without the proper credentials isn't right."

"I'm not lying—"

"Lies always find a way." The forlorn expression on her face matched the sadness of her tone as the fog wall dissipated. "I'm trying to spare you from more heartache and humiliation. I know you think I'm the strict one." She clasped my shoulders. "Lies destroy. You think you'll never be discovered and it's better this way, but it isn't. It's hard to hear, but I am thinking of what's best for you. Starting your business on a lie will hurt more than help."

My mother, the deliverer of harsh truths, never wasted an opportunity to point out what she thought I couldn't see. It wasn't a question of eyesight. If there was a fruit basket on the table, we would concentrate on different fruits and claim the rest didn't exist or that they didn't matter. The constant tug often blurred the definition of fact when we each insisted that we were right, yet the outcome always came with my concession.

"If I had mentioned I flunked out of matchmaking school, no one would hire me, Mom."

"I didn't say you had to declare it outright. All I said was that you shouldn't lie about it. Tonight, I did you a favor. I know you'll never thank me. Parenting is harder than you can imagine, especially when your daughter sees you only as a villain."

She walked away, leaving me standing alone.

Even though we disagreed often, I didn't want to hurt her.

But she had hurt my chances to succeed.

Matchmaking required clients. After tonight, I was ruined.

Where would I find anyone desperate enough to take a chance on me?

Chapter Seven

Though I scoured the lobby and the gardens over the next few days, Mabel and Flora, the two sweet old ladies with the fluffy perms, were nowhere to be found. No one called despite the many business cards I'd handed out at the Su-Winstons' event. I might as well have fed them to a shredder to make curly paper spaghetti.

Yanmei advised me to take a few days off to recover before going back on the hunt for clients, but my finances didn't have the luxury of waiting. Spending time building my website without any testimonials or referrals was also pointless.

But seniors were a growing demographic for matchmaking. This condo complex should be a ripe breeding ground for lonely people. By occupying one of the chairs in the lobby—the best location to eavesdrop on my neighbors—I might find a lead on someone interested in my services. And they would be conveniently located at my doorstep.

I grabbed my laptop and purse and headed for the elevator.

The lobby was empty with no one near the set of white leather club chairs by the revolving door. A lack of a cold draft from the spinning glass cylinder made the location ideal. I faced the entrance, making a census of the complex's residents.

Three children, between four and seven years old, raced out of the rotating glass doors giggling and screaming. They were followed by a couple in their late fifties, struggling to corral their wayward grandchildren. Tiny knots weighed down the red thread joining the pair. She laughed after he made a monster growl as they both hurried after the kids toward the elevators.

Already matched and happy.

I typed my observations on the open spreadsheet on the screen.

Two other couples entered the building, flashing red glowing threads. By the time the fourth pair arrived, I questioned my assumption that Flora and Mabel were typical residents instead of anomalies.

I closed my laptop and began packing up when three men emerged from the cold with unattached, thin red threads dangling from their chests.

Then a fourth, fifth, sixth . . . and a seventh!

They stood together chatting in a mix of English and Mandarin. The old men moved in unison—almost but not quite—in single file. They differed in age, shape, and size as they shuffled past. Also in smell. The faint but distinct smell of durian fruit assaulted my nostrils. I choked back tears and scrambled to my feet.

I kept a respectable distance to maintain my cover and also preserve my olfactory sense. Even though my father loved the fruit, Mom banned it from the house. That act was the only issue we agreed on.

The group migrated out of the lobby and down one of the corridors I hadn't yet explored. On the property tour, the manager mentioned private rooms and party rooms were available for booking—a month in advance for the former and at least three months or more for the latter. She also noted the numerous social clubs: from book clubs to baking to bird-watching.

One of the men unlocked a private room as they filed inside. There were no windows to see in other than the small rectangular glass insert in the door. It'd be too obvious. Since I couldn't lip-read, spying wouldn't help me anyway. I needed information, and eavesdropping was my best course of action.

I walked by the door, resisting the urge to press my ear against it.

"Come on . . . give that up. What about . . . ? Honestly, at your age . . . date."

Date! I pumped my fist and squealed.

The voices inside stopped.

I winced and flattened my body against the narrow wall beside the door, near the hinges in case they stepped out. Better squished than discovered.

"Probably Minji's grandkids. They never did grasp the concept of volume control." The voice was clear and so were the chuckles that followed.

"It's nice to have kids to play with. I can't be the only one who has entertained the idea."

"Don't you see how exhausting those tiny humans are? You're the furthest thing from a spring chicken. You're a gummy, fermented Silkie rooster."

"Your batteries leaked and rusted decades ago." This was accompanied by distinct laughter like that of a chittering dolphin.

"Old Ducks—none of this wishing for things you can't have. Accept what we've been dealt."

The chatter devolved into mundane gripes about parking near their favorite restaurant or grocery store, health issues, and the cold weather. The lull in the conversation gave me the opportunity to write short profiles of six different voices. One was being silent.

I wanted so much to start my classification system, but it'd be a disservice without meeting and interacting with them first.

"Are we still meeting on Thursday?"

"Yes, my dental appointment's been moved. We should be good to go. You'll need to bring those little cake square thingies you promised."

The shuffling of chairs inside the room grew louder. I rushed down the hall and pretended to browse on my phone near the western exit to the gardens. I counted the men again as they exited and headed for the elevators.

Seven.

Seven potential senior clients.

They'd want a discount rate—something low-risk, similar to the cost of a group lunch. Asking for a normal fee would lead to instant rejection. One of them might be contemplating dating, but paying for professional services showed commitment. These men may have been thinking about it for years, but never acted on it.

Older clients tended to be finicky and set in their ways despite longing for a match. Maybe they had already enlisted the services of a matchmaker with unsatisfactory results—which would hamper my efforts or, worse, prejudice them against the process.

If they detected my dire situation, any leverage I might have in financial negotiations would evaporate. They'd need to be at the same level of desperation as me. If they weren't, I'd have to convince them.

Even veterans like Madam Chieng or Madam Yeung would balk at these prospects. Easier matches helped build a fledgling matchmaker's reputation, but taking on difficult cases showcased a matchmaker's skill—impressing their peers and opening opportunities for referrals to more challenging and lucrative clients.

If successful, I'd be fielding calls from every available client in the city and fast-tracking my career. Testimonials to help build my case, paving the way to petition the Society for recertification. I had to show them I was able to make worthy matches and keep happy clients.

These old farts were my key to success—and my only hope.

Chapter Eight

Waiting the two days until the next Old Ducks meeting might have been eventful had Mom not outed me as a fraud in front of Toronto's Asian high society. I should have been fielding calls or meeting with Mr. Particular, who hadn't contacted me. Even Yanmei was scarce—only checking in a couple of times per day. She insisted she was giving me space to reassess while cautioning me to keep my impulsiveness in check. "You have options. Don't think about moving back in with your parents."

I hadn't told her about the grumpy old men. Yanmei's disappointment would hurt more than my own parents'. If this ludicrous plan didn't pan out, I'd live with the shame, but only if Yanmei didn't know about it. Plus, my best friend couldn't dissuade me from something she had no knowledge of.

My left pocket held seven business cards while my right bulged with minty Storck candies. The Filipino eucalyptus pastilles would combat the durian. My intention was to pitch my services after their meeting. I couldn't afford to hold off for another opening.

I waited in the lobby at the same time as before and rehearsed my sales pitch in my head: what skills I would bring, how I'd change their lives, and the convenience of having me in the building. My laptop contained the proposal, the process, and the breakdown of costs. After telling her that I wanted to keep my skills sharp, Yanmei looked over the sample package this morning and signed off with minor notes. Of course, she couldn't let me off the hook without yet another nag to think about my accreditation application. Once I had more clients and matches, I would start the process, but not before. Better to be overprepared.

Spontaneity was the best way to conquer timidity—leaving no room for doubt to make itself comfortable enough to multiply and occupy every waking thought. I learned this from a young age. My parents had conditioned me to obey, which I did until I saw the red threads. Those magical, glowing strands changed my life from ordinary to extraordinary. Without thinking, I'd let go of my mother's hand and run to Madam Chieng. That single act of civil disobedience created the chasm between Mom and me.

If I went back, I'd rebel again; consequences didn't matter. Life involved risks, and without them, rewards had no value or meaning. Yanmei took chances, but according to her, they were minuscule compared to what I considered reasonable. She viewed my impulsivity with equal parts admiration and terror and assigned herself as my designated antivirus software—knowing when to send out alerts and when to shut the program down before infection.

The men appeared right on time at the revolving doors. They didn't carry any takeout boxes today. Group lunch must be only on Tuesdays. They shuffled toward the entrance with snow-covered boots, stomping on the industrial-grade mats outside to shed the excess slush. The group moved inside. The grumbling, grousing, and griping about the short outdoor walk in subzero temperatures ramped up in volume—all directed toward the tallest of the bunch, who dismissed it with a wave.

Since I already knew where they were heading, I took a few extra minutes reviewing the proposal. The hour-long meeting afforded me time to get my pitch right. When I was ready, I packed everything up, headed toward the private rooms, and assumed my position by the wall on the other side of the door. I waited while playing my latest Match 3 addiction.

This would work.

I had a solid plan.

Of course they would hire me.

One of the grumpy old men was staring at me. Outside of the room. Outside . . . I hadn't heard the door open! I gasped as my phone and laptop bag fell from my hands.

"I didn't mean to startle you. Are you waiting for someone inside? Do you want me to get them?" he asked.

All thought scattered from my brain like spilled marbles on an uneven parquet floor. He repeated the question with a gentle tone.

The door rattled, and the tall one stepped out. "I heard a noise. What the hell is going on here?"

"I think I surprised her. Get her things and we'll have her sit down."

The kind one led me to a chair while the others watched with concern. A barrage of questions circled me. Speculation was directed toward the nice one who brought me in.

"What was she doing there?"

"Do any of you recognize her?"

"Is she looking for one of us?"

"Did you bring the cakes?" one of the men asked the one who helped me inside.

The last ridiculous question snapped me out of my temporary stupor.

"Cakes?" I asked.

"Petits fours." My rescuer produced a medium-sized domed plastic container with a grid layout. He lifted the lid to uncover an array of exquisite mini squares decorated with tiger lilies and gerbera daisies made of sugar paste. A cheerful color palette of golds, yellows, and oranges. He offered me one topped with a pink lily.

"Thank you. They're beautiful."

He placed the tray in the center of the round table where the other men helped themselves.

The tall one took a sharp bite of his delicate pastry, destroying the lime-green daisy topper. "Now that you can talk, why are you here? What do you want?"

"Honestly, I was looking for all of you."

The seven men, up close, confirmed how complex their cases would be.

The talented baker had kind brown eyes with the corners tipping down as if sadness or regret claimed responsibility for the weight. Mr. Regret.

The tall one's mouth formed a deepening scowl. His dark eyes narrowed into slits behind his black horn-rimmed glasses. He hated me on sight. His glare sent needle pricks traveling along my skin. Mr. Porcupine.

The source of the durian stench wafted from a pair talking to each other. The iconic dolphin laugh echoed, rising above the din. Mr. Durian and Mr. Dolphin.

To the left of the pair, another man wore a charcoal-gray tweed flat cap. His chair was pushed farther out, close to the wall, angled in such a way that he received a degree of isolation in such a small space. His face was obscured by a large, majestic Himalayan—the cover model of this month's *Modern Cat* magazine. Mr. Wolf: a feline reference would be too obvious.

The bachelor beside him was even quieter. If Mr. Regret had a trace of sadness, this man hoarded an ocean within him. It dripped from the shape of his eyes to the solemn line of his mouth to the sunken slope of his shoulders and spine in his chair. Mr. Sorrow.

The last man was examining me while I conducted my own assessment. Silver glasses glinted from the overhead fluorescent light. While I assessed and judged these men as if I were buying a car—but for their love lives—his motivations were unclear. I met his eyes and he smiled, transforming his pleasant features into handsome. Mr. Moon. His radiant grin gave me hope that he'd be one of the easier prospects.

Mr. Regret, Mr. Porcupine, Mr. Durian, Mr. Dolphin, Mr. Wolf, Mr. Sorrow, and Mr. Moon.

All with drooping, unconnected red threads.

"I recently moved into the building." I hid my shaking fingers under the table. The careful pitch I'd crafted last night hadn't returned. Anything would be improvised at this point. "I wanted to meet my neighbors."

"Huh." Mr. Porcupine cupped his chin. "Could it be that you're trying to sell us something?"

"No, I mean . . ."

"You don't know who we are. All you see are retirees willing to part with their hard-earned money. What is it? A stupid time-share?"

"No, it's not that. I—"

Mr. Porcupine slammed his palms against the tabletop. The movement jostled the remaining petits fours in the container.

"Come on, we shouldn't jump to conclusions," Mr. Regret interjected. "You haven't even allowed her to talk."

"Then why are you here?" Mr. Porcupine asked.

All seven pairs of eyes were on me. I gulped, trying to find a good way to introduce matchmaking, and failing. "I'm a match-maker."

Mr. Moon gasped as Mr. Dolphin laughed. Mr. Wolf continued to read his cat magazine.

Mr. Porcupine dragged his hand down his face to his neck. "Who do you think you are? Snow White?"

Chapter Nine

※

A hysterical giggle escaped my mouth. I clamped my hand over my lips to force it back in. The men continued to gawk, waiting for my rebuttal.

Calm down.

Sell yourself as their matchmaker.

My rehearsed pitch remained nowhere to be found.

"I only want to help." My voice stabilized, losing its earlier shakiness. "I heard that one of you wants to date."

"More like eavesdropped," Mr. Porcupine accused. "No one wants the scam you're selling. Leave us alone."

"I think you should let us decide." Mr. Wolf glanced up from his reading. His statement seemed to surprise the group.

He blushed and yanked the magazine up to cover his entire face.

Mr. Porcupine seethed as Mr. Regret tried to calm him down. Mr. Moon spoke to the rest. Although I was too far away to hear the entire conversation, it seemed as if Mr. Moon was convincing them to take this opportunity. Mr. Sorrow, like Mr. Wolf, kept to himself, watching and listening to the others.

"If you choose my services, I can facilitate dates and suitable matches for you. The process is simple. After an initial interview, I will search for a suitable match and, with your consent, arrange it. Follow-ups and in-progress check-ins are encouraged," I explained. "Since I'm starting out, I can't provide any references or testimonials. I'm hoping that one of you will be my first successful match."

"And how much will your fee be?" Mr. Porcupine asked.

He wielded his sharp voice as a sword, with the intention to intimidate, but desperation shielded me from any fear. I straightened my shoulders, sitting up in my seat to present a confident facade. "The standard rate for a matchmaker is five thousand for a period of six months with a certain number of matches monthly—tailored to the client's preferences. Of course, an exceptional matchmaker will command their own rates, due to limited availability."

"You're not either of those. Expecting to charge that much is ridiculous. You have no reputation, and you expect us to be your guinea pigs."

"I'm willing to negotiate a hefty discount."

He clapped his hands and sneered. "You said yourself that you have no references. Why should we trust you? Even after your discount the rate is still thousands of dollars. We're supposed to hand it over based on your word?"

The surrounding chatter died down. There were only two voices in the room—Mr. Porcupine's and mine—and his arguments were taking hold. Even Mr. Moon, whose initial palpable excitement had given me hope, sobered into a neutral expression.

I was losing them.

Matching one of these old men would define my career.

"I'll do it for free!"

Shocked gasps reverberated through the room. Mr. Porcupine

pushed his chair back, the caster wheels squeaking from the sudden movement. The silence broke with multiple voices speaking, each asking to take me up on my offer.

The second my brain processed the gravity of my words, something inside me short-circuited—fizzing, sizzling—from the loss of revenue. The discount I'd expected to offer had been a painful concession necessary to obtain them as clients. This form of charity would only benefit me if I managed to secure a quick match.

"It's only for one." I raised my voice above the blather. "I'll match one of you for free as a gesture of goodwill in hopes that the rest see my abilities and consider hiring me. You decide who."

Dragging Mr. Regret by the arm, Mr. Porcupine rose from his seat and herded the rest of the men into a huddle at the back of the room. Low whispers of deliberation rumbled across the space.

These ancient bachelors held my future in their wrinkled hands.

Anything other than a yes would be devastating. No one else in the city would take a risk hiring me. Gossip traveled as fast as sound—some of the faces I recognized at the Su-Winston gala were notorious for their vast networks. One of the classes I'd enjoyed at matchmaking school was Madam Yeung's lesson in gossip management—how to befriend and cultivate gossips—for networking opportunities. Unfortunately, the three professional gossips I introduced myself to at the anniversary banquet would never talk to me again—they would talk *about* me.

These men hadn't been in attendance. By the time they learned what happened, I would have already made my first match.

Who would it be? Best-case scenario: Mr. Regret or Mr. Moon. Worst-case: Mr. Durian.

Russian roulette.

I wiped my sweaty palms against my black pants.

They disbanded. As the group's designated leader, Mr. Porcupine stepped forward. "We considered your proposal, and despite my warnings and misgivings, these old fools decided to give you a chance. It looks like you have your first volunteer."

Oh God, please not him.

He stepped back, revealing Mr. Wolf. The shy man lowered his eyes, but his tentative smile was unmistakable. He whispered something in Mr. Regret's ear. "He wants to know if you have a business card."

I stuffed my hand into my pockets and pulled out a fistful of Storck mints. The green-wrapped candies tumbled and scattered across the table, followed by a smattering of chuckles.

Blushing, I pulled out my cards and laid them out. "You can keep the candy." I cleared my throat. "I'll need the phone number of my client so I can set up an interview as soon as possible."

Mr. Regret pulled a small spiral notebook with a pen from his back pocket and handed it to Mr. Wolf, who jotted down his number. Mr. Regret tugged the page loose, shearing it from the metal coil, and handed it over.

"I won't let you hurt my friend. We'll be watching you. Now, since you got what you wanted, leave." Mr. Porcupine pointed to the door.

I grabbed my laptop bag, phone, and the paper with Mr. Wolf's number. "It was nice meeting you all."

Back in the lobby, my heart returned to its normal pace: a steady drumbeat with a happy tilt as if I were skipping through an undersea octopus's garden. My buoyant steps produced an occasional bubble, which I relished popping with my index finger.

I did it.

I had my first client.

Mr. Wolf had enough courage to volunteer. His shyness was a minor inconvenience at worst. Matching him should be straightforward. The upcoming questionnaire and subsequent interview would reveal more about this quiet man. One way to break through his timidity might be through cats. I'd need to expand my limited knowledge of felines beyond the funny GIFs and memes that Yanmei and I exchanged.

I had to tell Yanmei about this important victory, though I debated disclosing the pro bono aspect of the deal. Given the twelve-hour time difference, she should be getting ready for bed. Back in my apartment, I messaged her for a video chat.

My friend appeared on my screen with her long hair in a messy bun and wearing an Innisfree sheet mask. Her nighttime skin care routine took a full hour. She tried to convert me, going as far as to offer a spa and shopping vacation to Jeju Island. I embraced moisturizers and face masks but couldn't adopt the full regimen. Underneath the beauty armor was a face that turned heads. Her delicate features were the embodiment of a perfect Asian daughter. That was until she opened her pixie mouth to hurl her trademark honesty.

"Guess what?" I asked.

"You got a hot date."

"No. Even better."

Yanmei sat up, shifting the screen capture. "Did my girl get her first client?"

"I did!" I explained what transpired with the Old Ducks, with every embarrassing detail, and the fact that it was free.

"It's not ideal to be putting all that work into something that doesn't pay your rent. You're hoping the rest of the geezers will sign up after you make your first match? For your sake, I hope they do and that the next client isn't the one that smells like durian. One of my clients has a body odor issue that requires all the tact that I don't have. I made the match. Not sure if she has anosmia. Anyway, you're doing great."

"Thanks. I need this to work. Can you imagine what will happen if I can match these unmatchables?"

"Your mother will finally shut up and realize how awesome you are." Yanmei's tender smile shone through the slot of her mask. "Though it's more important that you understand how awesome you are. You don't know how happy I'll be when I hear you say that you're proud of yourself."

I sniffled. "I'm not there yet, but I hope I'll get there this year."

"You will. I gotta go. I have a client appointment early tomorrow morning. She's a busy corporate type with scheduled free time. Anything personal is planned between six and seven a.m. Lucky me."

"Good luck."

"You too."

I formulated a tentative plan for Mr. Wolf and set a reminder for myself to call him in the early evening to schedule the interview.

My phone buzzed with an unfamiliar local number. I picked up, hoping for another of the Old Ducks while bracing myself for some sort of unsolicited spam caller.

"This is Sophie Go."

"I want a meeting. Are you free this afternoon?"

I almost dropped my phone.

It was Mr. Particular.

Chapter Ten

✠

Y ou're still interested in my services?"

"Yes. Are you free at two p.m.?"

Three hours from now. "Yes."

"Good. I'll send you the details of the meeting. I'll see you then."

The designated location was in the city. If I left in half an hour, using transit, I'd get there thirty minutes early. Driving to downtown Toronto in this weather and trying to find parking on a weekday for an important client was a recipe for a self-inflicted disaster.

Mr. Particular might be my first paying client.

I left twenty minutes later. No room for error. Only a fool or tourist would expect punctuality from Toronto's transit system.

CASA LOMA, THE CASTLE IN the city, had stood as a romantic landmark since 1914. A fairy-tale location for weddings, galas, and the rite-of-passage field trip of Toronto's students. The facade's varying tones of creams and light golden browns reminded me of Sans Rival—a buttercream layered meringue cake topped with cashews. A Gothic-style manor, it was the closest thing to a palace the area had. My first visit was a sixth grade field trip. I hadn't been back since. I asked my parents to go back, but Mom's answer was, "Why should we go see that when we've already been to Versailles?"

I couldn't imagine the opulence of having this property as a private residence. Buying my condo sufficed as a huge financial goal. The fact I no longer lived at home continued to give me endless amounts of comfort.

Arriving twenty-four minutes prior to our agreed-upon time, I followed the instructions and introduced myself as a guest of Mr. Particular at the information desk. I was escorted to the library on the main floor, where a wedding was scheduled to take place later that evening.

This large room, with its wall-to-wall bookcases and dark panels, was the heart of this place. During my class trip, I got in trouble for lying down on the floor to better take in the view of the architectural geometric off-white ceiling. As I walked into the space now, the crowded wedding setup of tables stamped out the urge to repeat the offense.

Crystal chandeliers hung over round tables draped with cream linens and fuchsia orchid and periwinkle hydrangea bouquets. In the center of it all stood Mr. Particular in a sharp deep plum custom suit. Once he noticed my presence, he waved me over. "Glad you could make it on short notice."

He pulled out a chair for me before taking a seat. "My cousin's wedding is tonight. I wanted to tell my mother that I've secured the services of a matchmaker."

"Honestly, I can't believe you're still interested." I winced as soon as these words escaped my lips.

He laughed. "This. This is why I'm hiring you."

"The lack of a filter?"

"No, the raw honesty. I don't care about what your mother said. After hiring three different matchmakers with no positive results, I'm open to unconventional, if not radical, options. Before we proceed, I need to know what happened. It will not affect my decision to hire you."

I chewed on my lower lip. Disclosing the pain of the past wasn't what I imagined I'd be doing.

He sensed my hesitation. "You have my word. I'll sign the contract now if you don't trust me."

This man had called me. He still viewed me as a viable match-maker despite what had happened during our last encounter. With-holding the truth meant losing him as a valuable client. I opened myself up: unzipping my bag of secrets and laying out every detail under the painful light.

"Every matchmaker presents their gift at a young age before they are mentored by a local matchmaker. Formal education is at the matchmaking school in Shanghai. In my first year with clients, I made a mistake in signing someone I shouldn't have."

"You mean like an unsuitable candidate?"

"Yes. I was taught what signs to look for. I should have seen them, but my eagerness to help her made me a fool. She was young, around the same age as me. She already had a match in mind for herself, and that glaring fact should have made me cut the contract. My teacher, Madam Yeung, oversaw the interviews and advised me to drop her. I did, but Fanny managed to get my private number and address."

Fanny Liang was obsessed with Jin, her high school classmate. She was convinced he was her soul mate—that their red threads linked. She used me to justify that they were meant to be together—that I'd seen their joined threads—though I didn't see a connection. She kept insisting I did. Matching her with other men didn't dislodge her fixation. Fanny disguised her neediness and desperation as friendship. Yanmei had warned me to stay away from her.

"Did she have you removed from matchmaking school?"

"No. I should have stopped seeing her after hours. When Fanny realized that Jin didn't reciprocate, she committed suicide. The school and Madam Yeung dismissed me when they found out I was still talking to her after I was supposed to have cut all contact. If Fanny had gotten help with her issues, she'd still be alive."

He leaned back in his chair and rubbed his left temple. "From a liability perspective, I can see why they had to dismiss you. However, you were caught in a terrible situation—it's as much your teacher's fault as it was yours. The screening process should have identified her as unsuitable from the beginning, and her case should never have been presented to a novice."

Yanmei had expressed a similar view but with more colorful language.

"Does this mean you're an independent contractor outside the Society?"

"Yes. I'm not technically sanctioned." I tugged at the hem of the table linen, squeezing it between my fingers. "They will allow me to practice, for now, as long as I stay under the radar."

"That doesn't seem tenable. Can you petition to have your license?"

"That's the short-term goal. If I can build a positive reputation on my own, perhaps I can change their minds."

Someone peeked in from the doorway and waved. Mr. Particular returned the gesture and rose from his seat. "I'm sorry, I have to go."

I gathered my purse. Disclosure had been a long shot. He might not have reservations about why I wasn't certified, but the fact that I wasn't might be the deal breaker.

At least I didn't pay the thirty-dollar admission fee to get into this place.

He pulled out his phone, fingertips dancing across the smooth surface. "Send me the paperwork. I'll forward you my schedule tonight so we can set up another meeting for the interview."

"I haven't scared you off?"

"Unless you find me unsuitable, I don't see why we shouldn't proceed."

Handsome, rich, and practical. He was the type that would leave me tongue-tied if we interacted outside a business setting. One of Yanmei's running practical jokes was to introduce me to the most gorgeous men she knew or came across, calling it exposure therapy. Despite years of this in Shanghai, it hadn't worked. When I flew back home, a hot flight attendant flustered me so much that I pretended to sleep—and missed two snack offerings—to avoid him.

Mr. Particular would be an easy match, and after the interview, I'd have a better grasp of what I was dealing with. "We're proceeding. You're officially my client."

I waved goodbye before leaving the library behind.

Two clients!

My phone buzzed with a text from Mr. Regret requesting a meeting this evening. He wanted to sign on as a client as well.

Three! And two of them paying!

I reached into my coat pocket, pulled out a baggie of konpeito, and popped a handful of the tiny star candies into my mouth to celebrate.

Chapter Eleven

By the time I arrived back at my place, I had left a message for Mr. Wolf to ask him for a meeting, sent the documents for Mr. Particular to sign and narrowed down a time next week for the formal interview, and confirmed the visit with Mr. Regret.

I overindulged and swallowed an entire universe of konpeito stars. I folded the reusable plastic bag, tucking it away in a nearby drawer. Mr. Regret's invitation to his seventh-floor apartment requested I bring an appetite. It'd be foolish to turn down an offer of free food when subsisting on a diet of candy and ramen—this was one of the main reasons why I still attended family dinners: to receive proper nutrition.

I checked the time and freshened up before heading to the seventh floor to meet my newest client.

APARTMENT 7B WAS THE SAME size as mine, but opposite in terms of contents. My space was empty due to frugality and my appreciation for minimalism; Mr. Regret's was crammed with wanton indiscrimination. Square and circular rugs rested on top of the cream carpet. Oil and watercolor paintings of flowers and flower gardens decorated the walls. Books, decorative boxes, plastic-covered photo albums, and ceramic baubles burdened floating shelves. Money plants and lucky bamboo peeked from red, green, and gold ceramic pots.

I wriggled into a spot on the raspberry velvet sofa with its crocheted doilies draped over the backs and arms. Mr. Regret sat in a matching armchair to my left. A cinnamon roll in human form—round, warm, with white hair frosting. He leaned forward to cut two slices off a glazed matcha chiffon cake resting on the coffee table. The scent of sugar, tea, and the heat from a well-used oven hung heavy in the air.

He handed me a slice. "Thank you for making the time to see me tonight."

"Thank you for this. It smells amazing." I took a bite. The fluffiness of the cake along with the creamy coconut glaze melted in my mouth. "This is delicious."

"My hobby is baking, and I always make too much. Thank goodness I have good friends to help me with this problem."

"If you're this good, I'm surprised you haven't been asked out on a date." I polished off the rest of the light pastry, wiping the corners of the mouth with a sunflower-yellow paper napkin. "Have you been married before?"

"Never." A slight pink crept into his full cheeks. "No long-term relationships either."

I pulled out my notebook to jot down notes. "What do you look for in a partner?"

"A woman near my age. Someone who knows how to laugh and appreciate French pastries. I prefer that she is Chinese, or at least Asian. She can be taller than me but not too tall because I want hugs to be comfortable for us both." He paused. "Is it strange to feel like I'm making an order at a restaurant?"

"No. This is normal." I smiled. "You must be specific. This is an important part of the process."

"I thought I would only be filling out a long questionnaire."

"You'll still be doing that. The extensive questionnaire fills in all the tiny details. The in-person interview is part of my process. They are both important to get a full picture of your profile."

Mr. Regret's hands rested on his knees as they bounced to an inaudible melody. His reedy red thread bobbed with every movement.

"I ask three questions, one of which you've already answered. Don't worry, it's not a rigorous interview by any means. Second question: What kind of relationship are you looking for?"

This simple yet innocuous query often revealed more than the interviewee intended. For those who approached it as a rhetorical question, their hubris and sense of entitlement revealed itself. I asked this question with no expectations or assumptions of how my client would answer.

"My life is one of missed opportunities, and this is one I'd like to say I've taken advantage of. I want someone to spend the rest of my days with, making up for a lifetime's worth of memories and experiences."

It was an answer true to his nickname. I wanted to find him the perfect partner—a Ms. Longing, one capable of creating so much joy as to drain his well of wistfulness.

"Last question. Do you believe in love?"

He tilted his head. "What do you mean by that? Are you referring to romantic love or . . . ?"

"It's up to you to interpret the question and how you want to answer."

Initially, I'd designed the vague question to satisfy my curiosity. It was my way to root out the romantics. In this business, only the most successful and busiest matchmakers choose their clients. Asking about love gave me a measure of control and insight.

"You mean that there is no right or wrong answer?"

"Correct. Take your time. There's no rush."

He squished his face, tugging his puckered lips to the side. Underneath the comical expression was a herculean effort to produce his response. As a gesture to help him relax, I leaned forward and helped myself to another slice of the delicious cake.

I was halfway to finishing it when he found his answer.

"I suppose love is one of those things that you don't pay attention to when you have it so abundantly in your life. Like good health, you take it for granted. For me, when it comes to romantic love, I believe in it even though I've never seen or experienced it for myself."

"This is a wonderful answer; thank you. You can relax. The formal interview is over." I finished taking my notes, closed my notebook, and tucked it into my purse.

Mr. Regret picked up the cake and the plates. "I have leftover lo mein noodles and barbecued duck if you want to stay."

Not wanting to sound too desperate, I waited three whole seconds before blurting out an emphatic affirmative.

Appliances occupied all of the counter space in his kitchen. The bright teal stand-up mixer was the showpiece. Cupboards, with their glass inserts, were at full capacity—dinnerware and crystal glasses took up one while the rest were crammed full of canned goods, baking ingredients, and variegated biscuit tins. An ornate farmhouse kitchen cabinet housed rows of colorful cookie jars and an extensive collection of recipe books. Assorted Asian salty snacks and potato chips filled the cupboards below. The cozy square kitchen table had two chairs. After declining my offer to help set the table, I took my seat as he reheated the meal.

"Can you tell me more about the Old Ducks club?"

"The club started a decade ago. For years, our clubroom was at Steeles library branch before we all moved here. The plaza had our favorite barbecue restaurant and noodle shop. We all know one another from the local Chinese business association. We don't have kids, and a lot of us don't have much family left, but we have one another." Mr. Regret placed the bowl of steaming-hot lo mein in the center of the table before returning to check on the barbecued duck broiling in the toaster oven. "I think that having you in our lives would be a good change. Some of us want to be married or remarried."

Remarried. One or more of them might be a widower or divorced. If this was Mr. Porcupine, I'd eat my own shoe.

"Do you have any tips on how to approach your friend who volunteered earlier?"

Mr. Regret laughed as he transferred the sizzling pieces of duck onto a plate. "He doesn't talk a lot. You'll need to learn to speak cat."

"I suspected as much."

My phone buzzed. The number was Mr. Wolf's and the text message: No.

Did this mean he didn't want to proceed? I never asked him a question in the voice mail that I left earlier—I asked for a proper time to meet.

"Are you all right?" Mr. Regret placed the duck plate on the table and settled into the seat across from me. "Bad news?"

"Your friend told me no." I held up my phone. "I don't know what this means."

"Did you call him?"

"Yes. I need a time for our meeting."

He filled my glass with ice water—ice cubes clinked against the sides. "He doesn't like the phone."

"Then why did he give me his number?"

"Because he'll send the occasional text. He's very shy. Good thing it's not fatal."

"It might be for me." I murmured my thanks as he offered me the bowl of noodles. "I can't make a match if he won't talk to me, or worse, if he can't talk to the person he is matched with."

"If you're adamant about speaking to him, you'll find him at the indoor rooftop garden at eight tomorrow morning. He's up there at that time every day."

"Thank you. I'll do that."

The building manager told me about the garden during the welcome tour. Mr. Wolf wouldn't be able to evade me.

Chapter Twelve

Spying on clients wasn't a lesson that was taught in matchmaking school.

Mr. Wolf had both a desire to be matched and an allergy to strangers.

It couldn't be helped.

After coming home from dinner at Mr. Regret's, I brushed up on cats. If I had to speak the language, I had to learn about breeds, behavior, and beauty. Cat culture was intense—no wonder they ruled the internet. The rabbit hole led to conventions, costumes, and cinematic documentaries. The type of glamour shots for felines rivaled those of Instagram models and influencers. My rudimentary research warmed me up to the idea of having one. Yanmei had a Pomeranian and a chinchilla. My parents had banned all pets. They had their hands full with me, they had declared, and didn't want to be responsible for yet another living creature in the house.

The building's rooftop garden was a botanical cathedral—a

place to worship nature—with its arched glass roof and large windows that preserved a semblance of summer during harsh Canadian winters. A perk for the building's residents, the space was rented out on weekends as the backdrop to engagement and wedding photoshoots. By day, the walls were near invisible, providing a panoramic view of the city, while at night, camouflaged spotlights transformed the venue into a glittering evening carnival.

A large mural depicting a local artist's interpretation of music flanked the entrance. Tiny squares and dots of purples, reds, pinks, and canary yellow blended into swirls and starbursts, giving the illusion of movement and energy. When I first saw it, I must have examined it for at least ten minutes as the colors came alive and danced to my favorite Beatles songs.

Cherry blossom trees, topiaries, evergreen shrubs, and a profusion of tropical flowers accented two parallel walkways leading to a waterfall. The engineered, fourteen-foot element was divided into three staggered drops with rough stone blocks as ledges. Management increased the force of the water for special functions, but on normal days, the stream was steady, creating subtle froth in the small pool below.

The square, flat area in front of the cascade hosted a small yoga class when I arrived. A nearby group practiced tai chi, moving in fluid unison. Ant-like gardeners in dark brown coveralls drifted among the foliage and shrubbery, snipping with manual hedge trimmers. They sculpted leaves and twigs into zoo animals—giraffe, sloth, panda, bird of paradise, lion. During my welcome tour, I had posed with each and sent the selfies to Yanmei.

Six comfortable yet sculptural benches made of recycled plastics and reclaimed wood provided opportunities to admire the scenery.

I occupied one of the benches facing the entrance to the garden. Despite the activities close by, the garden was peaceful and quiet. I made a mental note to visit the garden more often.

The entrance doors opened, revealing Mr. Wolf pushing a beautiful pram, an antique, deep navy blue carriage with pairs of white wheels in two different sizes. He leaned over, cooing to the passenger inside, and pushed it along the pathway by my bench.

A grandchild or some younger relative. He had been so consumed with entertaining his guest that he never noticed my presence as he drew closer. I stood up, straightened my shoulders, and silently practiced my gentle greeting.

"Good morning." I waved before approaching his pram. "Is this your . . . ?"

Three pancake-faced, cotton candy–furred cats sat where I had expected a baby.

"Cats. Persians. Long-hair breed with beautiful, sweet expressions and dispositions." I blurted out everything I had read on the various breeder association websites. The verbal diarrhea was a cover to divert his attention from my flabbergasted reaction.

He pointed to each of his cats, calling out their names. Rose, a cream one with the sweetest face. Dorothy was silver with the grumpy expression and displeased brows. Blanche, a regal, majestic creature sitting in the front to get the best view of their cat daddy.

Mr. Wolf continued to push the carriage. I walked alongside, hoping to get a chance to talk to him about his interview. All the while, Dorothy's beady golden eyes glared into my soul.

"I've thought about getting one. It might be nice to have someone to come home to."

Mr. Wolf grinned. His oval face glowed, illuminating his plain features, transforming them into something remarkable. His but-

ton nose and heavy-lidded eyes resembled his precious pets—
lending credence to the adage that pets and their owners looked
alike. His soft voice expanded as he talked about the joys of cat
ownership and companionship. This man had never spoken a word
before now.

By the time we reached the waterfall, he had pointed me to
shelters, possible breeders if I wanted to go that route, and a short
list of veterinarians. I listened the entire time, increasing my limited knowledge on the subject. The more I listened, the more concerned I became.

He wanted to be matched, but he hadn't asked me anything
about matchmaking. His commitment to his cats might interfere
with his ability to accept another human into his life. His match
would need to be first approved by his cats. Judging by the way
Dorothy wanted to murder me with her eyes, my worry seemed
justified.

"I'm sorry to interrupt, but we need to arrange a time for the
interview. I can't arrange a match if we don't talk."

Mr. Wolf came to a gentle stop. His thin red thread dangled
from his chest, and if it were visible, the cats would have been de-
lighted with their new toy. "Is it really necessary? Can't I fill out
a questionnaire instead?"

The comfort of the client superseded any personal preference
of mine. Having him fill out the answers left more legwork—to
fill the gaps that the verbal, in-person interview would have provided. "If that is what you wish, then yes. I can send you the paperwork."

"Yes. I have to go now. My girls are due for their grooming
session." He pulled a folded paper from the side of the carriage
and handed it to me. "Since you love cats, you might want to
come."

I thanked him as he headed out.

The flyer advertised a cat show in Kingston this weekend. The two-and-a-half-hour drive would be a dent to the wallet. On the other hand, there would be no better way to get to know Mr. Wolf or find those who were like-minded than at the cat show.

A familiar figure walked toward me dressed in a ruby-red cardigan and tan chinos. Mr. Regret's round face broke into a smile. "Did you talk to him?"

"I did, thanks to you. He won't consent to the interview, so I'm going to have to attend a cat show this weekend." I covered my eyes. "It's not what I had planned to do, but it's necessary."

"Do you want company?"

ROAD TRIPS WITH MY FAMILY never ended well. I never had control over the music. Dad always found a way to get lost, sparking a quarrel with Mom. She'd yell at him to ask for directions. He'd force me to get out of the car and ask someone at a nearby coffee shop or store.

I hated those idyllic families on TV singing along in harmony as they headed down the highway.

Mr. Regret as a driving companion made those TV shows seem real. He never touched the console to change the music. Best of all, he brought snacks: a large container of assorted Calbee potato chips and Nongshim shrimp crackers.

I'd been studying Mr. Wolf's completed questionnaire before the weekend. His concise answers displayed a yearning for a female partner who wanted a quiet life with him and his cats. He approached life as being almost full—filling the vacancy left by an absent soul mate would complete his being.

In contrast, Mr. Regret's answers were extensive. His desire for a mate stemmed from an emptiness long hollowed by decades of wishing. He considered his life incomplete without that special person to love—to find acceptance for the imperfect being he thought he was.

I needed to find matches for them both. It didn't matter that one was pro bono and the other paid. With my help, they both deserved to find happiness on their terms.

"Do you and the Old Ducks go on road trips often?" I asked.

"Only once. I think you know that one of us has an addiction to durian. No amount of air freshener will correct that." Mr. Regret adjusted the fan near his passenger window. "We tend to go in smaller groups."

"Have you been to a cat show before?"

"I haven't, but we all have our little quirks. You'll see when you get to know us."

"I appreciate your talents in baking. I find it hard to believe that you weren't a pastry chef."

"Baking is what I want to do, while cooking was what I had to do. I worked at the family restaurant for most of my life. I mean, I'm good at it, but being great at something doesn't mean that you enjoy it. It's something I learned as I got older. Did you always want to be a matchmaker?"

"Yes, even though it's not what my parents wanted."

He pressed his fingertips against the dashboard. "I understand the need to please your parents. My father died when I was young. I did everything to make my mother happy. In the end, she was. She called me the perfect son."

"I'm sorry for your loss." I switched lanes to prepare for the upcoming exit. "I can never see my parents calling me that. If they called me adequate or mediocre, I'd consider it a win."

"Be aware that pleasing them doesn't mean it'll make you happy. My mother died last year. Why do you think I needed to hire a matchmaker in the first place?"

Devoting all his energy to his mother explained the aura of

heartbreak that haunted him. "Who did you lose when you chose your mother?"

"Annie Chung. She was a waitress at the restaurant. I asked her to marry me and she said yes. My mother found out about the relationship and threatened to disown me. I was caught in a terrible situation and made the wrong choice. I loved Annie. I'm ashamed to say that I still love her to this day."

"Is it too late? Can you still talk to her?"

"She died four years ago. I read her obituary. She lived a full life—husband, three children, and many more grandchildren. She moved on."

"It must have been bittersweet to discover that."

"I know you'll find me a match." He traced a heart on the passenger window.

"I will. Love is infinite—therefore soul mates are as well. The red threads connecting people adapt to the rivers of life. They don't die when your loved one does. The capacity to love and be loved keeps matchmakers like me employed."

"Love is infinite," Mr. Regret repeated. "Even for an old goat like me?"

"Yes, and you're not a goat. If anything, you're a fluffy sheep."

"It's the belly, isn't it?"

"Maybe, but it's more like the lack of horns."

He laughed. The happy sound rumbled from the core of his being.

I smiled for the rest of the drive.

Chapter Thirteen

⊁⊰

The reconnaissance mission to track Mr. Wolf was underway. We found him behind the largest stage where the competitors prepped their cats. The sound and fury of ten hair dryers drowned out any other noise in the area. The blasts of heat sent tendrils of fur in every direction, puffing them until they resembled earthbound clouds. Amidst the chaos, every little pancake-faced feline exhibited a sense of serenity from a lifetime of being pampered and praised.

Mr. Wolf wielded a pair of sharp grooming scissors as he trimmed away the stray hairs from between Blanche's silver-pointed ears. Glacial blue eyes forward and chin up, the regal feline lay on a plush aubergine velvet pillow. Various ribbons already decorated Blanche's spot.

"This is like nothing I've ever seen." I leaned forward against the barrier. "It's a beauty pageant for teeny, tiny furry toddlers."

Mr. Regret laughed and gestured toward a mountain of caramel-brown fur two spots to the left of Blanche. "I can't even tell where the head is on that one. I can't tell if it's a large wig or a small rug."

"We could always look it up in the IKEA catalog to be sure." I giggled.

We were two of the many spectators. Mr. Wolf commanded his own battalion of female fans, complete with large flower pins with a drawing of his likeness in the center. The women's ages remained golden—from early fifties to eighties.

"He has his own fan club. Why does he need my help?"

Mr. Regret lowered his voice. "I don't think he sees them. You've noticed that he lives in his world. For people like that, they only acknowledge the existence of those they choose to invite into their lives."

One woman stood away from the others. Diminutive with a silver bob, she reminded me of a cactus houseplant, but instead of the prickles, she exuded a warm fuzziness. The large flower pin was attached to her dove-gray cable-knit sweater. She clutched a blue spiral notebook to her chest. Her eyes never left Mr. Wolf. A delicate red thread rose up, undulating, pointing toward the one she admired.

Mr. Regret tapped my arm. "We better find our seats. The best in show is about to begin."

The best in show wasn't a parade like I expected. Granted, I'd only watched a few of the Westminster videos and assumed cats got similar treatment. My hope to see these ridiculous creatures in motion, doing tricks, was dashed.

"If you think they're going to let these beasts run around, you've never been around cats before. It's similar to seeing toddlers on a sugar high, except tiny humans can't compare to the strong territorial instinct cats have."

"Oh. They'll fight. I read about this. You've seen a cat fight before?"

"Yes. I've also seen young children who ate too many sweets and the crash that happens as a consequence." He gestured toward

Mr. Wolf and Blanche. "I think he's going to win. Has he invited you to his place yet?"

"We barely spoke about anything other than cats."

"You'll see what I mean when he asks you over."

When our favorite competitors walked onto the stage, we clapped. Mr. Wolf's fan club drowned out our modest applause with their raucous hollers. These enthusiastic ladies even threw in wolf whistles.

The bald judge with an impressive white curled mustache lifted Blanche. His thorough examination almost made me chuckle. She remained statue-still and nonplussed as though no one was actively groping or measuring her furry parts. The seriousness of the situation seemed to be shared by everyone except me. Even Mr. Regret watched with solemn dignity. I sobered up by reliving one of Mom's lectures about the evils of candy and sugar.

After each cat was evaluated, the judge tabulated their scores. "I am pleased to declare Ladyship Eternal Blanche Dubois Deveraux is the winner for best in show."

The fan club roared. Mr. Regret and I stood up and offered our polite applause.

"When I was introduced to the winner, she only had one name." I showed Mr. Regret my crossed fingers. "It means we're close."

He laughed. "I'll take your word on it."

After the requisite photos were taken, Mr. Wolf returned offstage with Blanche in his arms. The haughty cat might as well have been crowned the queen of England. But as rabid as his fans were, they respected his privacy and kept their distance.

The mysterious woman from before had positioned herself away from the others. She watched Mr. Wolf praise Blanche as the others snapped their pictures of the pair. I had to speak to her; however, from where I was standing, the fan club blocked the way.

"Let's congratulate him." Mr. Regret moved toward his friend. "I'm sure he'll be happy to see us."

I joined him while keeping my eye on my person of interest.

"Congratulations! Best in show again."

"Yes, congratulations! Blanche was perfection," I added.

"Thank you both." Mr. Wolf beamed. "She is a true winner. She thrives on the competition."

Mr. Regret leaned in to admire the large ribbons that Blanche won. "Make sure you bring these to the next meeting. The rest of the Old Ducks will want to see them."

Mr. Wolf pulled one of the ribbons off and began explaining them to Mr. Regret. While they discussed the merits and politics of cat show judges, I wandered off in search of the woman who was the potential match for Mr. Wolf.

Her gaze switched back and forth between Mr. Wolf and his cat. I moved to block her view. "Hi!"

She bent her body to look around me. I mirrored her action. After a moment or two of coordinated shadowboxing, she let out a snort of frustration.

"Hi! I saw that you're part of some club. I want to know how to join."

"Talk to Rena. She's the president."

I stepped out of the way, and the ensuing smile on her face matched the eagerness of the red thread emanating from her chest with a tiny spark bursting from the end.

This might be the one. I wouldn't be certain until I put her in the same room, alone, as Mr. Wolf.

In an instant, the woman's eyes grew wide as the smile vanished from her face. She looked past my shoulder. The lady tucked her notebook into her tote and began to unpin her flower brooch. Her skilled movements preserved the petal ribbons and the integrity of her knitted sweater.

I followed the source of her alarm and came face-to-face with Mr. Porcupine.

"Beatrice, are you ready to go home?"

Chapter Fourteen

※

Mr. Porcupine spared me a pointed glare before directing his attention back to her. The gentle tone of his voice surprised me. "We should leave soon. You still want to pick up groceries, yes? We can still make that bakery before they close."

"I guess." Her eyes wandered toward Mr. Wolf before she lowered them. "We should get going."

Mr. Porcupine waved at Mr. Wolf and Mr. Regret before he and the woman departed.

As Mr. Regret finished up with Mr. Wolf and joined my side, the fan club moved in to talk to their idol.

"Do you know the woman I was talking to? I never got a chance to get her name."

"That's Beatrice. Our leader's sister. She runs a flower shop in North York. She isn't comfortable driving on the highway, so he brings her to these cat shows."

Beatrice. Sister meant she might be available. I still needed to speak with her to determine if the match was viable. My worry wasn't about Beatrice's compatibility though—it was the tall, prickly fence in my way.

Mr. Porcupine.

He'd object for a thousand reasons, but number one would be me and my matchmaking. I was sure he loved his sister and cared about her happiness, but my involvement would be a problem.

Mr. Porcupine seemed to have the type of stubbornness of never admitting he was anything but right—even when confronted with the facts. This obstinacy developed with age, fed with disenchantment, and its existence was further justified and ingrained by pettiness. He wielded his with authority while Mom used hers as a weapon.

"Hypothetically, if I matched Beatrice with our cat lover, do you think it would be a good match?"

Mr. Regret pursed his lips. "It could. I never thought about it. Beatrice has never said anything about that, but she is very quiet."

"I think it might work. Words are only one of many ways to communicate. I'm more worried about her brother."

"You should be. He's protective of her."

"How protective are we talking about? Gothic-novel-level protective or the normal kind?"

"He has watched over her for most of her life. Their parents were too busy working, putting a roof over their heads. I remember him mentioning that he had scared away a potential boyfriend or two. You'd think that he was some sort of hit man instead of an electrician before he retired."

"I see." I frowned. "Can you give me the name and address of Beatrice's floral shop?"

He dictated the information, which I jotted down on my phone.

"Have you been to the Vietnamese noodle place two blocks north of our condo?" he asked. "Along with the best pho, they have an amazing iced coffee and sugarcane shrimp."

"It's bothering you that no food is allowed in the building, isn't it?"

"Yes. Those snacks I brought weren't meant for the car alone. Can you imagine how much more fun this cat show would be if we were able to eat something?"

"All right, let's go. You had me at pho." I picked up the pace and headed for the exit.

My delightful excursion with Mr. Regret ended with giant bowls of beef noodle soup and clinking glasses of frothy iced coffee. Though he was my client first, he was also becoming a friend. The kindness in him reminded me of Yanmei.

When I rented my condo, I never imagined I'd also have the luxury of having more than one friend.

BEATRICE'S FLORAL SHOP WAS IN an older plaza with a gas station and a cracking asphalt parking lot beside a highway access ramp. A ruffled lavender-and-white awning hung over the big, spotless picture window. The hand-painted sign in white and cream read, "Once and Floral est. 1978." Scoops of violet hyacinths, pink peonies, and cream hydrangeas filled milk glass vases on a long sunshine-yellow counter by the window.

The softest shade of mint coated the interior of the small shop. A delicate floral perfume lingered in the air. Cone sconces and floating shelves with ceramic planters shaped like birds and rabbits lined the walls as a lamp fixture made from a cluster of glass bubbles hovered over the sales desk. I craned my neck to get a better look at the effervescent lights—the way they moved with the slightest of motions, thin walls vibrating while never popping.

"All You Need Is Love" swept in through the speakers, the bubbles overhead bobbing to the beat.

Beatrice brandished her scissors to make a cluster of ribbon corkscrews to decorate a Mylar baby sloth balloon nearby. The distinctive zip of the steel against the polypropylene rose above the music. She wore a navy blue smock over a striped merino wool sweater.

"Hello." I ventured forward.

"Are you here to pick up the Baby Gonzales order? You're much earlier than I expected, but I should be done in a few minutes."

"I'm not here to pick up anything. I'm here to talk to you."

"Oh." Beatrice set down her scissors. She studied my face. When the memory of the last time we met resurfaced, she let out a squeak. "You're from the cat show."

"My name is Sophie Go. I'm a matchmaker."

Her red thread perked up, rising from her chest as if I had called its name. "What do you want from me?"

"I'm reaching out because I have a client that I think would be a good match for you. Do you have time for a short chat?"

"How short?"

"Fifteen minutes at most."

"Am I being charged anything for this?"

"No, not at all."

She vibrated with nervous energy—like a skittish mouse pressed into a corner, her delicate nose twitching. Putting her at ease was my first priority. At the cat show, she'd exhibited the spark. I couldn't afford to lose her. "My client is the winner of the best in show—the man, not the fancy cat."

Beatrice blushed. "We can talk." She reached under the counter for a "Be Right Back" sign. She jotted down fifteen minutes on the whiteboard section and rushed to the entrance to hang it up while locking the door behind us.

We walked to a corner of the shop that wasn't visible from the front window.

"Is that why you were at the cat show?" she asked.

"Yes. I wanted to see him in his natural habitat, where he is comfortable and confident."

"The fan club crowded him too much. I understand. He has the most beautiful cats, and his record is spectacular. For the last eight years of competition, he's come away with more best in shows than anyone else." Her soft voice gained in volume as she rattled off his accomplishments, effusive in her praise for the person and his feline companions. Beatrice's transformation made her glow. Her red thread responded with a spark.

"Have you ever spoken to him?"

She shook her head and lowered her eyes. "He's private. I don't want to cross any boundaries unless I'm invited."

"If I arranged a meeting, would you be interested?"

Her hands fluttered to her collarbones. "Yes, but . . ."

"But?"

"My brother." Beatrice crossed her arms to hug herself tight.

Approaching her was supposed to make this process easier. I wasn't surprised that he would come up now. Mr. Porcupine wouldn't approve of this. Convincing Beatrice to take a chance and go against her sibling wouldn't happen today. Fomenting the seeds of rebellion took time—a luxury I didn't have. I had only one option.

"I'm sorry to hear that. I'll have to move on to the next prospect on my list."

Her brows creased, tightening to harness the tension across her face. The knuckles on her fingers flashed white from the rigid grip on her arms. She opened her mouth to speak, then closed it while shaking her head.

I pulled out a business card from my pocket and slid it toward her. "If you change your mind, this is my information. Thank you so much for your time, Beatrice."

Her silence contrasted against the thumping of my heart as I walked toward the exit. I unlocked the door, stepped outside, and headed to my car. My parking spot was across from the shop. I adjusted the rearview mirror to watch her through the front window.

She was as I'd left her—a statue contorted with indecision.

Pick it up, Beatrice. Take control of what you and your happiness want.

Her arms went slack as her cheeks puffed out the air trapped inside her. She braced her hands against the counter as she stared at my card.

Take it.

Choose yourself.

Beatrice grabbed the business card with both hands and pressed it against her heart. The smile and dreamy expression on her face—joy and longing radiating from the small gesture.

Inside my car, I squealed with joy, arms out in a confined victory dance, interrupted by a loud beep. My elbow struck the horn by accident, which sent me diving into the passenger seat for cover. It didn't matter. Beatrice agreed to the possible match.

Chapter Fifteen

Two days later and ten minutes before Mr. Wolf's daily walk, Beatrice tugged at the hem of her caramel-brown cardigan. Her hands, fingers intertwined as if in prayer, rested on her lap. Her small purse, dotted with embroidered daisies and pansies, lay on the ground near her tan loafers.

"It's normal to be nervous." I placed my hand on her shoulder. "Tell me what you're feeling."

"I'm afraid he won't like me. We've attended the same functions for years. Is it even possible for him to see me when I've been invisible for so long?"

"Yes, because now, he's looking to have someone in his life. Let me put it this way: You don't see the thing you need most until the time comes—like how you go to the grocery store and buy only what's on your list. This is now on his list. He'll see you."

She shifted in her seat.

"Do you have to go back to work soon? Are you pressed for time?"

"No. I have the whole day free. My assistant is watching the shop for me."

I dared not mention Mr. Porcupine or even hint at his presence. To do so would diminish her needs and the choice she'd made. I reached into my pocket to pull out a tin of Sakuma drops. After giving the can a good shake, a few candies tumbled onto my open palm. She picked the black currant while I chose the lemon.

"You'll do great. Remember that he's also agreed to this." I tucked the rest of the candy back into the tin. "You won't be alone. I'll be there for the formal introduction. And he's right on time."

Mr. Wolf appeared by the entrance, pushing his pram of cats.

We scrambled to our feet and walked together to meet him. Beatrice, to her credit, composed herself well, hiding any trace of her earlier apprehension. Her red thread sparked at the tip.

"Good morning," I addressed Mr. Wolf. "This is Beatrice. She is the potential match I talked to you about. I hope that you two can take the time to get to know each other."

I stepped back, leaving the opening for Beatrice to take my spot beside the pram.

She whispered her hello, and instead of looking down, she boldly stared into his eyes. Her thread floated up, a furious sparkler yearning to be linked to the man across from her. Mr. Wolf returned her unflinching gaze. He murmured his reply, earning him a small smile from her.

Beatrice peered into the carriage. She cooed at the cats inside. Dorothy, the crabby one, stood up, nuzzling Beatrice's hand for a pet. Mr. Wolf's red thread perked up, stretching, straining until it was an inch away from hers. The gap sparked. The threads wrapped around each other, twisting, twirling, growing thicker in size, and when they joined, the union ignited showers of fiery gold until the couple was enveloped by the blazing light. When the brightness ebbed, their joined thread danced between them, swinging in joyful rhythm.

This. This was why I was a matchmaker.

Nothing compared to seeing a match made, forged by instincts, and with a little help from my own hands.

They moved away, chatting. He stepped aside to make room as, together, they pushed the pram along the smooth path. No one else in their world existed, and this was how it should be.

Unable to conceal myself behind the bushes, I hid my face behind a copy of the *Globe and Mail*. I occupied one of the benches near the waterfall to observe my first successful match. Their linked thread swung, twirling itself into a thicker strand.

After three more minutes of respectful surveillance, I folded the newspaper and headed for the exit with the reassurance of a job well done.

DURING THE ELEVATOR RIDE DOWN, I reveled in my new match. Mr. Wolf had lived in his own comfortable bubble—seeing only who he wanted to see and devoting his time to his pretty cats. This might be the first time he *saw* Beatrice. She was no longer something mundane in his surroundings like the air he breathed or the color on the walls in our building.

When I stepped into the lobby, my phone rang.

Mom.

Ignoring this call would create more problems than answering it.

"Hi, Mom!" My greeting layered on the manufactured cheer. "How are you?"

"You can't miss the family dinner tomorrow."

My interview with Mr. Particular was tomorrow night. "Wait, tomorrow?"

"I moved it. Your father and I are going to the new Korean bar restaurant in Richmond Hill. We got reservations at the last minute."

"Mom, I have to meet with a client. It's important. This one is a paying customer."

"Paying . . . ? Are you otherwise giving away your services for free?"

Why did I say more than I should have? Mom would never let me get away with anything that she deemed problematic: lying to get clients, not getting paid.

Her uncanny ability to expose every crack and flaw contributed to her ascent as an average gossipmonger—good enough to be a local source for information, but lacking the social connections to important people on a regular basis. Mom's constant struggle to ascend to the upper tiers of high society was forever foiled by her lack of wealth and pedigree. My sins reflected heavily on her social rating.

"After what happened at the anniversary event, I had to hustle to drum up clients. I've taken on one pro bono client in hopes that it will translate to more clients."

"You're making everything more difficult for yourself. This unsteady job isn't worth the same as the one at the bank. You should reconsider. It's far less stress and trouble than what you're dealing with now."

"Mom, this is what I want to do."

"Well, we don't always get what we want, do we?"

I bit my lip. Arguing with her would be futile. I'd get more traction debating a brick wall. Be a little late for a client or incur my mother's wrath?

"No, Mom. I'll be there for dinner."

"Good. Don't be late. I'll be making you the spicy lemongrass pork chops you like."

"Thank you. I'll see you and Dad tomorrow."

"Your room will always be here."

If everything went terribly I'd have no choice but to crawl back to my mother. My lungs constricted, reacting to the need for more oxygen. I gripped my phone tight against my hip and took in a large gulp of air.

"I didn't mean to eavesdrop, but I was on my way up to the garden." Mr. Regret patted my upper arm. "Mothers have that effect on people. I'm not sure what's the best of course of action. If you fight, it won't end well. If you give in, you'll hate yourself."

"Outliving her seems to be the best solution."

He chuckled. "She's much younger than me. You'll need a better answer than that."

The elevator doors opened, revealing Mr. Wolf and Beatrice chatting. Mr. Regret and I raised our hands in greeting. The couple smiled in acknowledgment before strolling away, deep in conversation.

"Well done," Mr. Regret whispered. "They look happy already."

My smug smile stretched across my face. "They do, don't they?"

"The Old Ducks will be pleased with this! You'll get more sign-ups." He watched the couple head toward the main set of elevators. "Is this typical for you? I mean, the speed with which you made the match is astonishing."

"Oh no, Beatrice is a special case. I was lucky to find her at the cat show. Compatibility manifests itself as a spark. When I see a potential candidate, their red thread ignites." I snapped my fingers. "It's subtle. Consider it a visual sign that the rest of the homework I've done beforehand was effective."

"I suppose it'd be foolish to go looking for that alone. After all, there are over seven billion people in the world. I've changed my mind about a garden stroll. Want to come to my apartment for a visit? I was planning on baking madeleines and palmiers this morning for this afternoon's Old Ducks meeting."

"You know, you don't have to feed me every time. I can come over for a visit as your friend." I offered him the tin of Sakuma drops from my pocket. He accepted it and shook out a lemon drop.

"Feeding is an act of affection. It's how I show my fondness for my friends. You can't convince me otherwise."

I smiled. "Friends. I like this."

"Yes. We live in an overcrowded yet lonely world. The only way to make it bearable is to make connections, and you do important work—no matter what your mother tells you."

"I wish you could tell her that in person."

"You know she wouldn't listen to a stranger like me. It's vital that she hears it from you when you're ready. You're young; you have time."

I'd used up my reserves of defiance by moving out and pursuing my chosen career. Anything more revolutionary at this point would require emotional energy I didn't have. It took all my strength now to keep my defensive position while Mom did her best to get me to move back home in a tug-of-war to win all wars.

"I don't." I lowered my head. "I have enough savings to last me six months. If I don't have clients and successful matches, I can't maintain my independence. So much is riding on these matches."

"I have no doubt you'll succeed. Come. I'll teach you how to bake, and you'll feel much better afterward." He pressed the Down button. "On second thought, you might be happier being the taste tester."

"Hey! I can help with washing the dishes. I plan to earn my cookies."

"Here I thought your generation had no work ethic."

I made a face by scrunching my nose and sinking the corners of my lips down into a deep scowl. "Okay, boomer."

"What does that even mean?"

The doors opened following the sharp ding. We stepped inside, and in the gentlest of terms, I laid out the definition. His ensuing raucous laughter filled the small space.

The elevator's descent wasn't responsible for the lightness in my chest—it was the joy of having found a kindred spirit.

Chapter Sixteen

I carried the two plastic containers of baked goods into the club room. Not only had I done the dishes, but I'd been responsible for greasing the madeleine pans and the sugar snowfall decorating the palmiers.

The Old Ducks sat around the table in their usual places, except for Mr. Wolf. He stood before me, with his charcoal flat cap in his hand. The shy smile hung on his lips. He coaxed me over with a curled finger.

I dropped off the containers and walked to his side.

He cupped his mouth, leaned in, and whispered, "Thank you, Sophie. I really like her, and I think she likes me."

Mr. Wolf straightened and addressed the rest of the men. "I . . . have to go. I have a date." He placed his hat back on his head, adjusted the brim, and departed.

Mr. Porcupine stood up and clapped. The dark expression on his face didn't match his gesture. "So you managed to match one of us, and to my sister no less."

"Aren't you happy for her?"

"I am. Beatrice deserves all the joy in the world." He crossed his arms. His gaze swept across his friends before settling onto me. "What doesn't please me is how you lied."

"What lie? I did what I promised. I made a match."

"You're not a matchmaker. I know what happened in Shanghai."

All the blood rushed to my cheeks while my heart thrummed, speeding up to match my rising embarrassment. I explained my past to Mr. Particular, but I hadn't told the Old Ducks or my newest friend, Mr. Regret. My assumption that the velocity of gossip would slow down for old people was wrong.

"I might not be sanctioned by the Society, but I'm a matchmaker." The wobble in my voice made me even more self-conscious. "Besides, you've seen what I can do."

"You were kicked out! From what I heard, a girl died. My cousin was at the Su-Winstons' anniversary." Mr. Porcupine wagged his finger. "I know your kind. I've been swindled by this type of scheme before. Matchmaking disguised as financial fraud. You people taught me that love has a price and it's a steep one."

"I'm not charging ridiculous amounts. There aren't any hidden fees. I didn't even charge him! As for the girl, yes, I feel terrible. It was a tragedy. Fanny took her own life. It was my mistake and I wish I could go back and prevent it from happening, but I can't."

No matter what Yanmei or Madam Yeung had later said, I wouldn't absolve myself from Fanny's death. I vowed never to shrink from any accusation or refute my involvement. This was my penance.

"I don't trust you." He gestured to his friends. "We don't trust you. The match you made involved my sister. It was a convenient and easy setup. Until you can prove to us that you won't be relying on any shortcuts . . ."

He then continued to attack, disparaging my profession and my reputation.

I curled my hands into fists. I matched Mr. Wolf without charging any fees. I'd already proven myself. Mr. Porcupine was determined to test me again. I wanted him to be quiet, to stop talking, to stop badgering me.

Shut up.

Shut up.

Shut up!

"Fine! I'll match him in a week." I pointed to Mr. Sorrow. "But I won't do it for free."

Mr. Porcupine countered, "Full refund if you fail."

"I accept!" I rushed to the table and slammed my palms down in front of Mr. Sorrow. "Do you want to be matched?"

He flinched. "I suppose? Good luck, but I haven't loved anyone since my Janice died."

MOST PEOPLE BOUGHT A PACK of gum or a magazine at the grocery checkout line to express their impulsivity. Small acts without thinking, not resulting in any grave consequences. I never learned that lesson, or if I had, I continued to forget about its existence.

Mom cautioned me time and time again that my lack of impulse control would cause others to fall into a sinkhole I'd created. She was half-right. I dug a hole, but it was only big enough for me.

Mr. Regret had been more forgiving. He gave me some words of encouragement and promised to help me as best as he could while praising me for my courage in setting a motivational goal. Bless him, the poor man had rooted for the ugliest cat contestant at the cat show.

I arrived twenty minutes early at my parents' house, parking down the street to calm my nerves. Tried to call Mr. Particular, but his voice mail was full, and I ended up sending a frantic text instead about being late.

I called Yanmei for some moral support and levity.

She poured herself a cup of coffee on speakerphone. "Not the usual day for the family dinner?"

"Mom moved it up. She said that she and Dad have a date tomorrow night." I then proceeded to summarize the events since I'd last spoken with her.

"You get points for making a great match and getting two paying clients. I need to take those away because I want to reach through the screen to smack you. What were you thinking? A week? You don't even have the interview and preliminary questionnaire in hand."

"I live dangerously?" I shrugged. "I don't even know how I'm going to do this. I'm dealing with a widower."

"Girl, you're killing me."

"I'll make it work."

I had no choice. These men were the foundation to my plan of both reviving and establishing my reputation in this city. Everything I accomplished at this point was pushing a domino into another—the momentum building to my eventual redemption.

"If you need me, you know where to find me. Gotta go. Boss lady client wants a lunch meeting to perform a postmortem of her last date."

"You told me she wasn't happy."

"Yeah, because he's three inches shorter than she expected. I'll find out later what she means by this measurement."

I burst out laughing before hanging up.

My shoulders and neck loosened. I started the car and drove the fifty feet into my parents' driveway. The light coating of snow crunched under my boots. The sound matched my teeth finishing the last bits of the Chelsea butterscotch candy in my mouth.

I rang the doorbell and Dad answered. A few creases marred his smooth forehead along with a bead of sweat trickling down his left temple.

"Oh good! You're right on time." He let me in. "She's in a bit of a mood. Don't bring up anything controversial."

I grimaced. "I'll try. I have to leave a bit early tonight. I have a work meeting."

"That's not a problem. I doubt you'd want to stay longer than you have to." He tipped his head toward the living room. "She finished cooking about ten minutes ago. I suggested that she watch something before you arrive."

"What put her in a bad mood?"

"The credit company canceled one of our cards. It's her favorite—the one with the fancy travel perks. We'll manage. It means that we won't be able to go to Singapore this year."

My parents blurred their needs with their wants with no regard for the financial blowback. The addiction to credit, coded in my genes, was one I avoided. I didn't want to be buried under massive debt knowing full well I had no one to rescue me. My parents on the other hand . . .

"Do you think you can loan us a thousand?" he asked. "It will help lift your mother's mood. You want to make her happy, right? She really loves you. Why do you think she makes sure that when you visit your favorite food is on the table? Your mother shows her love through cooking."

I should have expected it. When I started working, the requests began—a little bit here, a little bit there. A small trickle, like helping with the grocery bill. Over the years, my increase in salary brought commensurate demands for rent, insurance, utilities, and the ever-important travel fund. Contributing to the household was a sign of adulthood. I believed it; never questioned it.

Yanmei classified it as a form of blackmail. "It's against the law to inherit your parents' debt. Why the hell should you be required to pay off their stupidity? If you want to, then fine. Them demanding is another thing. Sure, we love our parents and we're supposed to obey them, but it's a delicate balance to manage filial piety."

But the mileage on Dad's face when I left hadn't matched what greeted me when I returned. Aging both marked the passage of time and reflected duress. I had been gone for three years, but it must have felt like a ten-year prison sentence for him.

"I'll do it. It's no problem."

He patted my cheek. "You're a good girl, Sophie."

Then why didn't I feel like it?

Chapter Seventeen

Mom sliced into her grilled lemongrass pork chop. "Your father tells me that you have clients now. Ones that want to pay. Is this true?"

I already told her this. Repetition only worked if the other person chose to listen.

"Yes."

Keeping to one-word answers was safer. Providing more information than needed always led to trouble. I wasn't in the mood for another tongue-lashing.

"Good. We can't afford to pay for any of your expenses." Her knife slid through the meat and found the ceramic underneath. The squeaking sound sent an uncomfortable vibration throughout my spine. Both my father and I refused to say anything. Instead, we sat in visible discomfort.

"Do you know how humiliating it is to have your credit card declined when you're out shopping? I was at the Bay on my lunch break when I saw the perfect purse to bring on our trip to Singapore." She picked up her knife to continue the same process of cutting another strip. "Zeny was there. She saw it all. Of course, she's too savvy to say anything. Being judged like that in public is terrible."

"I'm sorry, Mom."

"You don't understand. I was humiliated. I can never show my face at that department store." Again, she struck the porcelain. The series of grating sounds jolted my shoulders to my ears. "It's one thing for people to suspect you're poor; it's another to have it confirmed."

I kept my eyes on my own plate.

Nothing I could say would placate her. My mother viewed her pain as a spectator sport—as if it wasn't real until Dad and I witnessed it for ourselves. The performative aspect of it was exhausting.

My meeting with Mr. Particular was in half an hour. If I left now, I might be able to make it on time. I had sent Mr. Particular a note earlier saying I might be late, but not this late. "Uh, Mom?"

"What?"

"I have to go. I have a client meeting uptown."

She narrowed her eyes. "So now that you're an important matchmaker, work is more important than family?"

There was no way to win. My fingers under the table dug into the scratchy denim of my jeans, clawing to express the trapped scream inside me. My phone was in my purse in the living room. No way to send a message to my client warning him how late I would be.

From across the table, Dad shot me a look of sympathy.

The next thirty minutes spent in the prison of my parents' home left me trembling. I made it to my car in the driveway, unable to stop shaking. This level of delay was unacceptable. I sent Mr. Particular another text apology saying that I was on the way.

I waited until I reached the highway to unleash the trapped screams from my throat.

FORTY-THREE MINUTES LATE.

I checked my reflection in the rearview mirror. Puffy eyes, a red nose. I couldn't even dismiss it as running in the cold to get some exercise.

The late-night traditional Taiwanese teahouse glimmered in the dark with its decorative paper lanterns. Last summer, during its grand opening, the ponds and gardens surrounding the building had been in full bloom. I'd been in Shanghai at the time, but I'd seen the pictures. The business was owned by two sister entrepreneurs from Taipei. Yanmei told me about this place and suggested a visit as soon as I returned home.

Mr. Particular's table was on the third floor in a private room. After the host escorted me, I stepped inside the screened-off space. Small picture frames of silk brocade embroidered with cranes and plum blossoms decorated the horizontal wooden paneled walls. A soft crimson rug warmed the dark composite hardwood floor.

In the lacquered table's center, alone, rested a full tea service.

I didn't sit down. "I apologize for my tardiness. I had family issues. This won't happen again, but if you choose to terminate our relationship, I will understand."

Attired in a dark dress shirt printed with tiny bicycles—the top two buttons undone—his sleeves were rolled to his elbows. He gestured for me to sit. "I get it. Some things you can't control." He pulled the iPad menu from its dock, swiping, fingers dancing across the surface as he placed his order. "I'm starving, so I ordered a ton of food. I hope you'll help me finish it all."

"It's the least I can do."

While Mom's cooking was excellent, she always spiced it with emotional carnage. I never enjoyed the food for what it was. Even now, my stomach grumbled around the dissatisfactory meal.

"After filling out the questionnaire, you mentioned an interview portion." He poured me a cup of steaming tea. "I'm wondering why it's a part of your process, since the questions were so thorough."

"The paperwork gives me the details I need while the in-person chat adds the extra—fills in the gaps that the written lacks. Matchmaking is built on nuances and being able to read what is said or isn't able to be said." I accepted the handleless earthenware cup and took a sip. Floral. Tikyuanyin.

"I'm not a people person. I prefer raw data and limited interactions. If I was in your industry, I'd probably program an algorithm into some app."

"Have you tried those?"

"I have. They're not effective for me. You know by the questionnaire that I work in IT, so it'll come as a surprise when I say that not everything can be solved with code. Even though matchmakers have failed before, I believe that traditional matchmaking is the solution."

The more I talked to him, the more he surprised me. I had pegged Mr. Particular as the type to be cold, or even awkward, because of his profession and idiosyncrasies. He wasn't one of those surprise jelly beans with gross flavors. Instead, he was a hard candy with a mysterious, delightful filling.

"There's something to be said about the human element and how it can be better than machines with certain tasks." I took out my notebook from my purse. "Shall we begin? What do you look for in a partner?"

He leaned forward, pressing his palms together, the sides of his fingers gently tapping his lips. "What are the parameters?"

"What do you mean? Like actual measurements, hairstyles,

et cetera? There are none. This question is designed for open interpretation."

"So, no guidelines." His dark brows smashed together, raising
the hill of skin trapped between them. "It makes it even trickier."

"I am not judging you at all for your answers. This isn't meant
to be a painful or stressful exercise." I reached over to pat his arm
but stopped myself. He was so deep in concentration that he failed
to notice.

"I always see the flaws first—in others, myself, the world. I
need someone who makes the rest of my life interesting by seeing
the beauty in the madness, the hope where there is none, and happiness in the ocean of blue."

I jotted his answer down and buried the follow-up questions
I wanted to ask: Why such a specific need to see the world in
this way? Why had he lost hope? Had he been unhappy? Did this
dissatisfaction from a lack of romance spread into all aspects of
his life?

The interview process had always been the chance for the client to be themselves without judgment—safe from any further
probing.

Observe.

Listen.

Stay impartial.

"Second question: What kind of relationship are you looking for?"

"Marriage. I want to get it right the first time and have it last."

Unlike the previous question, he delivered this answer with
ease.

"Last question: Do you believe in love?"

Tension crept back into his shoulders. He narrowed his eyes
at me and chuckled. "Difficult question, easy, and difficult again.

You do know the order is supposed to be easy, difficult, easy. It makes the sandwich more palatable."

I grinned. "When I devised this, I wasn't even thinking it would be this challenging."

"All right, you're going to have to wait for the answer for a bit. Our food is coming. I need to eat and use that time to think."

Two servers walked into the room carrying enough food for four people with an even distribution of bowls and plates. Extra dishes and chopsticks were provided for sharing. Mr. Particular hadn't exaggerated earlier when he'd claimed he'd ordered too much food. Puffs of steam rose from the center of the table. Wispy clouds bloomed upward into ethereal mushroom caps before dissipating.

For sharing: sliced roasted goose, flaky scallion pancakes, braised pork belly with brown tea eggs over steamed rice, popcorn chicken, and handmade fish balls bobbing in broth. Not for sharing: two bowls of beef noodle soup.

"This isn't all of it. I ordered mango shaved ice for dessert. They're holding off on delivering that until we finish all of this."

"They don't think we can finish?" I asked.

"No." He transferred three golden pieces of the popcorn chicken onto his plate. "They don't."

I heaped four slices of the goose into my bowl. "Challenge accepted. Let's prove them wrong."

Chapter Eighteen

⚜

We did finish everything. All the dishes the teahouse served were beyond reproach. A mountain of shaved ice with tender cubes of golden mango and topped with a generous drizzle of condensed milk arrived moments after our plates and bowls were cleared.

Mr. Particular sighed at the large dessert. "If only we could eat with our eyes."

"The worst part is that it will melt. You can't pack it to take home." I scooped a piece of mango and heap of condensed milk–drizzled fluffy shaved ice into my clean bowl. "Do you have your answer now for the third question?"

"Yes. Love exists. It isn't a drug or some magical force. It's real and can be quantified. If it didn't, then I wouldn't be seeing a matchmaker now."

I wrote down his answer in my book.

"I'm guessing that whatever conclusions you draw from this process, you don't tell your client about them."

"Correct." I snapped my notebook shut and shoved it into my purse. "Trust me, you don't want to know."

"You're right about that." He held up his palms. "Just like I don't want to see my therapist's notes."

"I have enough to go on now to arrange your first date. Since I do have your past dating history, I can avoid matching you with someone undesirable."

"That'll be good. My previous matchmaker insisted that I didn't give someone she chose enough of a chance. She was certain Tina Cheong was the right one. Tina thought the same thing."

"What ended up happening?"

"I fired her when I had to block Tina on my phone and on every platform." He carved a large chunk away from the ice mountain. "The matchmaker was so sure she was right. Even after I let her go, she still kept insisting. We get more than one soul mate, right?"

"We do. It'd be stupid to think you only have the one."

"Exactly. What happens if that perfect candidate dies? There should always be a built-in backup system."

I raised my spoon. "There is. Don't worry. I want what's best for you."

He spun the shaved ice until he found two perfect pieces of mango. "Good, because I don't want to be lonely anymore."

THE NEXT MORNING, I FOUND Mabel and Flora chatting by the building's mailboxes.

"Good morning, ladies." The genuine cheer in my voice reflected my hope that one of these two women would be a great fit for Mr. Regret.

"Are you still matchmaking?" Mabel asked. "I heard that—"

Flora elbowed her friend. "Don't be a gossip. We should get to know her first before jumping to any conclusions."

Mabel blushed. "I didn't mean to offend you. It's that we've been hearing things. You know how it is."

"I'm happy to answer any questions you may have."

The two ladies glanced at each other and declared in unison, "We'd like that."

We moved to one of the quieter corners of the lobby. Mabel's puffy white perm sported two jeweled barrettes, while Flora's pink flamingo rhinestone earrings peeked a hair below her chocolate perm line. Flora took a seat. Mabel pushed hers closer to her friend while I positioned myself opposite them. Both ladies placed their plump, giant satchels on their laps.

"Did you really match someone in the building?" Mabel asked before answering her own question for me. "Beatrice is a part of the volunteering committee at the children's hospital. We go to Sick Kids once a week. She let it slip when I kept badgering her about the smile on her face."

I grinned. "Yes, Beatrice is satisfied with the match I made for her."

"I told you!" Mabel swatted Flora on the arm. "Do you believe me now?"

Flora rubbed the spot. "I suppose. But what about the terrible stuff we heard?"

"I'm working toward getting certified by the Matchmaking Society. It will only be a matter of time." I met her eyes and addressed the elephant in the room head-on. "What happened in Shanghai was tragic."

"We're not blaming you, dear." Flora patted her chest. "People spread all sorts of stories, and trying to separate fact from fiction is always challenging. It's always best to confirm with the source."

"Yes, we can imagine how hard it must have been for you," Mabel added.

"Thank you for understanding." I took this as my opening to inquire about Mr. Regret and whether they were interested. Both of their red threads perked up, throwing off tiny sparks.

"The talented baker on the seventh floor?" Mabel asked.

A soft flush spread across Flora's powdered cheeks. She remained silent.

These two women were friends. Arranging a date with the same man was sure to cause friction in their friendship. I had thought that perhaps one of the two women might be compatible or interested—but not both. The only way forward in this scenario was to have them decide what would be most comfortable. I might lose them as potential matches for Mr. Regret, but I doubted he'd be happy if the process cost these women their special friendship.

"Yes, I can arrange a date if you so desire. However, I need you two to talk and see if this is what you both want."

Mabel bobbed her head and smiled while Flora lowered her eyes and clutched the handles of her purse tight.

"You have my information, yes?"

"We do," Mabel replied. "We'll get in touch with you soon."

I stood up and waved goodbye, leaving the cloud of whispers billowing between them.

My appointment with Mr. Sorrow was this afternoon. He'd been responsive when I'd sent the questionnaire and asked for a time to meet. I had my suspicions about this ill-fated meeting—Mr. Sorrow might prove to be trickier to match than I imagined.

APARTMENT 6E WAS EITHER A well-preserved shrine, a fan club, or whatever would justify showcasing close to a hundred pictures of the same woman, who I assumed to be Mr. Sorrow's deceased wife. A pretty lady with large eyes, blunt bangs, and a tight, crooked smile who exhibited such joy in these photographs.

She was his great love story.

I sipped my cup of oolong tea. "If I may ask, how long has she been gone?"

Mr. Sorrow drew out a long sigh. His round face didn't quite match his lean build.

"Janice left me twenty-three years ago."

"Oh." I leaned forward over the small, round table in the kitchen. "Just to be clear, are you sure you want to be matched?"

"Yes. I want you to find me someone who is as magnificent as Janice was."

Well, damn. I'd be using the ghost standard for this match.

I resisted the urge to smack my forehead. Widows and widowers tended to be easier to match unless they were like Mr. Sorrow. Still, he'd expressed his desire for my services, and I couldn't ignore that.

Losing the bet to Mr. Porcupine would end my chances with the Old Ducks. That grouchy old fart wouldn't win.

I pulled out my pen and opened my notebook. "Shall we proceed to the interview?"

He folded his hands in front of him on the table.

"What do you look for in a partner?"

"Janice. She was perfect in every way. She made me so happy that I found heaven in the years we were together. Her gracefulness transcended the dance floor to every aspect of my life. It's her sense of elegance that made me feel like the luckiest person in the world because she chose me."

The worry lines around Mr. Sorrow's eyes and mouth melted away. Happiness had this effect—to bring out the best in anyone. For a brief moment, the memory of his wife dispelled the aura of gloom haunting him, and his appeal shone through the sadness.

"What kind of relationship are you looking for?"

"A long marriage. My time with my wife was far too short. I don't want to bury my heart again. I'd thought I lost myself when she died, then I was angry that I was still alive. Now, the constant emptiness is there. I feel guilty for wanting to fill it."

"Do you believe in love?"

"Yes, it has to exist if you can lose it."

With those words, the melancholy returned—his features drooping down, even his snow-white hair exhibiting a tinge of blue. He was the misty-gray rain cloud before being pricked to unleash the rain.

A picture of Janice with Mr. Sorrow caught my eye. Dressed in a sparkling cobalt dress, she danced with her husband, who matched her attire in a traditional tuxedo. The spectators and setup in the background alluded to some sort of ballroom competition.

I gestured to the photo. "You both competed?"

"Yes. We won every year we entered. Our specialties were the foxtrot and the Viennese waltz. That one is the foxtrot."

"Does your ballroom club still exist?"

"It does. I haven't been there in decades, not since Janice . . ."

"I understand. Maybe we can visit?" Perhaps to find a match. He wanted another elegant woman in his life, and this lead might be the best shot I had. "You might be able to get back into it with a little help from your old friends. What do you say?"

He frowned. "No."

Chapter Nineteen

✣

Mr. Sorrow wouldn't dance.

The retired dentist refused to budge.

After all this time, he had not processed his grief. He still loved Janice and hadn't been able to let her go. He might have declared that he wanted to move on, but he would compare every woman to his late wife. Making a match was near impossible at this point—he was still looking for Janice, and she was gone.

In less than a week, I'd have to see Mr. Porcupine's smug face and listen to his gloating.

I'd live. I'd survived far worse than being bested by an old, grumpy man.

But if I couldn't match Mr. Sorrow, I would at least help him heal. I pulled out my laptop and searched for a local support group for widows and widowers. The first step to healing was attending one of these meetings.

After I gathered the right information, I called my client.

"Hi." I pressed the phone against my cheek. "I found this support group. They're meeting tomorrow. I think it'll be a good idea to go. You'll be with people who understand what you've been through and can help you."

"Honestly, I've thought about going to one for years." Mr. Sorrow's voice trembled. "But I don't want to go alone."

"I'll go with you. Heck, I'll drive you."

"Is this related to matchmaking?"

"Not at all. This is for you and what I believe is best. I'm already getting my kneepads ready for when I have to grovel to your leader at the next Old Ducks meeting. It's my fault. One week is not enough to unwind this. Only a master matchmaker can make it happen, and we know I'm far from that."

"You haven't gotten your chance yet. You're too hard on yourself. When Janice and I took our first class, I never thought I'd overcome my clumsy feet. My wife was naturally gifted. I did my best to make sure I kept up. You're like me."

As a chronic sufferer of klutziness, I related to Mr. Sorrow's story.

"You'll find your rhythm, and when you do, I want to be there to see it."

He believed in me.

I'd given him little reason to, but I'd take it.

THE WIDOWS AND WIDOWERS SUPPORT group was housed at a local public high school. Memories of my Catholic school kilt and the years spent at Mary Ward flooded in, accompanied by the distinct smell of strong body sprays, stale bread, and perfumes of teenage angst.

"I can't remember the last time I was in a high school." Mr. Sorrow stopped to examine the collection of framed graduates over the years. "Nothing much has changed, except there are more Asians. I was the only one in my school."

"My cohort in Scarborough was diverse. It was the white people that were the minority."

He laughed.

One of the homerooms doubled as the meeting space for the group. When we arrived at the door, Mr. Sorrow took a peek inside through the glass insert and hesitated.

"If you're not comfortable, we don't have to go in."

He held the door handle, squeezing to tighten his grip, then stopped. A faint instrumental version of "Some Enchanted Evening" drifted in from the opened doors down the hall. He abandoned the door to the support group and followed the music, picking up the pace until he froze at the doorway to the gymnasium.

An adult ballroom dance class was in progress—couples swirling in circles, men with their chins up and backs straight while their partners leaned back from the shoulders, one pair of hands linked as the other rested on shoulders and midbacks. Seven couples were on the floor, and a sprinkle of spectators sat on folding metal chairs by the side.

I placed my hand on Mr. Sorrow's arm. "Do you want to go inside? I'm sure it'll be okay if we want to sit and watch."

"Yes, I don't mind watching."

I escorted him in, linking my arm with his as we headed for the empty chairs by the wooden bleachers. I took a seat to his left and patted his hand. "Can you tell me what they're doing?"

"The waltz. It's the most recognizable of ballroom dances. The Viennese waltz, the one my wife and I specialized in, is much faster than this. That's the easiest difference to spot." His brown eyes sparkled under the overhead fluorescent lights. "There's a timing to it and the footwork."

"Did you ever lift her over your head?"

"I think you have ballroom dancing confused with pairs figure skating," he explained with a chuckle.

I laughed at my own silly mistake.

He then pointed out the intricacies of the sport, giving me a brief lesson on footwork.

From across the room, a slender, older woman with long, straight gray hair and round glasses watched us. The corners of her eyes tipped up as if they smiled. Her attention centered on my companion. She observed not from a place of recognition, but curiosity. By the time Mr. Sorrow had finished his impromptu lesson, the pretty lady made her way over to us.

"Hello and welcome. I'm Clara." Her radiant smile exuded warmth. "Are you looking to join the class with your granddaughter?"

Mr. Sorrow didn't reply.

"He's not my grandfather. He's a friend who used to dance."

Clara brightened at the revelation. "Then you should join us. It's even better than riding a bicycle after a long time. You remember all the steps and the joy. The way your body gets lost in the music."

Mr. Sorrow continued his longing gaze at the spinning partners.

"I don't know if he's ready yet," I said. "His wife was his dancing partner."

Clara adjusted her glasses. She took the seat on the other side of Mr. Sorrow. "Dancing is fun. When I lost my husband, I didn't think I was allowed to dance again because he wasn't there to dance with me. How long has it been?"

"I lost Janice twenty-three years ago." He tore his eyes away from the dance floor and said to her, "How did you deal with the guilt?"

"After Warren died, it took me five years to get the courage to try. He loved me, and I think he'd want me to dance again. I bet that your wife is similar. Something magical happens when we dance, don't you agree?"

A shy smile tugged at his lips. "Yes, I suppose so."

The strings of an instrumental version of "Hey Jude" echoed from the stereo system. Clara stood up and offered her hand. "Why don't we try?"

Mr. Sorrow hesitated, staring at her open hand. The second verse began. He rose and accompanied her to the floor. His tentative movements vanished when she assumed the perfect pose and position. The sharp tang of metal filled the air; tiny flecks of rust fell from his limbs. Clara moved with precision and lightness. How they danced—their feet rising three inches off the floor, equaling each other in skill.

Clara was correct. He completed his transformation into the most dashing of gentlemen. This was the man in those photographs with Janice, though they didn't do him justice. This man captured her heart with his charisma and starlight. He commanded the attention of all the souls in the gymnasium. Every dancer stopped. All eyes were on Clara and Mr. Sorrow.

Nothing else existed.

But when the music died, the spell was broken.

Mr. Sorrow let Clara go, sank to his knees, covered his face with his hands, and sobbed.

Chapter Twenty

I fished a plastic packet from my purse and offered Mr. Sorrow a Hello Kitty–printed tissue. He accepted it with a sniffle.

"How are you feeling?"

"Exhausted." He blew his nose and wiped it. "And guilty for enjoying myself as much as I did without her."

Clara stayed by his side—rubbing his back and offering quiet words of comfort. "Did you come to the building for the support group down the hall?"

We nodded.

"I was part of that group for three years. I left them when this ballroom club started. For me, dancing helped me heal more than the group ever did." She picked up the tissues and smiled at the cute design. "I reacted close to the same way as you. I cried because of the guilt. I cried because I found happiness again. It felt like a crime without Warren."

Mr. Sorrow grabbed another tissue to dab at his eyes. "That's how I feel."

"The crime is when we punish ourselves for feeling some measure of happiness. We already lost our loves, and we're still asked to give up more." She placed her hand on his arm. "Does that sound fair to you or like something she'd want?"

He closed his eyes. "No, it's not."

"What do you want?"

"I want to dance again. I haven't felt this alive in such a long time."

The red thread in Mr. Sorrow's chest came to life. The burnt end sparked as the red thread rose from his chest, seeking a connection, pointing toward the end of Clara's flickering strand. The two threads didn't link like I'd seen with Mr. Wolf and Beatrice; instead, they moved together with their ends in tiny blazes.

This was the start. In time and with patience, this connection would result in the joining of their threads.

Mr. Sorrow stood up and asked Clara, "When does the class end?"

"In two hours. We just started."

The look he gave me was the one a child gives his mother when he wants to stay and play longer. I laughed. "Yes, we can stay for the whole thing. I don't mind."

"Can you fox-trot?" he asked Clara.

"Of course," she replied with a dazzling smile.

BEFORE WE RETURNED HOME, HE asked for Clara's number and arranged to meet up for a date. The air of sadness hanging over him had lifted to reveal the man beneath.

By the time I crept back into my apartment, it was late, but not late enough for a phone call from my mother.

I stifled a yawn to chirp out, "Hi, Mom."

"I hear you've been getting clients. That's good news."

I'd told her this, yet she always checked with her own friends for verification. According to Mom, I was an unreliable source, ever the consummate liar.

"Is everything okay at home?"

"Sort of."

A heaviness settled in my stomach. My heartbeat sped up as I jolted up from my bed. "Is Dad all right?"

"He's in pain. You know how he gets with his joints. With the credit card canceled, we can't afford his acupuncture treatments anymore." She lowered her voice. "You know he would never ask anything for himself."

Dad wouldn't. The poor man would wear the same pair of shoes until they molted off his feet. Mom and I had to be on him for the basic stuff because he'd be too busy catering to everyone else's needs.

"How much do you need?"

"About eight hundred for now. It will pay for the weekly sessions for two months."

"I'll send the e-transfer tonight." I did a mental calculation of how much I had in my savings. "Mom, I don't know if I can keep this up though. Rent is pricey where I am."

"You should have considered that when you moved out. Life is never as easy as you see it. The world is a harsh, harsh place."

Not even a thank-you.

"Your father and I have worked hard to provide you with everything. The least you can do is help with your father's treatments."

"Mom, I am. I already said that I'd send the money you asked for."

"And what, after that I'm supposed to tell him that he can't get them anymore?"

Dad's health superseded my rent. It had to. I'd be a terrible daughter otherwise.

"You have nothing to say?" Mom's earlier cajoling tone vanished, replaced by one I knew best. "I find it disappointing you have to think about this. He loves you. It's never been a mystery concerning which parent you loved more."

"Mom, you can't—"

"What? Say the truth? I know what this is like."

The last time we visited Vancouver to see my grandmother, Amah Joan, Dad hadn't been able to come because of work. Both sisters were in attendance—Mom and Aunt Abigail. My aunt was a successful corporate accountant at one of the major national chemical companies, while her husband was a sharp litigator with his own firm. They lived in a four-million-dollar mansion in West Vancouver with an infinity pool and two Bentleys in the carriage house. Mom walked around that house like an appraiser—taking note of everything and tallying up the cost in her head. During the visit, my grandmother had barely acknowledged my mother's presence except with criticism. She had been too busy doting on her prettier, younger daughter with her perfect husband.

Mom had wilted under the scrutiny. She'd shriveled into someone I recognized in myself, with half replies when asked the occasional question. She swallowed her sorrow every minute she spent there. Instead of being validating, it made me sadder. I'd hoped that the experience would help mend our relationship or at least unite us against a common enemy. It did neither. Caught up in her own pain and turmoil, she failed to see how similar our situations were.

Mom didn't need to ask me to never speak of it again. When we returned home, the trip was struck from existence. Dad knew better than to ask for what Mom wouldn't give.

"Mom, I do love you. It's complicated."

"Why complicated?" Her hiss traveled through the phone, snaking its way around my bedroom. "I am your mother. I'm the only one you have. I loved my own mother without question. This is the way it is. What kind of a daughter are you?"

I tried to hold back the oncoming tears. "I'm sorry, Mom. I didn't mean to . . ."

"You never think, though, do you?"

"I'll send you the money tonight."

"This is the least you can do."

I dropped my phone onto the bed and cried.

You couldn't choose your parents.

You had to love the ones you had.

They loved you and you loved them.

The next morning I awoke with a depleted bank account and a message from Mr. Particular. He requested a meeting at an antique bookstore that evening. Though he hadn't disclosed the purpose of the appointment, it had to involve setting up a match as soon as possible.

After sending the money last night, I found an upcoming event featuring the launch of a line of wine spritzers by Sunny Tang, a local socialite from a family of successful Realtors. She would be a poor match, but her friends were in the right demographic and their social circles were far enough from Mr. Particular's to be compatible. I RSVP'd and added it to my calendar.

My parents' recent requests for money had taken a chunk off the profits from my paying clients. I'd need more to establish a comfortable buffer because I'd begun entertaining adding meat and vegetables to my candy and ramen diet.

My doorbell rang.

I had no deliveries scheduled and wasn't expecting anyone. I ran to the front door and squinted through the peephole. A cat stared back. The drawing of a cat on a Post-it note, to be exact.

I opened the door to remove the paper and stumbled upon a large, cellophane-wrapped basket—alone in the hallway. By the time I brought everything inside to the kitchen, I'd cataloged every single cat-shaped pastry, candy, and treat. A box of cat macarons in pastel colors, curry buns with drawn faces and whiskers, artisanal marshmallows, seven different kinds of Hello Kitty candies, and a set of three little cat plushies in gray, orange, and white. The enclosed note card said, "Thank you," signed by Mr. Wolf.

I unwrapped the package to hug the card and three kittens to my chest.

Such a sweet and thoughtful man.

I took too many pictures of the contents and sent them to Yanmei, labeling them as client swag. Yanmei responded with a video call.

Her smug smile was infectious. "Look at my baby getting swag!"

"I can't believe it. You'll think he's the sweetest if you ever meet him."

"With your new clients, you can start eating better. Vitamin S, as in starch and sugar, isn't ideal."

Yanmei and I often ate out when we'd lived together in Shanghai. The access to great food and Yanmei's endless generosity when it came to the groceries and food bill spoiled me. I ate well; the food didn't come with emotional baggage.

"About that . . ."

"God, did your parents ask you for more money?"

"Dad needed it for acupuncture treatments."

"They're adults. Yes, I get they ask for help, but the frequency and the way they do it isn't right. They'll bleed you dry, forcing you to move back home if you let them."

"I know."

"This is hard to hear, but you can't pay them to love you, Soph. They should do it unconditionally. You put up with a lot because it's cultural. The system is rigged for us to not question our parents, and to do what they tell us. Sometimes, though, what they want from us isn't necessarily the best thing."

Her words didn't hurt me as I already knew this. Giving money to my parents was an act of duty. It was my way of reminding them that I existed.

Yanmei smiled and raised her glass of mango juice. "If they acted properly, they'd be as proud of you as I am. That kitty present basket? You did that. This is the first of many."

"I hope so."

"It is. Now can I give you an update on boss lady?"

Chapter Twenty-One

Before I headed to meet with Mr. Particular, I received a message from Mabel and Flora. They both agreed to go on the dates. I'd need to talk to Mr. Regret to tell him the news when I returned.

The antique bookshop was north in Unionville, a picturesque former village in Markham. The quaint shops with their balconies, icing-covered angled roofs, and patterned gingerbread brick were a welcome sight compared to the steel and glass of modernity of my current neighborhood.

The little brass bell above the door tinkled when I entered the shop. The aroma of dusty books, leather, and polished wood permeated the cozy establishment. Copper rails for rolling ladders topped tall bookcases against the walls, while a single column of books dissected the main room in half. It wasn't one of those stuffy, claustrophobic spaces—instead, it was more like a museum with the occasional glass box housing a rare item. Across from the checkout desk a wrought-iron spiral staircase led to the second floor.

I walked through the first floor before deducing that my client was upstairs.

Mr. Particular stood over a glass case containing a set of illuminated books. His dark sports jacket stretched across his wide shoulders as he braced himself against the glass to get a better look. His charcoal winter wool coat and red cashmere scarf were draped over a nearby ottoman.

After unwrapping my pink-striped scarf, I took off my heavy peacoat and placed them beside his.

"What are you looking at?"

"I commissioned this set for my niece. Her twelfth birthday's coming up."

The collection of hardbound books with ethereal gilded illustrations of fairy tales caught my breath, holding it from my lungs until I remembered to exhale. I drank in the faeries, dragons, princes and princesses, and magical landscapes—fulfilling a childhood wish when these stories sustained me.

"Andrew Lang's *Fairy Books* except I asked a local artist to add in the gold leaf, with the help of this bookshop, of course."

"She is one lucky, lucky girl."

"She asked for the set. The modified illustrations are a surprise. She loves fairy tales. I know she'll take good care of these books." He leaned back from the glass case. "I think you might know why I asked for the meeting."

"I'm guessing it's to request a date."

"Wouldn't that be a breach of protocol?" A wry smile brightened his handsome face.

My hands slipped, and I landed hard on my elbows, almost smearing my face across the glass. I held up my left hand and laughed. "I'm okay!"

I sucked in air to compose myself and drain the blood flushing my face. By the time I was able to look up, he greeted me with a mixture of amusement and concern across his gorgeous features. "I have a plan to arrange dates for you soon. I'm attending an event that will yield great candidates."

"Good. I figured you already had something in the works." He moved to a nearby bookcase to scan the titles.

"Are you working on a time frame? Is there a due date or some deadline I should be aware of?"

"Maybe?" He retrieved a book from the shelf. The care he took in handling and opening the pages mirrored the way he'd folded his coat over the ottoman. "My grandmother died last year. On her deathbed, she told me that I wasn't someone who should be alone. It wasn't that she was nagging me like my mother to get married. It was more that she understood how difficult it is for me to connect with other people. Poh-poh wanted me to find my person."

"I'm sorry for your loss. It sounds like she was your person."

"She was. I don't make friends easily, and when I do, it's a select few."

Yanmei and, now, Mr. Regret were the only two good friends I had. The problem with human connections stemmed from the false assumption that finding friendship should be easy—that with the number of people on this planet, stumbling into meaningful relationships was a statistical guarantee.

"Don't worry, I will find a match for you. After matching two septuagenarians, I'd like to think that someone as good-looking as you with your great attributes should be a breeze."

His dark brows arched at my offhand compliment, causing me to blush again.

"It's the truth," I continued. "The majority of people are shallow and demand pictures ahead of time. I don't comply because more often than not it leads to trouble. A judgment is formed from the photo while personality and attributes are dismissed. It's helpful to have a pretty package, but what's inside is as important. In my opinion, the photo dehumanizes the person. For a quick hookup, sure, a picture will give the biological markers you need, but for a relationship? You have to get more information than what a person looks like."

"Interesting." He returned the book to its place on the shelf. "I'm curious, and please indulge me. Would you go on a date with someone you hadn't seen before?"

"I don't know. I never thought about it."

"You do go on dates, right? This isn't the case of a shoemaker too busy making shoes for everyone else to make their own?"

"No, I don't go on dates." I laughed. "I can't."

"Can't or won't?"

"Can't." I approached him. His red thread reacted, floating upward from its dormant state. "Like most people, you have a red thread. It indicates that you can be matched if you want; romantic love is available to you. I bet you hadn't heard of red threads before seeking a matchmaker. It doesn't tend to be common knowledge." I pressed my blank sternum. "Anyway, I wasn't born with one because I'm a matchmaker."

"That doesn't sound fair."

Yanmei railed against this and vowed to petition the Society to have her thread restored. Last year, it became possible, but the waitlist was massive. I put it out of my mind.

"I mean, I could change that, but right now, I'm fine."

He drew closer. "I wouldn't be. It's one thing if it were your choice. Instead, you were denied before you had a chance to choose."

My rising heartbeat thrummed against my chest as the distance between us dwindled. His subtle cologne, along with the intoxicating combination of Meiji Meltykiss chocolate cubes and Irish cream coffee, drifted to my nostrils. I wanted to bury my face in his sweater.

"Love has never been an option for me."

"I don't think you've allowed it to be."

The sound of a throat clearing in the distance caused me to jump back. It was the older gentleman with the argyle vest manning the front desk. "If you wish, we can pack your order and have it wrapped."

"Yes, please," Mr. Particular replied. "We'll be downstairs in a minute."

I grabbed my coat and purse from the ottoman. "I'll contact you soon about the match." Stabbing my arms into the sleeves, I contorted my body to fasten the buttons of the peacoat. My trembling fingers managed to wrestle three into their place before giving up on the last one at chest level.

"Sophie," he called out. "At least you have a course of action for the future if you change your mind."

I held up my hand in acknowledgment before descending the spiral staircase. I missed the last two steps and nearly face-planted into a nearby potted ficus. Escaping the bookshop with my dignity intact was a failure.

THE NEXT MORNING, I HEADED to Mr. Regret's apartment. The Old Ducks meeting was that afternoon, and I had volunteered to help in the kitchen and bring the goodies downstairs. We spent two hours preparing and baking tarte tatin. As the flat French-style apple pie cooled in its beautiful teal bakeware, I pointed to a ceramic blackbird on the counter.

"What is this?"

"Ah, that's a pie bird. I'd use that for apple pies and such.

There is no crust on a tarte tatin, so it remained caged." Mr. Regret picked up the bird and held it in his palm. "This little fellow acts as a vent for a crusted pie. Useful and decorative."

"It's lovely. Almost as lovely as the two women who agreed to go on a date with you."

Mr. Regret fumbled the ceramic. "At the same time?"

Chapter Twenty-Two

After I explained that the two dates were, in fact, spaced out and that he was under no pressure to decide until he was ready, Mr. Regret relaxed his death grip on the ceramic bird.

"You'll do great." I took the bird and placed it on the counter. "The two women are wonderful, and if you don't agree, I can make other matches. Remember, you're in control."

"Right." He ran his fingers through his gray hair, smoothing some unwanted spikes. "You're sure they'll like me?"

How did anyone resist this sweet marshmallow of a man? The interest from Flora and Mabel was immediate. They were drawn to his charm.

I smiled. "They already do. It's why they agreed to meet with you."

"I haven't been on a date in decades, and now I have two? I don't know if I have anything appropriate to wear. The last time I bought formal attire was before I committed to my love affair with pastries."

"I can help you sort through your closet later. If we need to, I'll go shopping with you."

He clasped my hands in his. "Thank you, Sophie."

THE PRIVATE ROOM WAS FULL when we arrived with the apple tart, disposable plates, and utensils. The other men had moved the table out of the way, setting it against one of the walls to leave more room for mingling. Mr. Wolf and Beatrice chatted with Mr. Sorrow and Clara while Mr. Durian and Mr. Dolphin huddled with Mr. Moon. Mr. Porcupine stood alone in the corner, his arms crossed. From behind those horn-rimmed glasses, his beady eyes tracked me.

Mr. Regret and I set up the food. He cut the tart. I helped distribute the plates. Out of sheer pettiness, I served Mr. Porcupine last.

Beatrice and Mr. Wolf were holding hands, their shoulders touching. A flower pin on Mr. Wolf's chest had Beatrice's picture on it. He was now the president of her fan club. I stifled a giggle. "How are you two getting along?"

Beatrice's shy smile matched Mr. Wolf's. "Very well. We're looking into a weekend getaway that will accommodate our girls."

"Thank you for the basket."

Mr. Wolf nodded, his eyes twinkling.

Their threads had braided together, casting a bright poppy glow around them.

Clara, dressed in a sharp blazer and cream pantsuit, tapped my arm. "I wanted to thank you as well. I haven't had this much fun in years."

Mr. Sorrow placed his hand on her arm. "We're even thinking of competing!"

"This is for you." He revealed a narrow box. "I know how much you love candy, but promise me that you'll use this so I can sleep better at night."

It was a high-end electric toothbrush. Long retired, yet still a dentist. I thanked him, revealing my pronounced toothy smile. "I'm glad you've found the joy in dancing again."

Their threads sparked, moving in unison. I hoped to be present to witness the moment they joined.

"It's so much easier when you have a great partner." He winked at Clara and twirled her into a dramatic dip. Both came up laughing.

This was the reward, the reason we trained, why we abandoned our own romance. Their lives were more full, more alive. Joy was exponential.

Mr. Moon began clapping. "Well done, Miss Matchmaker!"

The others joined in. Everyone except the old grump in the back.

"I want to sign on as a client." Mr. Moon called over to Mr. Dolphin and Mr. Durian. "So do they."

"Oh, this is wonderful!" I fished out my spiral notebook and a pen. "Write down your contact information and we can get the process started."

As the three men took turns scribbling, Mr. Regret approached. He grinned and looked to his friend in the back—the lone scowl in a sea of smiles. "I think it's time to cash out on the good karma."

"You're right. I am due." I gave him a wink and swaggered toward Mr. Porcupine.

My nemesis's frown deepened. Though he towered over me by at least a foot, my smugness made up for the height difference.

"What do you want?" he hissed through yellowed teeth.

"You've questioned me at every step, and each time, I've succeeded."

"So?"

"I think it's only fair that you sign up as a client. You mentioned before that you've used a similar service."

"Why should I?"

Mr. Regret piped in. "Oh, come on. You know she deserves a chance."

"She does," Mr. Sorrow added. "Sophie is an excellent matchmaker. Give her a chance."

Mr. Wolf vigorously nodded in agreement.

"What are you afraid of? That she'll find you a woman who will put up with your—"

Mr. Durian cut off Mr. Dolphin. "Baggage. He meant baggage. You should agree after what you put her through."

"I'm voting with them," Mr. Moon teased. "A few weeks ago, you were talking about how nice it would be to . . ."

Mr. Porcupine glared at his friends. They grinned back.

For the briefest moment, I pitied him. The poor bastard was trapped in a corner. He might have deserved it, but I'd been in that position far too often not to empathize. "It's my policy to offer a refund if you aren't satisfied. And if you don't want to do it—don't."

Mr. Porcupine snapped my olive branch and cast it aside. "I'll sign up. Doubt you'll follow through and find me a real match."

"Oh, I will. Might take me a lot longer though."

Mr. Dolphin slapped his knee and jabbed Mr. Durian in the ribs. Raucous laughter filled the room. Mr. Regret covered his mouth to hide his glee.

Mr. Moon handed the notebook and pen to Mr. Porcupine. He glowered with each stabbing stroke. When he finished, he returned the items.

"Thank you."

He grunted before getting another slice of apple tart.

"He'll come around." Mr. Regret patted my arm. "This will be good for him. Do you know why we founded this club?"

"No, I assumed you gathered because you're all Chinese and old."

He snorted. "Yes, we're Chinese, but we weren't always old. When we started meeting up, it was meant for companionship and friendship. Three of us frequented the same restaurant. That's how we ended up finding everyone. We're single. Most of us don't have much family left."

"Where does the Old Ducks name come from?"

"I read an article about a bunch of old bachelors living together in this small village in China with that name and found it appropriate. It's a lot better than some of the names we came up with ourselves."

I scanned the room, watching all of them laugh and interact. Even Mr. Porcupine broke his cranky exterior when engaging with the two couples.

"It's a good name."

"You're helping us with our loneliness. We're lucky to have you." The warmth in Mr. Regret's gentle voice soothed as much as the cups of tea he offered in his apartment. "We're a stubborn lot. Some more so than others. It's hard to ask for what we need."

"I can relate. I wanted to move out for so long, except now I can't talk to my parents about why. They don't understand. They see this whole endeavor as a financial mistake."

"If they're like most parents, you're stuck with them until you get married. And then you end up with in-laws, which can lead to more problems. Why do they see this as a mistake?"

"Because I'm house poor."

"That might be true now, but you've signed up four more clients. At this rate, you'll be able to buy your condo outright in two years."

"Ha!" I wrinkled my nose. "You're too kind."

"When you match our dear leader, all of Toronto will hear about it. You'll be so busy, you'll be turning down clients. If you were a politician, I'd say you're well on your way to getting the retiree vote and endorsement."

"I hope I'm not preying on your demographic."

He snorted. "You're not. We 'boomers' deserve to be catered to. We're no longer working, but we're not disposable."

"I didn't mean to offend." My cheeks turned pink. "I'm sorry."

"Don't apologize." Mr. Regret patted my shoulder. "The world believes that after a certain age, we should be hidden away. This is wrong. For a lot of us, this is the time of our lives—our golden years."

"And here I am just getting started."

"Yes, you still have a city to conquer. I can't wait for all your naysayers to eat their words."

"The first in line would be my mother."

"The next time you see her, ask her what being wrong tastes like."

Chapter Twenty-Three

✥

A quick shopping trip with Mr. Regret the next day yielded a modest selection of wardrobe choices that highlighted his warm golden-brown eyes and his huggable physique—his words, not mine.

As for my mother, I wouldn't be able to relay the good news. No dinner this week. No explanation given. I never deserved one. Family dinners always had one rule: my mandatory attendance. My parents canceled at any time without penalty, while my absence would only be excused by death or dismemberment.

My phone rang.

Mr. Particular.

"Is something wrong?" I asked.

"Yes, I have an emergency. Can you meet me today? I'll send over the details."

There was a palpable urgency in his voice. Something must have changed since our last meeting. I'd been planning to schedule the interview process with the rest of the Old Ducks but would need to shift that to the evening.

Mr. Particular requested to meet at the Royal Ontario Museum.

I HADN'T BEEN TO THE museum since leaving for Shanghai. The building was unusual. It had a stone facade and arched windows as one would expect from a traditional museum, except growing from its side, like a crystal formation, was a glass shard. The addition had been controversial. I thought it looked like a whimsical rock candy outgrowth. I visited on Tuesdays when it was free to the public. I tried to go once a month to see what had changed and the new exhibits on display. My recent favorite was the Iris van Herpen exhibition. The fantastical fashion made of unconventional materials equaled the fine art showcased in the lower floors. Mannequins dressed in the impossible—fog, sea-foam, an armor of bones.

The Gallery of Birds was located on the second level in the natural history section. The long glass hall contained flocks of taxidermy birds. They posed in midflight with glass eyes forward, staring into the unimaginable. I wished there were a gallery wall of eggs from every single creature in there. The magnificence of all those perfect shapes would have tickled the fancy of the Easter Bunny itself.

Mr. Particular stood before an albatross. He leaned in as close to the glass as possible without leaving a soft halo of moisture on the smooth surface. Close enough to count the feathers within the massive wingspan.

"What's the emergency?"

"I have to attend a work function in three days and I need a plus-one."

"Ah."

"I apologize for the increased pressure."

The wine launch was tomorrow night. I had to walk away with at least three prospects for him. From Sunny's Instagram feed, her friends were attractive and accomplished—not quintessential socialites found in more popular circles. I'd already prepared a targeted list.

"It's no trouble. Besides, it's a reasonable ask. Clients often have a deadline they need to meet."

"If love were so easily scheduled, your job would be redundant." The hint of a smile caused me to grin in return.

"I'm lucky it isn't. I have the ultimate job security."

"Yes, it's even better than mine." He walked toward the ostrich. "You know they eat stones?"

"No, why?"

"It helps with digestion. Ostriches have no teeth."

I didn't know if that was true, but I doubted he was the type to lie in general nor one who would do so to impress a girl, not that he was trying to impress me.

"Birds don't fart," I blurted.

"Really? And why is that?"

"Something to do with their diet and lack of gut bacteria. It kind of explains why bird poop doesn't stink."

Unlike everyone else in my past, he didn't laugh at me or sprint away to escape my awkwardness. Guess Mr. Particular had missed that memo. Mom winced whenever I strayed outside her preselected polite topics. Animal feces—shockingly—didn't fall into that list.

But he acted like we were conversing about something as normal as the weather.

We made our way toward the dinosaur exhibit. Naked lizard giants were assembled as I would arrange cleaned fish bones on a plate. Without the organs or skin, it was left to our imaginations how we'd fill in the empty spaces.

"Were you able to see the pandas at the zoo?" he asked.

The pandas had been on loan for five years. My father and I saw them before I left for Shanghai. My mother had no interest, but he had insisted on seeing the professional eaters of the animal world. We weren't disappointed.

"I have. They reminded me of lazy toddlers on a perpetual snack break."

"An accurate observation. I went with my grandparents. Poh-poh and Gung-gung had the best time comparing them to indolent relatives. They were always on the same wavelength."

"The pandas or your grandparents?"

He brushed a stray strand of dark hair from his forehead. "Both. My grandparents had this relationship full of inside jokes. They always had a good time no matter what they attended. I remember when I was covering my ears during a cousin's recorder concert, Poh-poh and Gung-gung were giggling to themselves. My parents ended up chastising them."

"That's what you want, isn't it?"

"Yes. Is that possible? I don't see it with the married friends I have. I don't know whether it's a matter of longevity or something else. One of my fears is growing old and not having what my grandparents had."

"Being old isn't a deterrent to love. You need to meet my other clients." I told him about the Old Ducks, of Mr. Wolf and Beatrice, and Mr. Sorrow and Clara.

"Mr. Wolf and Mr. Sorrow? Interesting code names."

"You should see the classification system my friend Yanmei uses. Hers are much more colorful. We use it to provide a semblance of anonymity for our clients."

"What's mine?"

I snorted. "As if I'll tell you."

He leaned down and whispered, "I want to know. What do I have to do to get this piece of information?"

"Maybe after I've matched you and you're living your happily ever after, it might be safe. Though, it's common to take these details to my grave. You can petition the Society to see my records, but I doubt they'd allow it." I gave him a soft jab to the arm. "Better to reconcile with not knowing."

He moved his hand to my elbow. I jumped at the warmth of his touch, careening backward into an exhibit, my butt inches from setting off the alarm. I'd done this once before when I was young and on a field trip. The ensuing noise and embarrassment was forever burned in my memory. My third grade teacher panicked; I ended up being the one to calm her down. My efforts weren't wasted—she kept the incident between us, sparing me a lecture from my parents.

I wasn't worried about my parents now—I did fear for my dignity.

This man, my client, had seen my awkwardness in its full glory.

Yet the alarm never went off.

I opened my eyes and found myself in his arms. The heat from my face spiked my internal temperature. This was bad. We weren't supposed to end up in the arms of our clients. Matchmakers maintained a level of professional detachment, and yet here I was grasping his sweater to pull myself up.

"Thank you for saving me from disaster."

"You're welcome."

My fingers dug into the softness of his sweater like kitten claws, but without the destructive sharpness. I left small indentations in the fabric.

"I'll find your match and be in touch in two days." My words ran together. I tightened my grip on my purse. "Do you need anything else?"

He wrinkled his brow. "No."

"Have a great evening."

I left him standing in the middle of the dinosaur ossuary with a mixture of confusion and sadness.

Chapter Twenty-Four

⋈

Sunny Tang had selected an upscale downtown nightclub in the entertainment district for the launch for her new line of wine. The decor paralleled the labels on the bottles: splashes of gold in the gold-leaf cocktails and trays of panfried dumpling hors d'oeuvres and crudités against bands of cream in the upholstery and puffs of hydrangeas and calla lilies.

I squeezed myself into the lone short, trendy dress I had in my closet. Yanmei insisted I have something that allowed me to blend in among different social circles. After a painful hour of learning how to apply formal makeup, I double-checked with my fashionable friend for her approval. She nitpicked my eyeliner application before giving me her thumbs-up.

I slicked down my short hair with gel to secure its obedience. Making the best first impression with these women guaranteed me an audience. Rumors of my matching two of the Old Ducks had helped repair some of my reputation.

Navigating through a crowd with nary a gray hair in sight felt foreign. My time with the Old Ducks and their lives had opened a world I never before considered. Thumping dance beats replaced the classical music Mr. Sorrow and Clara danced to. The rhythm of this room sucked my energy from me, one drop at a time. Any conversations would need to be moved outside—or anywhere I could hear my own heartbeat.

"Are you on the list?" the hostess at the podium asked.

"Oh, I thought this was an open event."

The event pages on several outlets indicated there were no restrictions. Given how busy the club appeared, I hadn't considered there would be a constraint based on capacity.

Damn it.

"Is there a waitlist?"

"No. You're either in or you're not." The hostess lifted the clipboard that contained the guest list and tapped it. "If you're not approved by Patty, you don't exist."

The event planner's name was displayed at the top corner. I recognized the last name. Staying here and debating the hostess was fruitless. I'd need to regroup and get myself on that list.

I retreated to a quiet corner of the hotel lobby. Sunny Tang wasn't at all within Yanmei's circle of influence. My own network so far consisted of the Old Ducks—but one shared the same family name as the event planner . . . It was worth a shot.

Mr. Particular's bachelorettes were inside. I needed to do whatever it took to get to them. Hopefully, it wouldn't involve breaking laws.

I dialed Mr. Sorrow's number.

"Ah, hello, Sophie."

"Hi! I'm downtown at a wine launch, but I'm not on the guest list so I haven't been able to get in. I'm hoping you can help me."

"Is this for business?"

"Yes. I'm here for a client. I'm certain that his potential match is inside." The vigilant hostess continued turning people away at the entrance. "Do you happen to have a niece who is a party planner?"

"Patty, yes. I had lunch with her and her mother last week. Of course Sheila was singing her daughter's praises. Patty landed her biggest account for some wine company."

I pumped my fist.

Magic.

When dealing with love, miracles were possible.

"Are you all right?" he asked. "Is there anything I can do help?"

"Yes!"

MR. SORROW CALLED HIS NIECE and Patty emerged from the bowels of the club to greet me. Dressed in a lamé tube dress with a white bolero jacket, she exuded the unlimited vibrant energy sucked from countless introverts like me.

"Sophie Go?"

"Yes."

"My uncle speaks highly of you. You're a matchmaker, right?" Patty's radiant smile was like her uncle's.

"I am."

"We're so happy he found Clara, and we have you to thank. For the longest time, we were worried he'd never find joy again. We all loved Aunt Janice, but he's not meant to be alone." She led me past the hostess, who was still busy turning people away. "My uncle mentioned you're here for business reasons."

"Yes, I'm here for a client."

Patty offered me a flute of sparkling wine from a nearby tray. I took a sip out of courtesy.

"He's not one of my uncle's friends, is he? Because that would be . . ." Her pretty face scrunched into a grimace.

I coughed up the liquid, wheezing. "No, it's for someone much, much younger."

"Oh good." She laughed. "Like, close to my age? I'm in the market."

Patty ticked the attractive and career factors, but everything else screamed incompatible with Mr. Particular. Much like the wine, I had to act out of courtesy. I plucked a card from my clutch. "Take my card and get in touch."

"Oh, I will." She winked, holding the business card. "Go. Mingle. Make sure you try the wine again. It tastes better when it goes down the right pipe." Patty spotted the hostess waving her over. "Gotta go. Duty calls."

I scanned the room for the four women I intended to meet. My intense research yielded personalities that would be compatible with my client, but gauging their interest was the final step before arranging a date.

Someone tapped my shoulder.

"Are you a friend of Sunny's?" asked a perky midtwenties Asian woman with feathery bangs. She had sparkling golden-brown eyes and a cheerful voice. Convenient. She was one of the prospects I had hoped to meet after studying her social media selfies and her posts about being woefully single.

"I'm not. I'm here to scope out the wine and the guests. I'm Sophie and I'm a matchmaker."

"Oooh." She tugged on my arm. "Come on. I'll introduce you. I'm Lindsay—Sunny's business partner slash operations manager. I haven't seen a matchmaker around since Madam Chieng. She and my mom used to have tea together. Are you looking for more clients, or do you have a current one you want to match?"

"Both, but I'm concentrating on the latter this evening. If you have time, however, I'd love to speak more in private."

"Wait. Me?" Lindsay smiled and pressed her hand over the sparkling diamond lariat on her chest. "I'm intrigued. I haven't had much luck in dating with the long hours leading up to this. With the launch almost over, I can't wait to get my life back."

I told her about Mr. Particular in statistical terms—his job, his personality. Lindsay listened, her red thread perking up with a small spark.

"Do you want to meet Sunny or should I let you circulate?" Lindsay motioned to the dense group surrounding her business partner. "I doubt we're the only ones you want to speak to. From what Madam Chieng told my mom, matchmaking involves a lot of throwing darts at the board until you get it right."

"It does, though Sunny isn't one of those darts. However, there are a few other potential matches who are supposed to be in attendance. As you noted, it's important to have a few options. There's no guarantee that who I think is perfect for my client matches his opinion."

"Well, if it doesn't work out with me, maybe I'll become a client. I don't want to deal with the hassle of browsing through profiles anymore. Don't get me started on my experiences in dating in Toronto."

"I hope I can make a match for you." I handed her my card. "I can get your details down now if you want."

Lindsay jotted down her information.

I spotted my next bachelorette and repeated my spiel about Mr. Particular. This continued all night. The women were receptive to my pitch and eager to meet with Mr. Particular. Each reacted with a spark.

A happy client was the goal.

By the time I returned home, I still felt the vibrating beats on my skin. I wanted to crawl into my bed and never see another soul again. But Mr. Dolphin, Mr. Durian, Mr. Moon, and Mr. Porcupine's interviews still needed to be scheduled. Lying in the fetal position, I messaged the four women to get their availability for Mr. Particular's date. Lindsay would meet him for a date beforehand, while Jenn would be his plus-one for his work event if Lindsay didn't work out.

Any of these women would make a great partner. He would make a great partner.

Get him matched.

He would be happy.

Chapter Twenty-Five

><┼<

After his dates with Lindsay and Jenn, Mr. Particular called.

I wedged my phone between my ear and my shoulder as I collated the completed questionnaire sheets from the Old Ducks into their separate folders. "How did they go?"

"They're unsuitable." The irritation in his voice was sand caught in a pair of sneakers after a stroll by the beach. "They're not terrible, but they're not right, at least for me."

"Okay . . ." I frowned. "I'm sorry to hear that. Can you tell me why? Be as specific as you can. The feedback will help me."

"Lindsay is nice, but she's too much of a workaholic. She was glued to her phone all lunch. Eye contact is important, don't you think?"

Lindsay must still be dealing with the residual work from the launch. I'd need to talk to her and get her take on the date in case it was something deeper. "And what about Jenn?"

There was an extended silence. "She eats weird."

"Excuse me, what?" I narrowed my eyes. "Clarify."

"It's the way she eats. The chewing ratio to the amount of

food is ridiculous. If it's a vegetable, it's three bites. Meat, six. Noodles, five."

Why the hell would he even be counting? I collected my irritation and swept it under the rug of professionalism. "I'm sorry to hear that she isn't an elegant masticator."

"It was the tipping point. There were other issues. That was the most glaring."

"Do you want me to continue arranging dates at restaurants or do you prefer meetings that don't involve food?"

"Avoiding meals will only delay the inevitable. Keep doing what you're doing."

"You are keeping an open mind, aren't you?"

"Of course. However, I know who I want. I'm not compromising."

There was a constant debate among matchmakers about which was worse—a client who possessed a clear picture of their perfect mate versus someone without a clue. Mr. Particular, true to his moniker, had an exacting vision. Anyone who didn't conform to his strict set of specifications was disqualified.

"Don't lose hope. I have more candidates you can meet."

"Good. My sister suspects my hiring a matchmaker is a lie. Like my mother, she thinks I'm commitment avoidant. I'm tired of arguing with them."

He wanted someone with whom to spend the rest of his life and had family pressuring him. I had no such pressure. We had no extended family in the area—just Dad, Mom, and me. Mom's side was in Vancouver, Dad's in Hong Kong. I'd always been given the impression that anywhere there was family were blackout and no-fly zones. Mom and Dad's bond excluded everyone.

"The sooner you can be matched, the sooner they'll stop, right?"

"Exactly."

"I'll send you the details soon for the next date."

"Thank you." There was a brief pause. "And Sophie?"

"Yes?"

"What happened at the museum?"

Oh, you mean that time where my client held me close in his arms? That little nothing? What was there to say? That I'd never been held like that before? Or that I enjoyed it? That it was wrong, and impossible, and glorious?

Instead, I bit my lip and lied. Lied in ways that were well-worn, like grooves in a record—to pacify, to spare other's feelings while protecting my own. "I had to meet my parents. I'm sorry for being so abrupt."

"Oh. I'll wait for your email then."

"It'll be soon. Bye."

I set the phone down and willed it to remain silent. The next date for Mr. Particular would be Trish Nguyen, a brilliant endocrinologist at Sick Kids. I'd met her at the wine launch, and of all the women I'd spoken to, she seemed the best candidate. My strategy was to save her for last—end with a bang. People were complicated; there was never a solid guarantee that anything would click.

Trish and Mr. Particular's date needed to be at a restaurant with two floors for me to spy on them and make sure it ended with the joining of their threads. The sooner he found his soul mate, the sooner I'd put my confused feelings behind me.

A LUCKY OPENING IN THEIR schedules aligned for Mr. Particular and Trish to meet that night at a casual Indonesian restaurant in Richmond Hill. Polished black tabletops and red chairs exuded modernity as gold gilded Buddhas perched in illuminated niches.

Hammered bronze pendant lamps hung over the square tables and light instrumental covers of the latest South Asian hits played in the background. While I waited, I followed up with Lindsay and Jenn. Lindsay was eager for a second date with the "hottie" and indicated nothing was amiss. Jenn, however, mentioned Mr. Particular's oral fixation and was disappointed there was no kiss by the night's end. I let them down gently.

The table I reserved for Mr. Particular was below mine. A quick peek over the balcony would be enough to gauge how the date was going. I ordered nasi goreng and sambal tumis sotong. The leftovers would feed me for at least two days.

They should be here in a few minutes.

He arrived first, dressed in a dark navy sports jacket and lemon-yellow dress shirt. Lindsay and Jenn were generous with their compliments of him—rightly so. When Trish was escorted to their table, he pulled her chair out for her then said something that made her laugh. The sparkle in her brown eyes was unmistakable.

Excellent. This was a good sign.

I relaxed into my seat.

When my food arrived—a sizzling bowl of fried egg over Indonesian fried rice and a plate of tender squid rings and tentacles in red sauce—I resisted the urge to wolf it down. After weeks of ramen, eating at a restaurant was a luxury. I justified tonight as a necessary business expense.

They laughed again. Trish touched his hand.

Such a handsome couple.

Her red thread sparked with excitement—his remained slack and unresponsive.

To anyone else, they were a young couple making a connection.

I knew otherwise.

What the hell was wrong with him?

BACK HOME, I TUCKED MY leftovers into the fridge and called Yanmei. It was early enough to catch her before she left for the day.

"Congrats on the four new geriatric clients!" She raised her glass of mango juice. "You're killing it with the gray demographic. You should be close to filling out your application for accreditation!"

I bowed. "Thank you! I called to get your advice. This is purely a shoptalk call."

"Oh really?" She raised her fork over her Thai breakfast omelet. "Go ahead. Shoot."

I told her about Mr. Particular, the failed dates, and Trish, who should have been a good match. Yanmei listened while she ate. Questions or advice came afterward. She was predictable that way.

"So no spark? Nothing from him?"

"Correct."

"Are you sure it's working? I mean, I've seen threads that can't react, but it's from deep-seated trauma or psychological issues."

Mr. Particular's thread had been active since I'd met him at the Su-Winstons' anniversary banquet. I wouldn't have taken him on as a client otherwise.

"I've seen it many times. It's normal."

Yanmei tapped her chin.

"You already have a theory?" I asked.

"I do."

"Spill."

"One: You've showed me his picture and the man is gorgeous, yet you seem otherwise at ease around him. Curious."

"He's a client, Yanmei. That's different."

She continued, ignoring my interjection. "Two: You said his thread is normal, yet at the date, it proved otherwise."

"Right. It hung limp."

We snickered.

"Three: It has reacted around you. Multiple times. Maybe it only responds to *you*."

I dropped my phone, my face ablaze. "No! That's ridiculous."

"You like him. I was right!" She clapped and pointed. "Can't hide it from me."

"I'm not hiding anything. Stop inventing stories. Just because you're a matchmaker doesn't mean you need to match me!"

"Listen. I'm not attacking you. I just . . . Sophie, it's great that you have a crush. We can restore our threads now. I mean, I don't have anyone yet, but I signed up anyway. I checked this morning. I've moved up five spots! You should start thinking that it's now possible—to be in love."

I sighed.

While I loved Yanmei to death, her tendency to control people was unquestionable; however, she had never tried it with me. Instead, she encouraged, nurtured, and coaxed me away from my destructive view of myself.

She always meant well, but once she latched onto an idea, she wouldn't let go.

"Be reasonable. When have I ever told you I was interested in anyone?"

"When have you not been scared by the idea? You don't think you deserve love."

When I was twelve, I hadn't learned how to recognize my mother's moods nor how to tune her out. If Mom was annoyed, she needed me and Dad to also be annoyed to validate her own feelings. She'd been in one of her dark moods when she told me,

"Marriage isn't for you. No husband would want the burden of taking care of such a selfish child."

"You're reaching with all of this." I splayed my hands flat on the kitchen counter. "Please. Let it go."

"Why? So you can deny something good for yourself? You're abstaining for no logical reason, thinking that you'll win a prize at the end. You're in the Self-Punishment Olympics, and all you're going to get is misery."

"And you think you know better than I do about what I need?"

"Yeah, I do. Fight me."

Chapter Twenty-Six

I never liked confrontation. Whenever Mom and I argued, I always lost. It's hard to win when your opponent is fueled by self-righteous zeal. Easier to concede than defend myself in a no-win situation.

"I don't want to fight."

"What's the worst that can happen? You end up being happy. Is that such a tragedy?"

Push.

Prod.

Poke.

My decisions—never good enough. What I wanted—never good enough. My life. Never. Good. Enough. They knew best, knew better than me.

"It's my life. I will do with it as I see fit. I get enough of this from my mother—I don't need it from you!"

I hung up.

For the next hour, tears drenched my face as I arranged a date between Mr. Particular and Patty.

Mr. Particular was my client.

Nothing more.

Yanmei was wrong. Bullying me into doing what she thought best without caring about what I wanted.

Match him and move on. Push as many prospects as possible his way.

I kept checking my phone for an apology—none came.

She was supposed to be my best friend, my rock. Was this how it ended?

Despite my personal tumult, my interviews with Mr. Dolphin and Mr. Durian were scheduled; however, it couldn't happen in my apartment as they insisted they go back-to-back. I sought a place with maximum ventilation: the condo's indoor rooftop garden.

Mr. Dolphin, the louder of the two, waited for me at a round table near the waterfall. Dressed in a busy-printed royal-blue silk shirt and charcoal pants, he patted unseen wrinkles on his trousers. The surrounding flowers accented his strong cologne. His family ran a successful fish sauce brewery in Malaysia that he visited often. He was a man who treated his appearance as one would curate a stock portfolio. His styled hair, perfect teeth, and smooth, unwrinkled skin belonged to a man at least two decades younger. The hint of a scar on his chin made him more interesting in the way a flaw distinguished a piece of art as created by human hands instead of a machine.

He offered me a seat. "I saw what you did for my friends. I hope you'll be as successful with me."

"Of course I intend to find the right man for you." I pulled out my notebook and placed it on the tabletop. "I'm going to ask you three questions. You can answer them however you please."

"Wasn't that the point of the paperwork? Why do I feel like

I've walked into a surprise oral exam?" He asked with a chuckle, "You're not going to fail me, are you?"

"I'm your matchmaker—not your teacher."

He cracked his knuckles. The sharp pops pinged in the air. "All right. I'm ready."

"What do you look for in a partner?"

"Someone who gets my sense of humor—like he needs to be able to laugh at my jokes. That's important." He paused, and his jovial expression sobered. "For my entire life, everyone turned to me when they needed to be cheered up. It was a lot of pressure when I was younger, but I've grown to accept it. I thought it would mean I didn't end up alone, yet here we are."

"What kind of relationship are you looking for?"

"A man to spend whatever remaining time I have left with. Someone to marry. It'd be nice to have a wedding after all these years. Any who might have disapproved are dead. I outlived them all with sheer pettiness."

I never reacted when listening to my clients' interviews, yet the last line coaxed a slight smile.

"Do you believe in love?"

"Yes. Always have. I believe in its expression—its many forms. It's a universal force that shouldn't be limited—especially not by people. We have enough crap to fix and deal with. If anything, more love would solve a lot of these problems."

I finished writing down his answers and shut my notebook.

"And we're done? That's it?" He leaned back in his chair, the front legs floating. "I thought it'd be harder."

"It all depends on one's point of view. Some find it difficult, while others, like you, know what they want."

He rubbed his hands together. "And when will I get my first date?"

My list of contacts had grown with each successful match.

Happy clients were generous with sharing their contacts—providing me with the first steps of my research.

"I'll need to double-check your social circles to make sure I find a prospect outside of them. I doubt you'd want a date with someone you already had a less-than-ideal experience with."

"Good point. No one wants another date with an ex."

Since Mr. Dolphin had been so candid, I decided to take a leap and ask him about the delicate issue that had been bothering me. "May I ask you something about your friend?"

"If it's about his addiction, I already know." He rolled his eyes and pursed his lips. "He likes what he likes and he's damned well entitled to it. If you grew up in Asia, it wouldn't be something you'd be so shocked by."

"I see."

"But good luck trying to get my friend away from his favorite food. No country on the planet would consider durian as anything but a biological weapon." He chuckled and waved to Mr. Durian, who stood near the garden's entrance. "Here's a tip for you: Don't bring it up unless you have a solution that doesn't involve him giving up what he loves."

I thanked him.

Right now, I had no idea how to tackle that pungent dilemma. Better let it rest until after I'd arranged the first date for him.

Mr. Dolphin and Mr. Durian exchanged a few chortles in passing.

Mr. Durian, sharply dressed with a tweed jacket, sage shirt, and matching tan slacks, approached me carrying a small plastic tub brimming with said golden fruit. The subdued stench of the durian rose above the heavy florals of the garden. None of the flowers wilted, unlike me.

He reminded me of my philosophy professor—relaxed and wholly unaware of his attractiveness. A slight gray shadow covered his jaw, matching the ruffled state of his short hair. A tiny birthmark, the shape of a streak, decorated his left temple.

I sank into my chair. "Thank you for coming to the interview."

He took the seat across from me.

Before he popped open the container, my hand covered the lid, keeping it shut. "It might be better to not eat in this case. This is an interview, and it's easier to enunciate without it. Plus, food can get stuck in your teeth, which is embarrassing for you, and for me."

"I guess I can have my snack later. This is Musang King. It's one of the best. I was going to offer you some."

I smiled. "I appreciate the gesture."

"Durian gets such a bad rap. People are so outraged by the smell that they overlook how delicious it is." He tapped his chest. "I'm being shunned as a connoisseur of this magnificent fruit."

"I understand your position. If only it smelled like a mango. I mean that would help, right?"

He crossed his arms over his chest and muttered, "Who the hell wants to be a boring mango?"

I tried my best to be an acceptable mango. It made navigating through relationships and society easier, though I feared I might be a durian disguised as a mango. "There are those out there who prefer to be more socially acceptable. It's not a moral judgment— it's a statement of fact."

"That's on them. They can live out their boring lives without knowing there's so much more out there. I've spent too many of my seventy-two years in existence to deny myself something that brings me joy. Can you imagine living like that?"

Joy was ephemeral—like chasing light, hoping to touch it. Security or financial stability were more important than joy.

Mr. Durian studied my face. He winked and snapped his fingers. "Ha! You're a mango, aren't you?"

Chapter Twenty-Seven

※

I might be?" I conceded. "Though mango is too flashy a fruit. I'm something quieter, like apple slices."

"Eat more durian. Get your chi up. Be flashy. Be bold. Live life! Trust me, I know all about this." Mr. Durian tapped the tabletop with his palm. "Have your voice heard."

My initial assessments of Mr. Dolphin and Mr. Durian hadn't been kind. We hadn't truly spoken—due in no small part to my olfactory prejudice—as they tended to keep to themselves. Their tight friendship made everyone else feel like an interloper.

That's how I had felt with Yanmei.

She hadn't sent any messages since our fight and neither had I.

"I guess we should get back to the interview. I'm sure you have more important things to do than to listen to me prattle on."

I took out my notebook and pen. "It will be three questions. You can answer any way you want."

"Is confidentiality a given?"

"Always."

He smacked the table, toppling the durian. "Drat. I wanted to know his answers. He has the worst talent for picking the wrong men. The idiot gets so distracted by whatever nice and shiny happens to be walking along."

"Have you told him this?"

"Yes. You can guess how well he listens."

I narrowed my eyes. "Have you two dated?"

Mr. Durian made a choking noise. Before I had a chance to get up or offer to help, he held out his hand to stop me. It took him a moment to recover. "Hell no!"

The emphatic answer invited no further polite probing, but his red thread had responded with gusto. I filed the information away for use at a future date.

"Okay, let's start. What do you look for in a partner?"

"A man who accepts me for who I am. He must be intelligent—someone I can talk to for hours without either of us getting bored. The best conversations are natural and sentient, starting off in one place with an unknown destination. I can never be with anyone I can't talk to. He needs to at least like durian, but it's not required that he love it as much as I do."

The biggest hurdle in his answer might be the last clause.

"What kind of relationship are you looking for?"

"I want forever. I won't settle for less."

"Last question: Do you believe in love?"

"It's the most powerful force in the universe. Nothing is more precious. Our existence hinges on the careful nourishment of love in our lives. The core of our humanity relies on it. As for romantic love, when reciprocated, it can be the most selfish and satisfying gift you can give yourself."

I finished writing down his answers and closed the book. "Thank you."

"I know I can't ask you about answers from specific people, but I'm curious if you see a pattern."

"Everyone answered that they believe in love." I tucked the notebook back into my purse. "It's a beautiful thought, isn't it?"

"Would someone cynical about love be looking for the services of a matchmaker though?"

"Your dear leader over there is such a person."

Mr. Durian leaned in closer to whisper, "If I offered you a bribe, would you show me his answers?"

"Ha! No."

The current subject of our discussion stood by the entrance, a scowl affixed to his long, narrow face. Mr. Porcupine leaned against one of the wooden boxed planters. He made eye contact with me and tapped his watch face.

I wasn't late. I'd budgeted enough time in between interviews. He was early.

"I better go. He looks like he's in a mood." Mr. Durian rushed to his feet. "If I were you, I'd run. You're younger, you should be faster."

As Mr. Porcupine sat down, the comfortable ambient temperature of the indoor garden became unbearable. I tugged at the collar of my blouse and wiped my sweaty hands on my jeans. His scowl seemed permanent, weighing down his narrow face. I longed to tug the corners of his mouth upward and see if it would soften his severe features. Of course, I'd also prefer to live to see another day.

"It shouldn't surprise me that you don't have a professional office. Conducting business here might be violating some building rules."

"I'm having meetings. Are you suggesting those are banned now?" The sarcasm in my voice matched his. "What about dancing? Or laughing?"

"Don't be ridiculous." His dark brown eyes glared at me from behind his glasses. "Of course you'd take the warning as some sort of criticism. Oh, there's plenty of that, but I doubt you'd have the mettle to hear it."

"Try me." My hands curled into fists under the table.

"This"—he made a sweeping gesture over me—"is why I shouldn't have signed up in the first place. You think you know what you're doing, but you don't. Those matches were pure luck or whomever you manage to bump into along the way. There's no skill involved."

I lifted my chin. "I delivered results."

"So you can go back and use the rest of us as some sort of example to lure more money from more desperate seniors?"

"Your friends are happy. Doesn't that mean anything?"

"They might be now. How long will it last?"

To some extent, I'd expected this from him. He had never shown anything but disdain for me. The old man acted as if he were the consumer protection bureau and I were some sort of predatory scammer. I cared about every single one of my clients, including him.

"There is no guarantee after the match. The couple is free to proceed however they please."

"Convenient how you take no responsibility after your 'work is done.' I can't understand how your Society allows you to operate under the table. It's unethical and until you get certified, you're not getting me as a client."

Though I was planning to petition the Society, he didn't need to know that. Mr. Porcupine had made his decision—I was unworthy. He would have been a pain to work with and, with that attitude, near impossible to match. After he was pressured into enlisting my services, this was buyer's remorse.

"That's fine. Consider yourself no longer my client."

He wrinkled his brow. "Good."

For a brief second, his narrow face softened—the way it was

when he was around the Old Ducks—before resuming its usual glower as he left the garden in brisk, efficient strides.

Losing him as a client sucked financially, but mental health–wise and stress-wise, I was better off. Mr. Porcupine concluded the set of interviews for this morning. Mr. Moon's meeting was later that afternoon. Of all the Old Ducks, he was the most eager to see me. One ungrateful former client wouldn't ruin my day.

My client roster was growing toward my goal of financial freedom and accreditation.

Each was a step to my dream.

Dad had sent me a message asking to meet for a dim sum lunch. I guessed he missed me after we skipped the family dinner this week. With my last appointment cut short, it was time to cleanse my palate with delicious wu gok dumplings.

Chapter Twenty-Eight

✳

Dad's wide smile made me forget the minus-twenty-four-degree windchill outside. Our dim sum haunt was in the heart of Scarborough at Brimley Road and Sheppard Avenue. The restaurant was sandwiched between an herbal shop and a dentist's office. Open twenty-four hours, we'd sneaked in here a few times at night after Mom had gone to bed—at Dad's suggestion, with which I happily complied. It was our secret happy place.

"I ordered three baskets of your favorite already." He lifted the teapot in the center of the table and filled my cup with jasmine tea. "I also got har gow, phoenix claws, soup dumplings, salted egg congee, and youtiao."

"Thanks, Dad." I took my seat and sipped the tea. "How's your arthritis?"

"It's much better. Thank you. Your mother mentioned you're responsible for the sessions."

He gripped his chopsticks with ease as my tense late-night exchange with Mom faded. He complained it was worse in winter.

A twinge of regret passed through me for having protested for even a moment.

"You know what's coming up soon, yes?"

I had no idea. Between work and research, there'd been no time to fit in anything resembling leisure. My brain scrambled to focus on this time with Dad instead of thinking about clients or worrying about Yanmei.

"I'm sorry, Dad, I've been a bit busy. What's going on?"

He scooped the steaming congee into his bowl. "Your mother's birthday. It's a big one, fifty-four."

Years that didn't end with a five were big, the rest, special. Those ending in zero, spectacular.

"Right. Has she told you what she wants?"

"Well." He formed his hands into a steeple and tapped his fingertips against each other. "We were out last weekend in Yorkville. She felt bad about that purse she missed out on, so I took her shopping. She came home with a beautiful limited-edition Coach handbag. It's much better than the purse. Anyway, she walked into a jewelry store, and she fell in love with a diamond tennis bracelet."

Of course she had. If Mom walked into a dollar store, she'd find the only item that sold for five. The woman's gift for finding the most expensive item anywhere was a game Dad and I kept track of. Factoring in the canceled credit card, their finances teetered, toppling, tipping in my direction . . . The mortgage was never paid off; they consolidated their consumer debt into it every two years.

They had tried using a financial adviser, once. Mom and Dad went into the meeting hoping for miracles; they walked out humiliated. The company's name was now used as a curse.

"How much?"

"Three thousand five hundred. I asked the shop to put it on hold until tomorrow. I had to talk to you first."

My monthly rent for a bangle. His income went straight into

their shared bank account Mom managed. She dispensed a small allowance to him. He couldn't afford this, but I couldn't either. I was living off savings that were depleting faster than my work replenished. If I agreed, I would only have four months left instead of six.

And that didn't even consider the other money I'd given them already.

"Dad, that's a lot . . . I mean—"

"You don't know how stressed she is. It'll make her so happy, you know?" He transferred some of the crispy squid onto my plate. "Jewelry is special. It perks her up. She'll know how much she's loved and valued. Without you being home, it's been tough. I just want to be . . . I want her to be happy."

He wanted to be happy, and if she wasn't, he wouldn't be.

My mother's happiness, and lack thereof, governed the house. Its absence infected us with misery while on rare occasions, its abundance elevated its residents. The most my father and I hoped for was her normal prevailing sense of seething dissatisfaction.

He lived with this every day. I understood his motivation to please her.

I'd been willing to spare his physical pain, so why balk now at easing his mental and emotional one? I'd do anything for Dad. No one in this world loved me more.

I patted his hand. "I'll make it work, Dad."

"Thank you." He squeezed my hand in return. "I love you. I'm lucky to have you as a daughter."

"I love you too."

AFTER LUNCH, I STOPPED BY Mr. Regret's apartment. Having gone on his dates with Mabel and Flora, he'd sent me a message requesting advice.

"Thank goodness you're free." Mr. Regret opened the door. Flour and sugar dusted the green apron tied around his waist. "I'm in desperate need of your advice."

I took off my shoes and placed them onto the mat by the door. "Why? Did the dates not go well?"

"Maybe too well? I like both of them. I don't want to choose." He wiped his forehead, smearing it white. "I'm so stressed."

I made a gesture across my forehead. "You have something . . ."

He reached for a nearby tea towel and wiped his face.

"You shouldn't be stressed. Tell me everything."

We settled at the kitchen table surrounded by trays of savory parmesan and leek Danish. The beautiful rectangular pastries contained crisscross windows of green, showcasing roasted bits of leek. The aroma aroused my appetite despite having already eaten lunch.

He began packing dozens of the cooling pastries into plastic containers. "Both ladies are lovely. Mabel and I went to see a foreign film and had dinner at a Korean grill. She's lively. She makes me think of all the things I haven't done yet."

"And Flora?"

"She's so sweet. Much quieter than Mabel. She's the type of person you can sit with and not have to say a word, like we're enjoying each other's presence without any pressure. It was wonderful. She then told me about the meaning of 'hygge.' It's a complex Danish concept relating to happiness."

His thread reacted both times he spoke about them. I didn't envy his decision. Both women messaged me after their date, eager for a next one. I wasn't surprised about the interest in Mr. Regret. He was the sweetest Old Duck.

"I can arrange another set of dates to help you decide. I do caution that prolonging the process isn't good for you, Mabel, or Flora."

"So after seeing them again I'll need to make my decision?" The fret in his voice matched the nervous energy in which he packed each container. He patted down each lid to ensure the air-tight lock.

"Not necessarily that quickly, but it's not a situation to dawdle over. And before you ask me, no, I won't tell you who I think you should be with. It's all up to you."

"What if I make the wrong choice?"

The corners of his eyes crinkled, dispersing to create miniature steps on his forehead. Even if I wanted to give him better advice, I couldn't relate to the situation, nor the agony of making the wrong choice. Not when it came to love. As for decisions, they never gave me any grief. Impulsiveness made sure of it.

On the other hand, Mr. Regret had made one wrong choice and it shaped him. He carried the consequences as a warning for all future decisions.

"You won't." I clasped his hands in mine. "You'll win in the end no matter what. Love is the prize in either path."

His worried expression deepened. "Maybe wait until next week to schedule the dates?"

"I can do that. It's whatever you are comfortable with."

My phone buzzed in my pocket from Mr. Moon confirming our meeting in ten minutes. "I need to go. I have another interview."

"Bring him a box for me and take two for yourself." Mr. Regret stacked three containers. "He's excited to see you."

"I think out of all of you, he's the keenest for my services."

AFTER DROPPING OFF THE TREATS at my apartment, I hurried to Mr. Moon's condo on the sixth floor. Out of all the questionnaires, his taste in women had no bounds. He was an unusual one.

Madam Yeung would have been fascinated and used him as a case study for her students. She'd have amazing advice, but shame kept me silent. Yanmei was the next best substitute. I would not apologize; to do so implied I had been in the wrong—that I was incapable of making my own decisions.

But I missed her.

I had chosen her and she had chosen me.

Before I changed my mind or overthought it, I sent a short message to her about my peculiar client.

Tell me all about it after your interview. Missed you.

But first, a chat with the charismatic Mr. Moon—the one I hoped would be the easiest to match.

Chapter Twenty-Nine

✥

Mr. Moon's condo was closer in style to my minimalistic sensibilities. He created a space meant to entertain—an antique liquor cabinet, spacious quartz countertops with leather barstools, a cubic sectional with draped plush throws and velvet pillows along with a tiled gas-insert fireplace. Popular magazines were stacked on the coffee table with playing cards, dominoes, and a mahjong set stored below. Before he retired, he was an insurance broker who held parties on a weekly basis for professional and personal reasons.

"Welcome, Sophie!" He greeted me at the door. "Come, let's talk in the living room."

"These are for you." I handed him the container of Danish from Mr. Regret. "I think you already know who they're from."

I took off my shoes and placed them on the mat by the door. He gestured to the guest slippers stacked nearby. I helped myself to a pair and followed him down the hall.

His round glasses reminded me of John Lennon's, framing his milk-chocolate-brown eyes. His long nose had a slight bump that created the perfect shelf for the bridge of his spectacles.

"I'm so impressed with the matches you've made with my friends." Mr. Moon set the Danish aside on the counter, pulled out a prepared charcuterie plate from the fridge, and set it on the modern coffee table in the living room. He poured me a drink from a glass carafe full of a homemade fruity beverage. "Strawberry lemonade made fresh this morning."

"Thank you so much."

His hosting skills were impeccable. Each piece of sliced meat was positioned at matching angles with equal spacing. He arranged heart-shaped folded paper napkins with damask patterns alongside spotless cutlery. Even the cold pitcher showed no sign of condensation. The care and presentation of everything showcased a meticulousness I hadn't expected.

These Old Ducks.

They never failed to surprise.

I prided myself in being an excellent judge of character. It was the trait that brought Yanmei and I together as we bonded over how well we sized up everyone in our cohort. She rationalized that this was a professional necessity—it was a skill we needed after school. "How are we supposed to match people if we can't assess them thoroughly? Finding the perfect person requires us to see all the warts, including in the places our clients don't want us to know about." The conversation devolved into which places on the human body were the worst spots, excluding the face of course.

"Are you having an easier time finding clients?"

The women I'd approached for Mr. Particular had expressed continued interest in my services. The ladies were impressed by my client.

"I think so. It's one of those businesses where having one successful client yields new contacts and testimonials. Similar to what you were doing before you retired."

"The insurance business is built on people."

I pulled out my notebook and readied my questions. My phone buzzed in my purse. My stomach wobbled. Mom.

Mr. Moon detected the subtle sound. "Do you need to take that?"

I wanted to say no. I wanted to proceed with the interview and ignore the call, but the consequences would be dire. "I'm sorry. It's my mother."

I picked up the phone and walked to the hallway to answer it. "Mom, I'm in the middle of an interview right now. Is something wrong?"

"Your father needs a ride to his acupuncture appointment to-night. I can't drive him because I have my book club. Transit isn't an option. It's uptown."

"I didn't know you had book club."

"This is my first meeting. It's at Zeny's penthouse. I've been waiting for an invite for close to six months. It's an exclusive gath-ering. I even read the book."

The excitement in her voice was palpable.

Saying no would lead to yet another argument. I sighed.

"I'll do it. Send me the details."

"My birthday is coming up in a few weeks. Your father and I—"

"Mom, I am in the middle of an interview with a client. I'll talk to you later, okay?"

"So selfish. Family should be your highest priority. Sophie, this is not the end of the discussion."

I allowed her the satisfaction of ending the call. I gathered the brewing storm of my emotions and buried it deep. Plastering a natural smile on my face, I returned to the living room. Years of practice. Suppression became a useful superpower.

"I hope everything is well?"

"As well as can be." I opened my notebook. "Now, where were we?"

"Parents are complicated, aren't they?"

Nothing wrong with his hearing.

"The day we find out our parents are flawed people is the first sign of adulthood. It isn't getting your first job or paying your bills. It's the moment you see the world for the first time on your own terms."

By that definition, I'd reached adulthood much earlier than most.

"I didn't mean to pry."

"No, it's all right." I settled into my seat. "My mother doesn't approve of my career. It's caused more friction than normal."

"She should be proud. Matchmakers are rare. The prestige and the status. The question then becomes, why isn't she happy?"

"Because she's rarely happy."

Mr. Moon filled my empty glass with more lemonade. "Ah, one of those. Then nothing will satisfy her. I hope you're not waiting for her to come around. It's healthier to not ask for what she can't give you."

Mom might not give me her approval, but, like any parent, at least she loved me.

"Sorry if I overstepped." He handed me a miniature fork meant for fancy pickles, cheese, and sliced meats, a patterned paper napkin, and a small plate. "The look on your face reminded me of myself when I was younger. My own family life wasn't like any of my friends."

"Same for me."

"And yet here we are—thriving in spite of them. When you get to my age, it's hard to justify worrying about what people expect of you, especially if it overrides your own happiness. And you're here right now to help me with mine."

"Yes, shall we start?" I smiled. "What do you look for in a partner?"

He made an exaggerated thinking gesture—tapping his temples, tightening his brows, and scrunching his mouth. A slight wink betrayed that the show was for my benefit.

I broke my impartiality and giggled.

"I want a woman I can't have. Someone who plays hard to get, makes me work to fit her schedule. There's something so compelling about chasing after the unattainable."

I jotted down the answer. As tempting as it was to explore this further, I refused to break my personal rule. Trust the process. Yanmei and I would discuss this later.

"What kind of relationship are you looking for?"

"I want something that is risky and exciting. It doesn't have to be permanent. I'd even prefer if it wasn't. You appreciate it even more when it is fleeting. Every second together is so precious that you can't waste it."

"Do you believe in love?"

He narrowed his eyes. "What do you mean? Love is a general and nebulous term."

"It's up to you to interpret the term. There is no right or wrong answer. Most clients find it to be a philosophical exercise."

He wrinkled his brow. The comical display of thinking he had exhibited before was a close portrayal of what he seemed to grapple with now. Mr. Moon seemed perplexed.

His hesitation might be related to his previous answers.

"Can I abstain? I'm afraid my answer might not be suitable."

Interesting. I'd never had someone respond like that before. I preferred if all my questions had answers, but the comfort of my client was my primary concern.

"Yes. This interview is about you."

He exhaled. The calming gesture returned his joviality.

"Thank you. Now that the hard part is over, I hope you can stay and help me finish off the food."

I relaxed into my seat and held out my empty plate.

YANMEI WORE A PAIR OF plush cat ears as a peace offering on our call. The silver sequins on the pink faux fur headband sparkled under her overhead lamp. I won them for her at an arcade in Shanghai. She appreciated the gift but never wore them, until now. I'd never felt more elated or relieved to have her back in my world again. "So, tell me about this weird case you have."

I told her about Mr. Moon and his unusual answers both in the questionnaire and the interview.

"How old is he again?"

"He's seventy."

"Vigorous old like my uncle Ollie." Yanmei tapped her chin. "This only means one thing. It can only be . . ."

Unavailable women.

Risk.

I winced. "Mr. Moon has a thing for affairs with married women."

Chapter Thirty

✳

There are services and websites that address this. He can use his own devices to find what he's looking for. I do wonder why he's chosen a matchmaker. This isn't something we do." Yanmei walked into her kitchen toward the stainless-steel fridge. She fetched three little Yakult containers and proceeded to peel the bright red foil covers. "Well, it's a gray area. We're supposed to build connections, not break them."

"There're a few matchmakers who do this though."

"Right, but they don't get much prestige. If you go down that route, they will be the majority of your clients. Is this what you want?"

When she and I had discussed our career trajectory, we never considered catering to those who wanted affairs. It was a niche market that, once you decided to dive in, barred you from having regular clientele. Facilitating extramarital affairs was a covert and often dangerous pursuit. Madam Yeung had been adamant about the potential lawsuits and consequences. The clients we took early on defined the shape of our careers, the kind of patrons we attracted, and our specialty. While Yanmei had been targeting the wealthy workaholics of Singapore and shaping her future, my success with the Old Ducks would send other seniors in my direction.

Neither of us wanted to facilitate infidelity.

She sucked down her Yakult. "What are you going to do?"

I liked Mr. Moon. Despite my hypothesis that he was attracted to and was looking for trysts with married women, I felt he had a deep-seated hope to find a connection.

If he had been Mr. Porcupine, I'd have walked away without a second thought.

"I have to see for myself. If we're right, then I'll decide if I still want to help him."

"Sounds fair." Yanmei finished the last container of her yogurt drink. She leaned forward as her expression sobered. "Are we going to talk about the other night?"

Was there a way to pretend that it had never happened? I'd live with ignoring an elephant in my bathtub, but Yanmei wouldn't let anything go unresolved. "Do we have to?"

"Yeah. I'm worried about you—you, not your career. I know you'll be a master one day. It's why I was drawn to you: you're the smartest kid with the most potential. I know that as soon as you file your petition to be accredited, Madam Yeung will vouch for you. It's everything else, Soph. The stuff outside of work."

"And what is it about my life that you have a problem with?"

"That you don't have one outside of the job. And because you don't, your family sees this as an opportunity to take advantage of you. I wouldn't be surprised if they saw your success as a reason to ask for more money. I mean, that's how you're supposed to prove that you love them, right?"

I bit my lip. Despite the distance, she knew exactly how my parents had acted. But she didn't understand why. She grew up in a happy family. She never had to wonder whether she was loved.

Whether she had been wanted. Whether they would have been happier without her.

"They do love me. I don't have to prove anything. Just because we're not as wealthy as you and your family doesn't mean it's wrong if I help them."

The moment the words slipped from my mouth, I wanted to cram them back in. Yanmei viewed her family's affluence as a millstone around her neck—that she needed to prove her success on her own terms. On good days, she acknowledged it and appreciated the opportunities it provided, and on the rare bad days, she questioned her identity outside of her family, the validity of her achievements.

"I'm sorry, that was a low blow." I held my forehead with my right hand. "It's complicated. My dad needs his acupuncture treatments, and there's always drama surrounding Mom."

Yanmei's voice softened. "You're not going to get ahead if you allow them to squeeze all your success out of you. You'll always be behind: their demands keeping pace with what you're making. And who knows what else they'll ask for besides money."

She didn't need me to agree.

"This is why it's important that you have a life outside of work. They need to see that they aren't your only priority. You can have it all, including a certain Mr. Particular."

"We've gone over this. I don't like him that way. He's just a client."

"You're too good a matchmaker to have failed to find him a match three times in a row! And every time he's with you, his thread reacts! If it were anyone else, you wouldn't question it. You would have matched him with yourself."

She had the right to criticize my troubled family life—I complained about it often enough—but I never talked about having a romantic relationship of any kind. Yet she kept pushing, never letting go.

"It's not the same. You need to stop this."

"Tell me that you don't care about him, haven't had thoughts about him, that—if you dared to allow yourself to—you haven't dreamed about a future with him."

I hadn't, wouldn't, couldn't. I had no spark. Mr. Particular was a gentleman. Our relationship was strictly professional.

Except when we touched.

And the way he looked at me.

It didn't matter. No red thread, no future, no point in wishing for things you can't have. It only leads to heartbreak.

He was a client. That's how it had to remain.

"It doesn't matter. I can't. It won't work."

"Give yourself permission. I mean, you won the fight to go to matchmaking school in Shanghai. Isn't this a similar battle?"

No. Going to Shanghai had been a matter of life and death. My career meant my independence—to move out, be on my own, to be away from Mom.

I was struggling to hold on to my freedom. There was no room left for anything else, especially Mr. Particular.

"He's being matched now. He'll be out of my life soon."

Yanmei rested her chin on her hands. "Is that what you want?"

I collapsed in bed. "Yes. He's a client. Nothing else."

"There's more to life than your career!"

"No, there isn't. I have to work my ass off to get accredited. My family is pressuring me, and I'm doing all I can to make sure I can stay in this condo. Moving back home will kill me, Yanmei!"

I almost screamed the last sentence. My chest heaved, letting out the underlying stress that threatened to suffocate me. I was treading water without any movement forward. All my efforts to stay afloat left little reserves to challenge my parents, let alone Yanmei.

"I'm saying that you can have it all. You deserve it. All of it. Don't push him away because you're afraid."

"I can't do this with you. I have to go take my dad to his acupuncture appointment."

"So you paid for his treatment and now you're his chauffeur. What's next? Their mortgage payments?"

"I'm not—"

"You will give them as much as they're willing to take, and what they want is everything. I'm not there to help stop them."

I straightened my back. "I can handle myself."

"When was the last time you told them no?"

My finger hovered over the red button. I wanted to end the call. Instead of giving me the support I wanted, she put me through an interrogation.

"You know I'm under so much stress right now. You should be on my side."

"I am! I always am. But you're deflecting. I'm trying to get you to see—"

"See what? That I'm making sacrifices because I love my parents? I know I complain about them, but I do love them. They're all I have. There's nothing wrong with being a good daughter."

"Yes there is when the cost is your own happiness!" Yanmei exploded as she leveled her gaze at me; even across continents, it was as if we were sitting together in the living room of our Shanghai apartment. "I push you because I love you and want the best for you. You have the biggest heart of anyone I know, but until you figure out that you deserve to put yourself first when it comes to love and happiness, we'll continue to argue. Call me when you decide to stop being a martyr."

She hung up, robbing me of the chance of having the last word.

I didn't have the opportunity to process how this conversation had played out. Dad had his appointment. I was a good daughter, and for now, it had to be enough.

Chapter Thirty-One

T hank you for taking me to my appointment." Dad patted my arm before unbuckling his seat belt. "Your mother told me how you've offered to take me to my sessions from now on because of her book club. It's kind of you. I know how busy you are."

I smiled.

I didn't have the heart to correct him. Mom never asked me, she simply assumed. Her excitement about her book club had been palpable on our call; nothing would prevent her from going. With Dad's appointments, my schedule on Thursday nights was full.

Free time was scarce. My downtime was spent researching, making calls, and expanding my contacts, in addition to being available for my clients.

"This book club is making her happy. I'm happy when she's happy," he declared, his last words materializing as a heart-shaped puff from the cold air.

I had wondered how deep his love for Mom went, as though quantified into strata layers like geologists excavate. He contorted himself into the worst knots to please and placate her. It wasn't that he was compelled to—he derived genuine pleasure when Mom praised him or appreciated his efforts. The red thread between them had always been a thick, heavy braid with an occasional minor knot. Their relationship baffled me. He loved her to his core, yet no one in the world had the power to make him more miserable.

"Dad, how much do you love Mom?"

He arched his brows. "Like, in quantity?"

"Yeah, like do you love her more than you love yourself?"

"I do. She means everything. I love her very much. Your mother is someone who I admire because she surpasses me in so many ways. I trust her more than anyone else. She always knows what's best."

"Mom was your first girlfriend, wasn't she?"

"Yes, and she chose me. There were other boys hanging around her, but I was the lucky one." He patted my cheek. "It hurts that you two don't get along. Know that she loves you and wants what's best for you."

This wasn't the first time Dad had told me this. This was one of many similar speeches—his way of trying to maintain peace. To him, a mother's love was as obvious as the sun in the sky. To question it was tantamount to blasphemy. The cost was mine to bear; I was expected to capitulate in every scenario.

"You should come inside for a minute. I have some ham and cheese buns I picked up at the bakery for you this morning." Dad opened the car door.

Those pastries were a childhood favorite. There was a Chinese bakery by his work. He often brought home a few for me as extra treats in my lunch. He continued until I left for Shanghai.

Because of him, I had forgiven my mother for a multitude of transgressions.

I grabbed my purse and followed my father inside.

Dad had packed up the box of buns in a plastic bag from the local Asian supermarket.

"I hope you're not planning to leave before speaking with me." Mom stood in the hallway in her batik nightgown.

"Mom," I blurted, juggling the box. "You're home?"

"The book club was canceled after I called you. It looks like I'll be making my debut next week." A glowing shine covered her smooth face—one of her expensive French night creams. Afterward, she massaged her face with retinol serums to promote blood flow. Gauging her mood after her skin care routine was trickier than usual.

I swallowed any retort or protest about consulting me before deciding it was my job to drive Dad to his acupuncture therapy.

"Raymond, why don't you take your shower. I need to talk to Sophie for a bit."

Dad headed upstairs.

I wanted nothing more than to run back to the car and drive away, winter tires squealing.

"Is this about your birthday?"

She placed her hands on her hips. "It is. Now that you're working and so successful, I think we can have the dinner at a nicer restaurant, don't you?"

She refused to acknowledge or praise my success—unless it benefited her. "Which one are you looking at?"

"That French restaurant with the Michelin star. What is it called? Papillon?"

Yanmei had visited the Tokyo location after making reservations six months ahead. The world-renowned chain originated in Paris. The innovative chef trained in classical French cuisine before spending two decades in Asia. The result: a beautiful fusion of East and West. The prix fixe menu started at five hundred per person. "That's too much just to poop out the gold they put in the food," she noted.

"The reservations will be hard to get. It might be a good idea to have an alternative." No point in mentioning the cost; that was my responsibility.

"I'm sure you can get us a table with your newfound connections. I mean, you do have two weeks."

"Mom, I can't guarantee—"

"Haven't you told me that you can make things happen? Your father thinks you can do it. He talks about how proud of you he is. He thinks you are destined for great things. You don't want to disappoint him, do you?"

Mom fought dirty. She dragged Dad into this because she knew I wouldn't say no. My failure would be his, for the crime of believing in me. "I'll try, but please don't tell anyone."

"I've already told Zeny. She's impressed. She said I'm lucky to have such a devoted daughter." Mom stroked my cheek. "Don't try. Do. Nothing in this world is accomplished without a measure of hard work, Sophie."

I RETURNED TO MY APARTMENT mentally exhausted. Spending time with my father had no expiration date, but the minutes with Mom did. Reservations for Papillon were at least five months out. After reviewing the comments on their Yelp page, where secured reservations were celebrated and envied, I emailed the restaurant and begged to be on their cancellation list. A reservation, even on the wrong day, had to be better than no reservation at all.

My financials were a mess. Line after line of negative entries without enough positive ones. I was losing money faster and faster. I needed more clients, but I didn't have enough time to cater to my current roster. Mr. Regret, Mr. Dolphin, Mr. Durian, Mr. Moon, and Mr. Particular. I had to hang on until they were matched and I was paid. It was going to be tight. White rice and luncheon meat, with one packet of ramen every two days as a treat. No more candy purchases.

For Mr. Dolphin and Mr. Durian, I contacted matchmakers outside of Toronto, hoping that they had compatible older gay clients. The practice of consulting with our brethren was beneficial to both parties; cooperation was encouraged by the Society as the reciprocity built rapport and expanded the pool of potential matches. My specialized hunt yielded connections with matchmakers in Vancouver, New York, and New Jersey, who promised to notify me if any potentials became available. I'd done some preliminary research into senior hobby groups and leisure clubs as both loved to travel and found a few leads. The issue became their preferences—Mr. Dolphin, through his questionnaire, expected to see pictures of his prospects first. It was a prerequisite I didn't agree with, one we'd need to sort out tomorrow morning.

My phone buzzed.

Mr. Particular.

"Hey, how did the date with Patty go?"

A crinkling static noise in the background muffled his voice.

"I'm sorry, I didn't get that. Can you repeat?"

The call dropped. Technology, got to love it.

Instead of calling back, he texted: The date was terrible. We need to talk in person. I may need to reassess. I'm losing confidence in your abilities to find me a match.

Chapter Thirty-Two

⋈

A droplet of doubt possessed the power to pollute a sea of confidence. The lights dimmed around me while the music from my record player quieted to match my darkening mood.

I'd never questioned my abilities as a matchmaker. What happened to Fanny was tragic, but it wasn't because of my skills or lack thereof. Everything else might detonate around me, but my calling as a matchmaker was my safe haven.

I'd waited my entire life; I was damned good at what I did.

I'd fix this.

It would be a full day of client meetings, beginning with Mr. Particular at a Japanese pancake shop five blocks from my building. The lure of fluffy, spongy soufflé pancakes bestowed a receptive atmosphere for my pleading to be given another chance.

I arrived early and secured the booth away from everyone. Round chestnut tables with upholstered cream chairs matched the stained benches while buttercream paint splashed with wide stripes of saffron decorated the interior walls. The little cafe was half-full: teens skipping morning classes, moms on stroller dates, a handful of seniors chattering at a long table across the room. The blend of cloudlike perms contrasted against the bristly tones of gray.

I smiled.

My time with the Old Ducks had made me more aware of this demographic. I'd grown to envy their freedom and vivacity. Catering to them was a specialty I never considered but now embraced.

Mr. Particular appeared by the entrance. I waved him over. He approached our table and hung his wool coat on a nearby hook on the wall.

"I'm glad you suggested this place." He scooted into the seat across from me. "I haven't had decent pancakes in a while."

We settled into a routine of perusing the menu and discussing safe topics like the cold weather to keep the conversation light. Nothing in his handsome face or his body language indicated agitation. Agony was in my knowing that the pleasantry was temporary.

Once the server took our orders, Mr. Particular leaned forward and threaded his fingers together. "I need you to walk me through your process. How you thought Patty was a good candidate."

"She's attractive and well-connected. I was hoping for an opposites attract situation. The other matches were well tailored to your tastes, yet they didn't work out. I tried something different."

His dark eyes studied me, weighing my words. There was nothing to do but face the intensity of his scrutiny. I believed in what I'd said. No other rational answer existed. Yanmei would protest, but she wasn't here. Thank God.

"You were off the mark with her." He pressed his palms together. His red thread perked up from his chest, active and curious. "I wonder if what I want is possible."

"What do you mean?"

"You know that my preferences are specific. Am I asking too much?"

The sincerity in his deep voice caught me off guard. If he were any other client, I would have grasped his hands and reassured him, but I was afraid that touching him would unravel me. "You want what you want. You shouldn't compromise."

"What if I wanted what I can't have?"

His eyes, unblinking, bore into my soul. His dark red thread glowed brighter and brighter; a desire to forge a connection. Like Mr. Wolf and Beatrice. Mr. Sorrow and Clara.

Mr. Particular and . . . me?

Our order arrived, breaking our communion.

Two plates of fruit-covered soufflé pancakes with miniature pitchers of cream and maple syrup. A dusting of superfine sugar painted the strawberries, blueberries, and raspberries. My fluffy pancake jiggled to the slightest pressure under my fork. This reminded me of mousse cakes and our first meeting.

"So, are you going to test the wiggle factor?"

He already was. Balancing the plate on his fingertips, Mr. Particular bopped the pancake. The slight wobble brought a smile to his face. "Perfect. Then again, the food here is stellar."

"I haven't been here since before I left for Shanghai." I cut a quarter wedge away and let the piece melt inside my mouth. The familiar buttery sweet flavor took me back to the nervous, yet excited, version of me getting ready for my big trip. "I wanted to leave so badly."

"But you came back."

"Yes, Toronto is home. This is where I wanted to be. I always dreamed of being a matchmaker here. Despite what happened in Shanghai or how difficult it might be, this is what I wanted. I cannot imagine it any other way." I slid in my knife, cutting away another section. "Earlier, you said you wanted what you can't have. What do you mean?"

He grew quiet, with an awkwardness I hadn't seen in him before.

"I want . . . to date you, to be with you, to see if what I feel is happening between us can turn into something more. I understand how unprofessional this is, but nothing else has felt right. The women you matched me with, they weren't right. But every time I'm with you, it feels right." His unflinching gaze locked me into place. "Is there any chance you feel the same?"

His red thread lifted from his chest, sparking in a glorious fire arcing toward me and my empty heart. Would a thread of mine have reacted the same? He was certain we were a match—I had no way to know.

First Yanmei, now Mr. Particular. The same question—one I refused to entertain: Was this what I wanted?

"Why me?"

"Aside from my grandparents, you're the person I feel the most comfortable with. You know how hard it is for me to be myself versus what other people expect of me. The days I know I'll see you are brighter. Most of all, you make me happy."

I was comfortable around him as well, more comfortable than I had a right to be. Mr. Particular was the only man I'd ever spent a prolonged period of time with without breaking out into hives or injuring myself by running away. But he was my client. I was fine around clients.

I'd never been in a relationship, never learned what it felt like to be in love. That door was closed long ago. I didn't know if I liked him. What did "liking someone" mean anyway? I enjoyed our time together, but was that the same?

I lowered my eyes. "Can I be honest?"

"Please."

"I don't know. I can't know. Matchmakers have no red thread. Romance is for others, not me. I never considered any of this. It was never an option, so why think about it, right?" I fidgeted with my fork, running my fingernail over the raised groove along its handle. "I'm not saying that I don't feel the same. I don't know what I'm feeling. I need time to figure me out."

"I understand. When you're ready, I'll be here to hear whichever way you decide."

"Thank you."

We ate the rest of our meal in silence, preserving the delicate détente. I promised that within a month, I'd tell him how I felt.

One month.

I didn't want him to wait forever for someone who wasn't the right match.

I was a matchmaker, after all, first and foremost.

I RETURNED TO MY CONDO and focused on my career. My coming-out at the Su-Winstons' event had bombed. I needed something else to put myself out there. Debutantes held balls to commemorate their entrance to society. No money for a ball nor the desire for something that extravagant. I needed something like . . . an open house?

The perfect opportunity to showcase my successful matches, yet intimate enough to mingle and meet new potential clients. I'd invite Patty, Lindsay, and the others who had expressed their desire to sign up.

My first instinct was to call Yanmei, but telling her about it would mean telling her about what had happened between me and Mr. Particular. Avoiding the topic would only make her more annoying.

Not wanting to deal with that, I called someone closer—Mr. Regret.

"I'm thinking about having an open house. Do you think it's a good idea?"

"It's a fantastic idea. You can have it here! We have party rooms. I can talk our property manager into renting you one at a reduced rate. She owes me a favor." He chuckled. "If she wants to continue getting her pastry delivery, she'll agree. Do you have a time in mind?"

"I'm thinking in a couple of weeks. That should be enough time to notify everyone and get the word out." And after Mom's birthday dinner. No way to deal with that and an open house at the same time. I needed time to recover from whatever Mom decided to be unhappy about on her special day.

"I want to provide the pastries, and I won't take no for an answer. It will give me an opportunity to practice."

"Practice?"

"There's this amateur baking competition this national morning TV show is hosting. I think I might be good enough to enter."

I grinned. "You are! When is the contest? Tell me all about it."

I leaned back and listened to my dear friend's excitement. For a little while, I didn't have to worry about what I should be doing or what decisions I needed to make.

I had my career, and a friend who didn't judge me.

For now, it was enough to ignore the little fires burning around me.

Chapter Thirty-Three

❋

That afternoon's client meetings involved Mr. Durian and Mr. Dolphin. These two were more complicated than they appeared.

Our meeting was set at Mr. Durian's condo with reassurances that there would be no trace of the fruit. I trusted my client and knocked on the door. He opened it with a flourish.

Lilacs. The perfume of a field of lilacs greeted me as I stepped across the threshold.

"Lampe Berger. My friends' acceptance of durian is considered a sign of affection. They love me for who I am, and what I love, but there are methods to neutralize the smell until they grow to love me or the fruit."

"I appreciate the gesture." I took off my shoes and followed him down the hall.

Vintage illustrated advertisement posters from the fifties hung on the walls, from back before photography killed the art form. His aesthetic choice matched his philosophical nature. An overflowing bookcase filled the longest wall in the living room. A photography book on the art of the tea ceremony rested on the wooden inlay coffee table. A short stack of three Ray Bradbury books with worn spines sat beside a basket of Bosc pears on the kitchen counter. An eclectic reading collection: science fiction to mystery, philosophy to meditation.

"I requested this meeting because I'm concerned." Mr. Durian sat on the chocolate leather love seat while I took my place in the modern lounge chair across from him. "Consider this a warning. He'll try to bully you into sending him pictures of his prospective dates."

He knew his friend well.

"I have a meeting with him after you. I intend to dissuade him from it." I placed my purse on the floor beside the chair. "If he had wanted pictures, there are other methods, apps even, that are cheaper than a matchmaker."

"He's tried those. The old fool." Mr. Durian rolled his eyes. "You'll need to branch out of the city. I think he's dated every gay Asian man over fifty in the GTA. To think of it, you might branch out of province to be safe."

"Why do you think he hasn't found his soul mate?"

"As if I could only limit myself to one reason." He started listing every minute flaw belonging to his best friend from his superficiality to his gregariousness to his vulgar sense of humor. As he continued, becoming more animated, his red thread burst into a shower of sparks—an undeniable display of pyrotechnics. This man harbored deep feelings toward his friend. The passion in his argument was an indication of the veracity of his emotions.

It's what I suspected after witnessing his thread during the interview. I had to investigate these feelings and see if they were reciprocated. A decades-long friendship was at stake if this were to go awry.

I cleared my throat. "I think it's time to talk about your match."

He leaned back in his chair. His thread calmed, flowing out from his chest with a slight undulating movement. "You have someone in mind for me already?"

"I do."

Mr. Durian's forehead creased as his brows arched upward. "Who is it?" The conflict in his voice matched the agitation of his thread.

"The man whose shortcomings you listed."

He cradled his face and shook his head, his agonized whispers muffled by his own hands.

I had stated the obvious: his heart spoke through his thread, but only he knew how long he'd kept his secret and how it devoured him from the inside.

As far as the world was concerned, they were friends, nothing more.

I waited.

The tremors of Mr. Durian's shoulders subsided into steady deep breaths and his flailing thread calmed, returning to its normal state.

The release of heart-locked secrets can be cathartic or devastating. "Only I know, and this will remain between you and me. I have no intention of telling anyone about this without your consent."

His eyes were bleary as the wrinkles deepened. "The truth can both cage you and set you free. I was married once. I thought that if I lived the life everyone expected me to have, I'd forget how I felt and who I was. I came out to my wife first, then to my family. They all cut me from their lives."

"And now you're afraid you'll lose him too. That's why you haven't told him after all these years."

"He's my best friend. There is no one else in the world I care about more. I love him. Being with him all this time as his close friend was enough. I thought it was . . . until it wasn't."

"What changed?"

"You."

It wasn't the response I had expected. "Me?"

"You've matched my friends and made them happy. The Old Ducks were founded on the principle that we were destined to be content in friendship and companionship because romantic love was no longer an option for us. Here you come, proving that this isn't true."

Kindness and awe radiated from his voice, enveloping me in a warm glow like a fuzzy fleece blanket.

"Seeing them happy made me realize that this might be possible for me. Even though what I want is complicated." He lowered his head. "Am I a fool?"

"For wanting love? No, it's what most people want—though not everyone."

"Perhaps, but for people like us." He stopped short. Something in my manner had aroused a newfound curiosity, replacing his earlier distress. Was it in how my eyes shifted, avoiding his gaze? Mr. Durian arched a brow. "Love is something you want, right?"

"I . . ."

I'd been a fool to let something slip around such a clever mind. He was older than me by decades, but that didn't mean anything. Nothing got by him. These Old Ducks continued to surprise me with their wit, warmth, and quirks.

"You're a beautiful, charming young woman. It is surprising that you don't have someone in your life already. Have you been too busy catering to everyone's love life to attend to your own? Like the shoemaker's children who have no shoes."

A flush crept across my cheeks.

"It's complicated."

I had worked hard to get here and yet it felt as though everything was unraveling. Ground I thought solid kept shifting, revealing wide cracks. I gripped the only constants available—my career and my family—the positive and the negative.

"A fine pair we make then."

"I can help you with your problem if you want."

Conflict returned to his face. He squirmed in his seat and wrung his hands. As his matchmaker, I knew my duty. He'd entrusted me with his heart and his red thread. There was only one thing to do.

"I want to take you up on your offer."

"What offer?"

"I'd love to try the Musang King. We can figure everything out while we eat durian."

The smile on his face outshone the ray of sunlight streaming in from the balcony windows. He glowed from inside out, radiating gold like his favorite fruit. With a flourish, he fetched a container from the fridge.

Chapter Thirty-Four

※

Mr. Durian insisted I take a tub of his fruit back to my apartment. Having tasted it after all these years of close encounters, I enjoyed it more than I had imagined. The combination of sweet and savory notes and the custard texture was spellbinding. It reminded me of a smoky garlic cream. I'd been proven wrong, once more, by prejudging something.

We came up with a tentative plan: I'd suss out whether Mr. Dolphin felt the same way and regroup from there.

The heartbreak of unrequited love was the purest form of rejection. If there was a landfill of discarded hearts with their red thread tails, it would be bigger than the plastic continent in the Pacific Ocean. The time invested in that love mirrored the weight of the throwaway heart—the longer we spent pining, the heavier the mass.

I hoped that Mr. Durian's love was reciprocated and that today's meeting with Mr. Dolphin would unearth some clue, while also dissuade him from demanding pictures of new prospective matches.

Back to the eighth floor once more. Mr. Dolphin and Mr. Durian were next-door neighbors—another sign of their deep friendship. I pressed my hand against the wall of their apartments. What was Mr. Durian feeling? Severing a friendship this old would resemble an acrimonious divorce. Nothing would escape the ensuing collateral damage. No amount of financial reparation would mend a broken heart.

Please let this work out for both their sakes.

I rapped my knuckles against the wood.

Mr. Dolphin opened the door and invited me in.

My client's decor was luxurious. Fine finishes and furnishings—marble counters, custom modern pieces, and the various oil paintings decorating the walls. A pricey console table topped with a series of Inuit soapstone carvings dominated the hallway. He was the wealthiest Old Duck and part owner of the building management company. He displayed his affluence in a tasteful, subtle manner. The Herman Miller Lispenard gray sofa that I was sitting on cost more than three months' rent. He had the whole set, including the chaise and ottoman.

"Thank you so much for agreeing to meet." I set down my purse on the empty seat beside me. "I need to talk to you about your request to see photos before your arranged dates."

"Why? Is it an issue?" He crossed his arms. "Physical attraction is important. I don't want to go on a date with someone I find ugly."

"It is important. It's why I'm following what you've written down as desirable attributes when finding you a match. However, an open mind, free of prejudgment, is more valuable."

"When you buy something, you need to see it first. How am I supposed to find a soul mate without knowing what they look like? You can't discount biological urges."

My phone buzzed in my purse. I ignored it.

"Yes, physical attraction is significant, but that is why you have the date and then make your decision. Viewing a photo beforehand can prejudice a person such that they don't give the date a fair chance."

"It's more efficient to weed out the potentials and not waste any time."

"I would not present a potential I didn't think would suit your requirements. Making a snap judgment based on their appearance might lead you to discarding someone you're compatible with."

Another incoming call. Mom. Anyone else would have left a voice mail and waited for a return call. My purse shifted from the vibrations, the pleather fabric undulating in small waves.

"Efficiency is key. I've wasted enough of my time sorting through all the dreck. I'm not getting any younger." He sank into the chaise. "I'm tired of waiting. You don't know what it's like to spend a lifetime wishing for that one person who understands you, thrills you, and makes everything more."

He was correct. I didn't. But listening to my clients and their yearning for romantic love offered me a deeper understanding.

"And you will get that. Trust in the system, in my skills. I will arrange a suitable match for you that adheres to your tastes." I stopped and pivoted in an effort to approach the problem from a different angle. "You're a foodie. Do you like sushi?"

"I do. Where are you going with this?"

"Have you ordered omakase before?"

"Of course. No self-respecting foodie passes up the opportunity to try it once."

"Think of me as your chef. I pick out the best fresh ingredients and instead of serving up sushi, I'm serving up men."

"Clever." He began pacing. "So, this premise of going in not knowing who I'll be meeting is supposed to be a pleasant experience?"

"Yes. This is still a controlled situation. It isn't a random stranger plucked off the street."

My phone buzzed again. The angry low sound bucked my purse off the seat and onto the floor. My bag wiggled as if it was asserting its angry sentience.

"Somebody really wants to get ahold of you. Boyfriend?"

"No, mother."

"Worse." He sucked in his teeth, grimacing. "You better answer that before she disowns you."

I excused myself and took the call in the hallway. Mom's name splashed across the black screen. When I bought my phone, I'd made the conscious decision to label my mother by her full name, "Irene Go," while calls from my father were "Dad." A petty measure of control.

Things would be better if I was someone who never disappointed her. Or if our conversations weren't ladened with criticism. My feelings for Mom were complicated.

You couldn't choose your parents.

They loved you and you loved them.

I kept my voice low. "Hi, Mom. I'm sorry. I'm with a client."

Apologies always came unprompted. I had an endless supply of them for Mom, who took them all, leaving none unclaimed. Saying sorry became the go-to tactic to mitigate damage. Contrition had lost its meaning, but the years of capitulating had made me reluctant to subjugate myself to anyone else.

"Your job doesn't excuse you from ignoring your parents." The hiss from her words slithered into my ear. "I could never get away with such behavior with your amah."

"I'm sorry, Mom."

She snorted. "Don't let it happen again. It's not often that I need to talk to you immediately."

"Why? Are you okay? Is Dad okay? Did something happen?"

"Yes! Rosalind and Talia agreed to join us for my birthday dinner. They're the leaders of my book club. You are still working on the reservation?"

I calmed myself. Those were two extra plates I'd have to pay for—if I was even able to make the reservation happen. She'd never bothered to ask. She decided and I had to make it happen. "Mom, the bigger the guest list, the harder it will be for me to secure a table."

"It'll be these two then. A cozy table of five." There was a rare, excited giggle from her. "This is going to be the best birthday ever."

Until next year, that is.

I fabricated my excitement. Glad it was a phone call, my facial muscles were spared from having to perform. "It sure will be."

"Make sure you call me the minute you've confirmed the reservation. Don't disappoint me."

An extra thousand dollars for the VIP guests.

My attendance was compulsory, and I couldn't stick to glasses of water and not order anything. However splendid this meal might be, it would be ashes on my tongue from the circumstances, the company, and the cost.

By the time I returned to Mr. Dolphin's side, I had contained the storm of rage and frustration behind a glass facade.

"I was thinking some more while you were gone. I don't like this idea. Even in an omakase situation, I know I'm getting fresh fish and the format. That's what the photos provide—context. I'm a visual man."

I wanted to scream. "It's a terrible idea."

"But I am your client." He grinned and winked. He had trapped me. "This is what I want."

"Fine." I gritted my teeth.

Helter-skelter. He'd be the death of this matchmaker.

Chapter Thirty-Five

⋊⋉

The battle lost to Mr. Dolphin hurt. I tossed and turned all night, unable to get it out of my head.

I shouldn't have capitulated.

I should have tried harder to convince him.

My client didn't know his shallowness would be his undoing.

The emails I'd sent out to matchmakers outside the area had yielded some potential matches for Mr. Dolphin. The bachelors were decent in the looks department, but it was up to Mr. Dolphin's discerning tastes. I'd sent him three prospects this morning, and within five minutes, he replied with criticism about complexion problems or dodgy dental hygiene.

Yanmei would have told him where to go and how to get there. I missed her, but not enough to apologize or admit she might be right.

Mr. Moon had invited me to a large party thrown by one of his old real estate buddies. The penthouse apartment in Markham was a twenty-minute drive from our building. I hopped into his silver Lexus and withdrew a pack of Mintia Chocomints, offering him first choice. He shook the flat container over his palm and the tiny pale circular mints tumbled out.

"Coffee is my favorite flavor. I used to keep three packs at my desk while working. Started with the regular flavor before graduating and exploring the rest until I found the one right for me. Thank you."

"You're welcome." I helped myself to four mints. "I love these, the juicy grape, and the salty ume."

"I made the mistake of eating too many of the umeboshi on my first try. I wasn't prepared for the saltiness of them when the rest of the flavors tended to be sweet or sour. Ended up spitting them out and have avoided them ever since."

I laughed. "They were an acquired taste for me too."

"I can't wait to introduce you to my other friends. It'll be a nice change from the boys' club that you already know."

"Maybe I don't want the change." I laughed again. "I have to admit that I'm starting to get attached to you Old Ducks."

"Can't blame you. We are a likable bunch. I imagine that you have your share of parties because of your career."

When not researching, I attended birthdays, engagements, and anniversaries. It was the only way to build my connections. Two recent functions involved lunches with matchmakers from out of town, whose clients Mr. Dolphin was so eager to decline. It was business, an unavoidable necessity that drained my introvert batteries. It was called work for a reason.

"Yes. I went to Charlene Huang's nineteenth birthday last weekend. Her parents introduced me to the birthday girl's three unwed older siblings in hopes that I'd take them on."

"The Huangs from Singapore? They moved here two years ago. I met Alfred and Yvonne when they hosted a charity golf tournament. Did you know that Yvonne is on the board of five charities? Her beauty matches the quality of her heart."

His thread sparked, bobbing against the leather steering wheel.

And there it was—my client was attracted to married women. But the why eluded me—he was seeking a genuine connection. Perhaps the party tonight would give me an opportunity to investigate further.

"It will be good to see the couple again. I enjoyed chatting with them last week."

"Did you sign any of their older children?"

"I didn't. My list is full. Unlike real estate or insurance, where the more, the better, I can't in good conscience take on more without neglecting my current clients. I don't want anyone to feel ignored."

"If it makes you feel better, I feel well taken care of. My friends share the sentiment. And we're here."

Mr. Moon pulled into the building's parking garage, spoke into the intercom, and was admitted moments later.

If I didn't find out more about his predilection for affairs tonight, I'd have no choice but to redirect him to another matchmaker better suited to his needs.

THE DEMOGRAPHIC FOR THE EVENING'S cocktail hour was in my wheelhouse—gray, white, and salt and pepper. The lavish penthouse was open concept—two spacious living rooms flanked a chef's kitchen with an elevated Calacatta marble island countertop that sat twenty people. Floor-to-ceiling panoramic windows displayed the striking skyline of office buildings and newly built condos. The spread of hors d'oeuvres included chhole samosas, grilled chicken satay skewers, tempura cauliflower florets, taquitos, and Korean popcorn chicken.

The aromas alone compelled me toward the spread. I promised myself that I would snag one of the coveted seats by the counter.

After meeting the hosts, Mr. Moon made a beeline for Mr. and Mrs. Huang, with me in tow. The lovely couple wore dark navy— him, a custom fitted suit with a plum dress shirt; her, a sleek off-the-shoulder cocktail dress.

Mr. Moon introduced me before striking up a conversation with Mr. Huang about golf vacations. Behind his round glasses, he sneaked glances at Mrs. Huang, his thread sparking in her direction. At least no one else saw the blatant display.

Yvonne Huang turned her attention to me. "It's so wonderful to see you again, Sophie. You will let me know when you're accredited. You must be building a healthy waitlist."

At least six potential clients in the queue, not counting her three older offspring. Once I was accredited, I'd have my choice of clients. It was a source of pride and reassurance to know my services were wanted, despite my rocky start.

"It's getting there." I beamed. "More matches, meeting more people, growing my network—all to increase my value as a matchmaker."

"Of course." A pretty, older Asian woman with the complexion of a twenty-five-year-old tapped her on the shoulder. "Oh, Rosalind, so good to see you."

Rosalind leaned in and patted Yvonne's upper arm. "I came back from Tokyo two weeks ago after visiting Aaron. He's doing well."

"I find it fascinating that he's studying seismology." Yvonne introduced me. "Rosalind Jeong, this is Sophie Go. She's agreed to match my three oldest after her recertification. I understand that she's having an open house soon; a coming-out party for her profession."

Rosalind narrowed her eyes as her penciled brows arched in

an unnatural curve. She assessed me as though trying to make sense of how I fit into her existing logic—like I'd taken the place of someone who better fit who she assumed I was.

Rosalind Jeong. One of the two people Mom had invited to her expensive birthday dinner. She was the coleader of the exclusive book club along with Talia Pham, Mom's other guest.

Whatever this woman thought of my mother, I was certain I'd hear it soon.

"Ah, Sophie. Your mother is in my book club. She's our newest member."

"Why don't you two chat?" Yvonne waved and headed back to her husband and Mr. Moon.

Rosalind motioned toward the less crowded area near the gas fireplace. "Shall we?"

We took the two seats. The area was empty for a reason: the heat from the gas insert intensified the already warm penthouse. Rosalind set down her black calfskin Birkin beside her Jimmy Choo pumps. In her short dress, she seemed more comfortable than I was in my cable-knit boatneck sweater and dark slacks.

"It was Zeny Acosta who nominated and vouched for your mother's membership. Zeny's like that—always charitable." Rosalind examined her manicured nails. "The book club has been around for fifty years. It was founded by my grandmother. I was unsure about Irene until she invited me and Talia to Papillon. It was a casual invite too. A nice ladies' night out, though you and your father are also attending? Irene did want us to meet you."

She hadn't told them it was her birthday. Doing so would have revealed how out of the ordinary the situation was and spoiled her fictitious narrative.

Nothing my mother did would ever impress this entitled woman.

"Mom is sweet like that. She cares that her friends meet her family." I resisted the urge to tug at my neckline. The heavy sweater was roasting me rotisserie style. "She's looking forward to the book club and speaks highly of it and you."

"I'm sure she does." Rosalind paused. "Your mother is eager to please. She seems invested in something that isn't guaranteed—I hope she understands that. We are very selective about our members. Irene still needs to pass our trial period. I'm not sure she's up to the task, but we'll see. She might surprise me."

Mom and I did share this sick need for approval from those who were unwilling to give it.

"She hasn't said much about you, however. A matchmaker in the family is a remarkable achievement. The ability to recognize and appreciate the rare, finer things in life is innate from birth. People think you can develop it, as if education can make up for the lack of pedigree. It can't. It's the same principle as your special career."

I disagreed with everything except for the last part.

"I look forward to seeing you again at Papillon, Sophie." She got up and departed into the crowd.

Mr. Moon emerged from the other end of the room. "Why are you sitting here? You can't be comfortable."

I got up and aired out my neckline—a discreet fanning motion—without being indecent or drawing attention to myself. "I had a chat with my mother's friend, Rosalind Jeong. You have perfect timing. I was about to look for you. We need to talk."

"Excellent. You'll agree to facilitating an affair between me and Yvonne Huang? If she's interested, that is?"

Oh shit, this was bad.

Chapter Thirty-Six

⊰⊱

I asked my client to join me in a more private place to talk, but he decided to ditch the party and head to a nearby Krispy Kreme. I selected a table by the large glass window showcasing their signature donuts coming off the conveyor belt.

The smell of sugar and fried dough softened the tough conversation I was about to have. Mr. Moon looked hopeful that I would accommodate his request.

"So this is possible, yes? I know matchmakers do this."

"Okay, yes, there are some matchmakers who do this, but I am not one of them." I folded my hands on the tabletop. "But I also believe that this isn't what you truly want."

"How so?"

"Your attraction to married women is real, but why? I believe it's psychological, though only you can confirm this. However, if you choose to pursue married women, I'll have to refer you to a colleague who can help you."

He opened a box of donuts and offered me one using a napkin. "What makes you think it's psychological?"

I took a bite. It was so soft and warm. "Your questionnaire—specifically, your family background. You mentioned your parents both had separate affairs and were happy because of them. The marriage itself was miserable."

"They stayed together out of obligation. It was for convenience, not love."

"Affairs were thus normalized as sources of happiness. Have you ever tried dating an unattached woman?"

He creased his brow, causing his glasses to dislodge from their perch and slide down the bridge of his nose. "I never thought about it. It's more exciting to sneak around and have this special secret. Is this all strange to you?"

He had no idea, but I had to dig deeper. Get him to think about why and not to accept what he believed was second nature. Answering aloud was an exercise toward self-awareness. "It's not. Remember, I'm not judging. I'm here to provide you with what I believe is best for you and something you want at the same time. Both aren't mutually exclusive."

He laughed. "Are you sure you're a matchmaker and not a therapist?"

Madam Yeung had insisted that this career was both. After what happened with Fanny, I understood firsthand that the psychology classes provided by the school were as important as the rest of the curriculum.

"A matchmaker wears many hats. We're trained to listen first and foremost and to treat everyone with empathy."

"Kindness in any profession is a welcome trait."

I mustered my best stern look and repeated the question. "Why do you think you haven't given single ladies a chance?"

"I don't know. You seem to think you do; I'd love for you to enlighten me."

"What I think isn't important. You need to discover it for

yourself. If you do, it means you want my help. If you don't, or decide the question isn't important, I'll make the referral."

He grew quiet and took a sip of his coffee. Our drive home wasn't tense, but he was lost in thought—not enough to be distracted, but enough that he was clearly contemplating my words. He didn't say anything until he bid me good night.

I'm sure Mr. Moon had never thought it possible to be in a normal relationship because of his parents. His negative views on marriage came from a place of fear rather than personal experience, like an acrimonious divorce. I wasn't certain if he'd sought me out because he wanted to change or because he considered me a skillful facilitator for his affairs.

I hoped it was the former. I wanted to help.

I wanted to help all of the Old Ducks, if they'd let me.

ALL WEEK, I MADE MY daily check-in with Anya, the hostess of Papillon, who, by now, must have cursed my name when my phone number showed up on her caller ID. After I changed the number of guests for the reservation, she warned that it was unlikely a table would free up in the near future. Anya gave me more kindness and patience than I deserved. She mentioned I was a refreshing change from the verbal abuse she received from wealthier patrons. In desperation, I joked about bribing her. She replied, "I don't take bribes, and if I did, you couldn't afford the price."

She wasn't wrong.

My encounter with Rosalind Jeong confirmed how much Mom needed this dinner to happen. If I couldn't get the reservation, Mom would be humiliated—and I didn't want to fathom the consequences for me.

My phone buzzed from Mr. Dolphin: Can we meet? You need to stop sending me stock pictures for retirement homes.

I dragged my fingers down my face, pulling my eyes and cheeks downward. Gathering myself, I texted him to meet me at the rooftop garden in fifteen minutes.

On the way to the elevator, Mom called.

"Did you get the reservation yet? Rosalind called me, telling me how much she's looking forward to the dinner."

Her calls came daily. Mom asked the same question over and over. I became the watched kettle she was waiting to boil. The urgency in her voice increased each passing day with the immovable deadline looming over our heads.

"I haven't heard anything. You know that I'll call you as soon as I do."

"People cancel all the time. I don't understand why the line isn't moving."

No point telling her about the two tables for three that had been available. She'd insisted on inviting her "friends."

"It's a table of five now. That's more difficult to accommodate."

"Are you trying hard enough?"

I was approaching my breaking point. "I'd be more than happy to turn over the task if you think you can do it better."

I don't think she heard the sarcasm. "No, I don't have time for that—and it's for my birthday. Make this happen, Sophie."

I'd be late for my meeting with Mr. Dolphin if I didn't get off the call. "Mom, I'm sorry, but I have to go. I have a client meeting."

"Of course you do. Always so busy. Better not be too busy to follow up on this."

She ended the call.

Mr. Dolphin waited for me near the garden's entrance. He wore a buttoned lemon-yellow sweater with dark khakis. His bold color choices never failed to surprise me.

We strolled through the garden together.

"I need you to find me better-looking men. What you've been sending me is no good." He sliced the air with his hand. "There's always something wrong with them."

"Did you even read their profiles?"

"Why bother if I can't get past their faces?"

I grimaced. "This is what I warned you about. You are dismissing someone who might be a great match for you. Like Edward."

"Edward. You mean the one with the snaggletooth? I mean, if he smiled with his mouth closed in the photo, then it wouldn't be an issue. I'd still see it in person, though, because you can't hide something like that for long."

"His teeth are fine. He took courses to be a sommelier and is an accomplished actor with a theater group. Why didn't you see that?"

"What did he act in? *Phantom of the Opera*, where he never smiled or he wore a mask to hide his toothy disfigurement?"

"And Vincent. What was wrong with him? He's an accomplished pianist."

"With a big mole."

"It isn't a mole; it's a birthmark," I corrected him. "You're being too picky."

"Why can't I be? This is my life we're talking about. I don't want to settle. I want the best for me. Love is the grandest adventure out there. You can't waste time on clunkers."

I was running out of potential matches. I was already consulting out-of-province colleagues because Mr. Dolphin's dating history eliminated most of the gay men in his desired age range in the vicinity. Gay septuagenarians are rare.

This was becoming a bigger problem than I'd expected.

If Mr. Durian wasn't his love match, I'd have to go international.

Chapter Thirty-Seven

※

The problem with arguing with your elder was that they had more years of practice at being stubborn. Mr. Dolphin and I had been embroiled in an exhausting circular argument for the past thirty minutes—me trying to convince him to drop this unproductive selection process while he insisted it was necessary.

"You're reducing an already small pool." I pressed my fingertips against my temples. "You can't be this picky. It isn't tenable."

Mr. Dolphin snorted. "That's your dilemma, not mine."

"At this rate, you'll reject every potential bachelor on the planet by summer."

"Not if you find my match first!"

I let out a drawn-out sigh. It welled from the core of my being, and upon its escape, I was left deflated. "Why is appearance so important to you? What drives you to find this perfect physical specimen who may not exist?"

"He exists."

He had placed an emphasis on the first word that piqued my interest. Mr. Dolphin seemed to have someone specific in mind.

This person may no longer be around, but they existed once. My client had adored someone at one point in his life, but he had never divulged this fact in either his questionnaire or interview.

What else was he hiding?

"Tell me his name so I can speed up the process and get you two together."

Mr. Dolphin made a choking noise then blushed, fidgeting with his hands.

I switched to a softer, more gentle tone. "I hope you're able to trust me, to confide in me. I want to help, but I can't do so without your assistance."

"Appearance is the only thing I can be certain of. You can't be sure about anything else, but with looks, what you see is what you get." He tapped the wooden surface of the round table.

"About your type, let's see if we can narrow this down." This was my opening—to see if his feelings for his friend ran deep below the surface. "Why don't we start with someone we know? You have a wonderful friendship with a certain Old Duck. He's handsome. Hypothetically, is he more your type?"

Mr. Dolphin locked eyes with mine. "He is my type—or was—but I screwed it all up."

Behind us, the waterfall and its soothing sounds muffled our conversation. Mist from the foot of the falls widened and condensed, providing more privacy.

"Is it a mistake that you can fix?"

"No, it's too late. It was all my fault." The usual shell of confidence I'd come to associate with him had cracked. "I moved to Toronto to attend university, and then I discovered the gay scene downtown. That's where I met him."

I scooted closer and leaned in to not miss a syllable.

"We were intimate, but it didn't work out because I couldn't . . . I was more concerned with seeing what else was out there. Having come from Malaysia, I was just starting to live my true life. I refused to settle down with the first man I met. He . . . didn't take it well. We ran into each other a year later and became friends. We pretended it had never happened and moved on."

His red thread floated upward, sparking at the tip.

He still loved him.

They had loved each other—for all these long, lonely decades—but had been too afraid to compromise their friendship.

I needed a plan to join them together.

MR. REGRET HAD GONE ON his two most recent dates with Mabel and Flora. I visited to see if he had made up his mind. The heavy aroma of toasted meringue filled the air. God, this man was magical.

"I'm making pavlova," he called from the warm kitchen. "I made two cakes. One is for the property manager and the other is for us to share."

"Is this the bribe for the party room?"

"Yes. It was her request. After I deliver this, the date is yours and so is the use of the space." He smiled with pride. "Bartering is still an effective tactic."

"You mean bribing." I kissed his cheek. "Thank you. This is so wonderful of you."

Jewellike raspberries, strawberries, blueberries, and bright green mint leaves decorated the two beautiful cakes with the swirly meringue base. I would only have a slice—or two.

"I hadn't made this before, but my experience with meringue made it much easier." He tucked a cake into the fridge and brought the other to the kitchen table.

I had already begun pulling out the dessert plates and utensils from the cupboards.

"I added a layer of coconut whipped cream inside. You'll see when I cut it. She asked for a vanilla-based one, but for us, we get coconut." He reached into the knife block and pulled out a sharp blade. "Our version is better. Trust me."

"Did you hand in your application for that baking competition you wanted to enter?"

"Not yet. It's not due until closer to the open house. I have time to figure out what kind of cake I want to make." The meringue snapped with a crunch as it met Mr. Regret's knife. "It won't be this one. This is far too plain and the difficulty factor isn't that high."

"Speaking of difficulty, have you made up your mind yet between Mabel and Flora?"

He transferred two generous slices of cake to both our plates, then sat down across from me.

"Your silence is very reassuring," I joked. "Anything I can do to help?"

"I still worry that I will make the wrong choice." His fork slipped, clattering against the plate. "Both are so nice. I don't want to hurt their feelings."

I patted his shaking hands. "You can't think about that. Focusing on the fallout is unproductive. You'll give yourself an ulcer, or worse."

"My doctor did tell me to watch my stress levels."

"Did you make the requisite list? You know the type where you break down each option into their positive and negative traits. It allows you to see everything. If you don't like that, there's always the simple way. Ask yourself: Who can't you live without?"

"Huh." His hands steadied as he rested them, palms down, on either side of his plate. "I like the second method better. For such a young person, you're wise."

I laughed. "No, I'm not. Maybe for other people, but not when it comes to my life."

I took the plunge and told him about Mr. Particular and the choice I needed to make. The confession eased the tension I'd been so busy ignoring. He listened without judgment—something Yanmei never did.

"Why are you procrastinating? Are you afraid of hurting his feelings?"

"I don't need this in my life right now. Between my full client list and what my family needs, there isn't room for anything else. I mean, yes, a part of me doesn't want to hurt him. I think he sees me as someone I'm not. Going on a date with him will only lead to disaster."

"Have you thought that maybe he sees you for who you really are?" Mr. Regret stabbed a sliced strawberry with his fork. "It's how I think the two ladies see me. I don't have to try to be anyone I'm not. They want to be with me. It's odd. Other than the Old Ducks and you, I haven't had this. It's such a wonderful feeling."

"Can you describe it?"

"I feel wanted." A blissful smile stretched across his lips. It wasn't generated by the delicious cake we ate; it stemmed from the surety of being loved—something I'd never felt for myself.

Perhaps there was a tiny part missing from my life.

Chapter Thirty-Eight

When I was little, I used to smash my dolls together as practice for when I became a matchmaker. "Red threads unite," I'd declare with religious fervor.

I found myself in a similar situation with Mr. Dolphin and Mr. Durian. Now that I was older and wiser, I would use tact instead of force. They'd never told one another how they truly felt, for legitimate reasons. But I had to bring them together in one place and allow the magic to happen. I hoped.

If I arranged a date for them, but without telling them it was with the other, they'd attend, but would they divulge their secrets? Would they embrace the experience as a real date?

They needed privacy, nothing to impede or interrupt them. If I invited them to my condo, I'd have them arrive staggered, so it would be a surprise.

The best matchmakers were attuned to the whispers of the heart, no matter how soft.

This must work—for their sakes and mine.

. . .

FIGURING OUT WHO WOULD ARRIVE last was easy: Mr. Dolphin. If he was the one waiting, he and I would argue. Mr. Durian would be more patient.

When I finished my draft, I called them both and delivered the same speech. "I've arranged a date with someone who has confessed their deep feelings for you. It will be up to you whether you want to continue or pursue anything beyond the meeting, but this is a guaranteed opportunity. I witnessed their red thread exhibiting a spark."

As expected, they had different reactions.

Mr. Durian: "This is interesting. I guess we'll see what happens."

Mr. Dolphin: "What does he look like?"

I'd never wanted to strangle someone over the phone more than this man. "If you're that curious, come to my condo and find out. This is a no-obligation scenario. You can walk in then walk out if you want."

He agreed only because of the exit clause.

I scheduled their meeting for that evening and contemplated setting a trap or blocking the door to prevent Mr. Dolphin's escape.

Three hours until Mr. Durian; fifteen minutes after, Mr. Dolphin.

Every possible worst-case scenario ran through my brain: them hating this, their friendship being ruined, blaming me. The latter didn't matter. I'd survive—to live with the guilt for the rest of my life.

They'd been friends for decades—far longer than I'd been alive. Would the language of love emerge after so many years of being buried?

The truth was made subjective by the most stubborn of minds.

Mr. Dolphin's and Mr. Durian's threads spoke their truths, but it hadn't been done with words. I was its sole witness. The truth might die before it had a chance to live.

I paced and tidied what little furniture I had to "Penny Lane" on repeat. I arranged and rearranged my candy jars, lastly by color, before plucking a few from every container and placing them in a Hello Kitty–shaped candy dish on the counter.

While sucking on two sour watermelon Hi-Chews, I pulled the chair that doubled as a nightstand from my bedroom into the living room. The other chair was always in the kitchen where I ate ramen at the counter. Both wooden chairs were from Goodwill and were the only two that matched when I went shopping that day.

Yanmei offered to buy me new ones as housewarming gifts, but I declined. She'd already been generous in buying me a wardrobe before I returned to Canada. She'd wanted me to look the part when starting my dream career.

I was a matchmaker on the verge of matching two best friends who'd never told each other how they felt. I rushed to the bathroom and threw up. When was the last time I was this anxious?

If I matched Mr. Dolphin with Mr. Durian, I would be two successful matches away from having enough clients to list on my application submission. All the worries about the future were bundled into this match between these old men.

The knock on my door jarred me from my thoughts. I turned off the music and straightened my shoulders.

Mr. Durian had arrived.

There was no trace of his favorite fruit; instead, a strong ocean-themed cologne teased my nostrils.

"How are you feeling?" I asked.

"Nervous." He rubbed his fingertips together as he followed me down the hallway to the living room. "Nervous about how this person will react and what they'll say when we meet."

"Rest assured that this match is viable. I wouldn't bring in someone incompatible."

Mr. Durian took the seat to the right. I offered him the full candy dish, and he picked out all the Classic Series guava hard candies. The bright green foil wrappers crinkled in his palm as he emptied three successive pieces into his mouth.

I fetched a tissue paper. "It might be good to get rid of at least one. You don't want to choke while you're talking."

He spit out two into the paper, which I discarded along with the wrappers. "Good idea. What if it's not who I want it to be?"

"What do you mean?"

"I'm in love with my best friend. How can I change that and be open to loving someone else?" His thread sparked. "Do you know that the only dose of culture my friend gets is when I drag him to things? He hates it like a child refusing to eat his vegetables, but he still goes anyway. He even makes donations without me asking."

Love.

The grandness of this emotion grew exponentially when reciprocated.

"Everything will work out," I said. "Be open-minded."

"He never caught on in all the times I've hinted at it. It's gotten so flagrant that it's turned into a habitual joke between us." He pushed the small candy against his cheek, making a marble-sized bump. "Maybe with this new man, I will be seen in a different light."

"When light shines into darkness, the world is changed. You will be seen."

The knock on the door drew our attention.

Mr. Durian closed his eyes and sucked in a ragged breath.

It was time.

Chapter Thirty-Nine

※

I better get the male supermodel I've been asking for." Mr. Dolphin grinned and wagged his finger. "Otherwise, I'm out of here."

"I've brought you the most beautiful man."

I had hid Mr. Durian's shoes in my bedroom. Nothing to spoil the surprise. Mr. Dolphin took off his shoes and walked inside without a clue.

I emptied a tiny carton of Marukawa strawberry bubble gum into my mouth. Chewing helped calm my nerves—not only because it gave me something productive to do, but because the bright artificial strawberry scent comforted me.

Mr. Dolphin froze. His best friend sat, waiting.

Mr. Durian leaned forward, elbows on his knees, hands clasped together. His red thread sparking and pointing toward Mr. Dolphin. He laughed—a dry sound devoid of mirth. "Not the supermodel you were hoping for, am I?"

Mr. Dolphin staggered into the room and collapsed into the empty chair.

"Disappointed?" Mr. Durian asked. "It's okay to say so. I've seen the parade of your former lovers. Never been and never will be as beautiful as them."

"This has to be a joke," Mr. Dolphin cracked. "You sure you're in the right place?"

"I am, and as usual, you're avoiding the subject. You and I aren't getting any younger, yet you insist on chasing the perfect physical specimen." Mr. Durian clenched his hands. "Why? You're not as shallow as you portray yourself to be."

"I like what I like." Mr. Dolphin spread his hands. "What can I say?"

"But *why*?" The anguish in that one word constricted my heart.

Mr. Dolphin slumped against his chair. The semblance of levity he'd been trying to maintain slipped away, stripping the jovial smile from his face. All to avoid this fundamental question.

A rawness lingered in the air, like a sting from an open cut when sprayed with antiseptic. My exposed arms throbbed from the sensation. It was a palpable pain in its purest form—one released after being incarcerated for so many years.

Mr. Dolphin lowered his eyes and whispered, "I'm sorry."

I would have missed it had I not been standing in my kitchen, halfway between pretending to be a statue and trying to blend into the white subway tile backsplash.

"What?" Mr. Durian asked, rubbing his ear. An exaggerated gesture that wasn't from a lack of hearing.

"I'm sorry," Mr. Dolphin declared in a louder voice. "I didn't mean to hurt you."

"I appreciate the apology, but you didn't answer the question." Mr. Durian's shoulders slumped down from the release of tension in his body. "Don't you think that after all these years of friendship, you owe me this much?"

"You're going to think it's stupid."

"Try me."

"Because . . ." Mr. Dolphin stood up and began pacing. "If you can . . . Perfection is . . . No, no, no. Why is this so hard?"

"Maybe because I'm confronting you with something that you should have been thinking about instead of ignoring all this time. Thinking with your brain is more preferable than the other body parts you use."

"Hey! I'm using my brain right now and it's rusty." Mr. Dolphin cupped his hands over his mouth and nose as he continued pacing. His loud breathing was amplified by the makeshift mask.

"If you had exercised it like the way you jog on the treadmill, it wouldn't react so damned slow."

Mr. Dolphin dropped his hands, making a dismissive waving gesture. "You're not helping."

"This isn't a dissertation. How complicated can it be?"

"This isn't what you think it is. Be quiet for a minute. Let me think."

"Fine." Mr. Durian crossed his arms. The sour expression on his face was that of the puckered end of a lemon.

It took a minute. The subtle ding hovering in the air as Mr. Dolphin glowed like a filament. His red thread swinging wildly. "You've always had a way with words; you know I don't have your eloquence. I make jokes because that's more natural. What I'm about to say is serious. I can't diminish it with humor."

Mr. Durian raised a brow but kept his silence.

"It's all on purpose—this hunt to find physical beauty. I wanted the best."

His best friend rolled his eyes.

"I know it's not what you want to hear. I wanted this because it was the closest to you." Mr. Dolphin glared at the man seated below him. "I swear, you're the stupidest smartest man I know."

"I'm not beautiful. Now you're just mocking me." Tears welled up in Mr. Durian's eyes, and he dashed them away.

Mr. Dolphin knelt before his friend, taking his hands in his. "I thought that finding a pale substitute for what I couldn't have would make me forget how stupid I was." He squeezed, almost as if to make sure all of this was real and that he didn't intend to let go. "You're the most beautiful person I've ever met. Such a beautiful mind to accompany a beautiful soul and body. You're my first thought when I wake up in the morning and the last when I go to sleep. I love you."

His red thread sparked into a massive blaze enveloping them both, stretching toward Mr. Durian's, who leaned forward to kiss him. Their threads became one, splitting into a thousand tiny fibers, all flaring out in spirals until they fused into stronger braids, shifting, changing from reds to golds and back. The new thick thread they shared undulated, dancing to a silent song, shedding shimmering gold dust.

Oh, the kiss. The golden kiss lingered and shone so bright. I turned away and wiped the tears streaming down my cheeks.

Romantic love: so beautiful and dazzling to behold.

This was decades in the making, brewing, hidden by fear, until today—where it burst into fireworks of joy.

A strange thought fluttered like a butterfly landing on my fingertips quivering with fear.

Was romantic love a basic right that I, myself, was entitled to?

Yanmei and the others who had petitioned to have their threads restored thought as much.

Was this a possibility for me?

This magnificent joy?

When the glowing illumination receded, I found them both touching each other's faces, foreheads pressed together. Their joined red thread braided three times over into the strongest of cords.

Again, my heart clenched. "I'm happy for both of you."

Mr. Dolphin placed his hand on Mr. Durian's arm. "Thank you, Sophie, for getting me together again with my first love."

"Thank you for teaching me that the patience of love transcends time." Mr. Durian glanced toward the hallway. "We better go."

I escorted them out.

THREE MINUTES AFTER MY NEWEST successes had left, my phone rang.

Anya from Papillon.

"Please tell me you have a cancellation."

"I do, but only if you can put me on your waitlist."

"My waitlist? You want to be a client?"

"I googled you, and I'm interested. I'd prefer a person instead of an app." A beep interrupted her. "I have to go. I have two other people on hold. Will send you the details and all you have to do is text confirmation. Congratulations, Sophie! You got your table."

"Thanks, Anya! I can't wait to meet you at the restaurant."

The day and time for the reservation came in a minute later. It was three days after Mom's birthday, but it had to be good enough. I had no doubt Anya had moved mountains to get this cancellation so close to the date I'd requested—it was her bargaining chip to get on and move up on my waitlist.

Once I confirmed, I called Mom and left her a voice message.

She was probably on the subway heading home. I'd get a call when she arrived at Finch Station and got on the 42B bus. I took that bus as part of my tedious commute working at the bank. An hour and a half to cross town. Since I wasn't able to read in motion, it was hundreds of wasted hours that I'd never get back. My parents hated the commute, but they couldn't afford driving to work themselves.

I was in the middle of typing up my report for Mr. Dolphin and Mr. Durian and answering social invites when she called.

"Did you get the table?"

"Yes!"

She paused as though shocked I'd managed to deliver.

"I can't wait to tell Rosalind and Talia. They will be impressed. Your father will be pleased as well. He knew you could do it." She sighed. "For once, my birthday will be how I wanted it to be."

She placed so much importance on one day each year where she seemed to demand everything from the universe (which included from Dad and me).

"It won't be on the exact day—"

"What?" The sharpness of this word contrasted with her previous honeyed tone.

"It's three days after your birthday. I already confirmed."

"No, it has to be the day of. Tell them to move it."

I gripped the edge of my seat, fingernails digging into the soft wood. "Mom, that's not how it works. We're fortunate that this happened. I can't guarantee that—"

"It has to be on my birthday. Otherwise, it won't do."

"Mom, please. This is the best case. We have a reservation so close to the date."

Your friends won't know that it wasn't on the right day anyway since you never told them.

"It's unacceptable. Move the date."

I gathered my resolve. "If we move the date, you won't get a table. It's better to have a table a bit late than no table at all."

"It's my special day. Having the dinner at the time I want is important."

Appeal to her ego.

"Think about your friends. I met Rosalind at a party and she mentioned you and the dinner. They're looking forward to this and getting to know you more."

Silence.

This could go either way.

Chapter Forty

·)(·

Negotiating with Mom wasn't a chess game—it was a hostage situation. I had lost most of the captives; getting one out alive would be a win. Mom always did what she wanted, and if I happened to ask for something that aligned with that, I had a better chance of getting it.

I don't know how I made it to Shanghai without her disowning me. I'd been so grateful to be gone that I never probed into why she had said yes. Years later, I regretted not asking. It was her biggest act of kindness.

"You are sure you can't get a better date?"

"Yes. If I hadn't confirmed, we would have lost this table too."

"It's not perfect or ideal, but fine."

She hung up.

Mom wasn't pleased.

Her ability to be dissatisfied never failed to astound me.

It wasn't ever enough.

I was never enough.

A message came in from Mr. Moon, asking for a meeting. Nothing like work to kill any time wasted on self-pity. My career saved my sanity and provided in more ways imaginable.

Life as a matchmaker was everything I wanted it to be.

Mr. Moon wanted to meet at his place first thing in the morning. These septuagenarians, they sure loved to be up before the sunrise. My clients had conditioned me to sleep earlier to match their schedule. Messages and calls lit up my phone at six a.m. Old Ducks quack early.

After finishing a mug of instant coffee, I stuffed two packets of Little Mantou into my purse. These small, round Taiwanese egg biscuits melted in my mouth when I needed to savor them or crunch them into oblivion, depending on my mood.

Mr. Moon welcomed me into his condo with the aromas of breakfast coming from the kitchen. Should have known my client would have prepared something delicious. Mr. Moon's hosting skills were unparalleled.

"I made my specialty breakfast sandwich: egg white omelets, wilted spinach, Havarti, and shaved ham on toasted English muffins." He opened the fridge. "Grapefruit juice, orange juice, or coffee?"

I settled onto one of the barstools against the counter. "Orange juice, please. Thank you for breakfast. You shouldn't have."

"It's the least I can do for asking you to meet me at this time. You young ones hate early mornings."

I hid my sheepish smile.

Mr. Moon slid over a plate with an open-faced sandwich. The wilted greens rested over melted cheese and ham. He added a sprinkling of cracked pepper with his electric pepper mill at the last second. "Enjoy."

"This looks amazing." I cut it into quarters, stabbed my fork into a portion, and took a bite. Delicious.

"I've been thinking about what you said." He took the seat beside me and started picking at his plate. "My parents were happy, but not with each other. There was a ten-year difference between them, and it was a marriage of convenience—done to please my grandparents. They never hid their affairs from each other. As long as it never went public, it was business as usual."

"They kept it private?"

He took a sip of his coffee. "They were good at what they did. With all this in mind, I asked myself what I wanted."

Discretion or indiscretion.

"And?"

"I think it's time to try something different. It might be a nice change to have my lady meet my friends and attend parties by my side."

"What's prompted you to see this in a different way?"

"My friends. They're so happy with their partners. I realized I could never have it for myself the way I've always done it. It didn't sink in until now." He paused to refill my half-empty glass with more orange juice. "I was part of the club because I was still a bachelor. Despite the affairs, I was still one."

"Does this mean you want to retain my services?"

"Yes. I want you to find a match for me."

I raised my glass. "It will be my pleasure."

At Mr. Moon's request, I checked my database and found a potential at a nearby hospital. Dr. Adeline Tiangco was a retired radiologist who still volunteered at Scarborough Grace Hospital. Her full social calendar and arresting looks made her a perfect candidate for Mr. Moon.

She remembered me from the Liangs' Winter Soiree, an annual party held by the founders of the Filipino-Chinese Association of Scarborough. Her red thread reacted when I mentioned Mr. Moon, and it was all the confirmation I needed to arrange the date.

As I exited the hospital lobby, I recognized a tall, wiry figure in a thick wool jacket and trapper hat by the front doors. His upper left sleeve displayed the emblem of a Japanese automotive factory.

Mr. Porcupine.

I hadn't spoken to him since I'd let him go as a client. The other Old Ducks had mentioned that his crankiness had increased after each of my successes. Though he'd never liked me, I still wanted to help him. My intuition sensed a person who wanted to be matched.

A bolt of worry threaded through me as I walked alongside him. "I hope everything is fine with you."

He frowned and picked up the pace, but I matched it while huffing and puffing. The windchill and brisk weather tightened my nostrils and transformed my breath into trumpet-like clouds, air tiger lilies.

Mr. Porcupine groaned when he realized he and I were heading to the same bus stop. Ignoring me for the forty-minute ride back to our building would become a challenge if I decided to sit beside him.

"What do you want? Aren't you busy matching every geriatric in the vicinity?"

"I was at the hospital on client business." I decided to forgo inquiring about his health again. He never replied to the initial question, and I doubted he'd tell me anything anyway. "The Old Ducks tell me you're grumpier than usual."

He snorted. The red trapper hat, when paired with his narrow face, made him look like a disgruntled strawberry.

"I haven't been to the last few meetings," I continued. "Because of my busy schedule."

"Why are you talking? Don't you have something better to do?"

"Consider this my form of community service."

I spied a slight upward tip of his lips. Humor. A way through his prickles.

The almost-empty bus pulled up, and we boarded with our Presto cards. He chose a seat at the back, and I took the spot beside him. His glasses fogged over, hiding his eyes.

He crossed his arms. "I'm not signing up as a client, no matter how much you pester me."

"I don't recall me asking. Besides, even if you were interested, I can't take you on right now. You'll need to be on the waitlist."

"Is that so?"

I fished out a package of chocolate Yan Yan from my purse. I peeled off the lid, shook the biscuit sticks inside, and offered it to my seatmate. "No double-dipping."

He took one and swirled the stick into the little compartment of chocolate sauce. He devoured the snack in two bites. "Your dental bills must be astronomical. All I see you eat is candy."

"I have an electric toothbrush. It keeps the cavities away."

He took another piece, without dipping this time. "This waitlist. How long is it? Not that I'm interested."

His red thread undulated. Mr. Porcupine wanted to be matched, despite his insistence otherwise.

"It's starting to get longer by the day—about eight." I dipped a biscuit with a generous dollop of chocolate. "I don't want to overextend myself. I can refer you to a colleague if you're still interested in getting a matchmaker."

"It's too late for me."

"You're old, not dead. It's never too late until you're the latter."

He laughed. "I wonder what your parents think of your smart mouth."

"My mother is very disappointed in me. She can provide you a long itemized list if you ask her."

"Sometimes you can't please them, but it's your duty as their child to try. Your parents are the most important people in your life."

They were, yet trying to please them seemed impossible. My bank account hemorrhaged money from my devotion. I was running on a hamster wheel—keep my place, earn enough, pay my parents, repeat.

"You don't agree?" Mr. Porcupine plucked another biscuit from the container. "Think of all the sacrifices they've made for you. They had to go without to give you what you wanted or take you on family trips. Listening and honoring your parents' wishes is important. We wouldn't be authentic Chinese otherwise."

I almost laughed. "I'm not saying I don't love them or appreciate them. My mother's birthday is in a week. She wanted this pricey dinner, and I snagged the reservation last night. I'd like to think that she's happy, but I'm not so sure."

"Showing emotion isn't something we do. Gratitude falls into that. She knows what you're doing. I'm sure she appreciates it. You'll see."

Even sitting down, he towered over me. "Please tell me you played basketball or volleyball at one point. It'd be a shame otherwise to waste that height."

"Basketball. I played center in college." He paused. "The height also helped when climbing hydro poles."

This side of him was what the Old Ducks and Beatrice knew

well. Mr. Porcupine and I had not talked until now. He used his crankiness as an armor. This squirrel managed to crack the nutshell. I yearned to see more.

"What was that like?"

"Do you have more snacks in that purse of yours?"

Chapter Forty-One

In life, pleasant unpredictabilities were like a welcome rain shower on a hot, muggy day. The conversation with Mr. Porcupine from the bus ride cooled our previous hostilities. I garnered a few smiles by being my most brutally honest self. Amazingly, his face didn't break when doing so. We spoke the language of frankness. It was liberating.

"I prefer you this way." Mr. Porcupine pressed the button for the elevators. "In your line of work, you have the habit of measuring your words. You can understand why I was suspicious."

"With all due respect, you don't need an excuse to be suspicious."

"You're right." He chuckled. "I'll give you that."

We stepped into the elevator. "I'm serious about the offer. If you want to be matched, I can refer you to a colleague."

"I'll think about it."

Progress. I smiled—not too wide, as not to appear smug, but enough to express the ray of joy singing inside me.

"It was nice talking to you." As I exited, he held my sleeve.

His dark eyes softened behind those glasses. "My sister is happy."

MOM CALLED EVERY DAY WITH the same question: Is the reservation at seven p.m. on Thursday? The answer never changed: Yes. Don't be late. It's a set meal—it's scheduled to be served at our arrival time.

She grew more anxious by the day. It must have been torture deciding what to wear or what purse to bring. In addition to her dictating Dad's wardrobe, she demanded pictures of my closet. I let her choose the knee-length copper sparkle A-line—one of the two cocktail dresses Yanmei had gifted me to wear on special occasions. It was Mom's birthday after all.

The day before the big dinner, she called three times. I answered each with borrowed patience, a cash advance from the future.

When my phone rang yet again, I almost cried in relief.

Mr. Regret.

"Are you free? I need help filling out the last bits of my competition application."

"Of course. I'll be right over."

I left my despair in my apartment when I locked up.

By the time I arrived at my client's doorstep, my bad mood had evaporated. I knocked and tried to guess what my friend had been baking inside. He'd been practicing all sorts of treats of various difficulty—the tasty results I partook in as evidenced by the clean, empty stacked containers I carried.

"What are you making today? The last batch of curry chicken buns was excellent. I—ah!"

Mr. Porcupine blocked the entrance.

I juggled the stack in my arms. Lids came flying off, scattering like Frisbees across the hallway.

He narrowed his eyes. "And here I thought we had parted on better terms."

"We did." I laughed, passing him the containers as I gathered the matching lids littering the carpet. "I just wasn't expecting you. You've seen how well I react when surprised."

I gathered all the tops. "These will need to be washed again."

Mr. Porcupine held the door open. I took off my shoes, slipped into guest slippers, and headed to the kitchen. "Does he know what he's making for the contest yet?"

"Getting him to make a decision is like trying to pull apart two industrial-grade magnets." He grunted. "He worries too much about it when in reality, any choice he makes will be a solid one. His baking skills have come a long way since he retired."

"He was bad at one point?"

"The first biscuits he made used baking soda instead of baking powder. You can imagine how much of a disaster that was. Inflated so much it exploded all over his oven. I had to help him clean it up."

I laughed. "When I'm here, it's dish duty."

Mr. Regret sat at the kitchen table with the printed form. A blue pen was tucked behind his left ear while his fingers massaged his temples. He reminded me of myself during my high school physics final exam.

I deposited the lids into the sink to be washed.

"Sophie, what did you think of the curry buns? Were they good enough or should I do the Asiago and blue crab soufflé?" Mr. Regret tapped the form.

"Both were excellent."

"When is the deadline?" Mr. Porcupine asked.

"In less than a week. It's the day after Sophie's open house. I want to hand it in before I deliver the goodies to the event."

The two men discussed the details of the form while I finished washing the lids. After I'd done my task, I retrieved a teakettle from the lower cupboards, filled it with water, and placed it on the stove to boil. Mr. Regret loved having tea with company.

"Jasmine or pu-erh? Or do you want oolong?" I asked.

"What do you think?" he asked Mr. Porcupine.

"Oolong."

I fetched a tin and set it by the stove. "So, did you pick the right lady yet?"

Mr. Regret blushed and wrung his hands.

Mr. Porcupine guffawed.

"I'm guessing no. They've been hounding me. You need to decide by the open house." I set three teacups on the counter. "You can tell them then."

"What is the matter with you? You're sitting on an embarrassment of riches. Two women!" Mr. Porcupine chastised his friend. "Make a damned decision. Think of those poor women."

"I am thinking about them. Constantly." The groove in his forehead deepened. "Every time I think I've chosen one, I get this fear—that I'm making a mistake."

Annie continued to haunt him.

"If you don't pick one, they'll have your hide, then tell their friends, and you'll make Sophie's life harder."

"I mean . . . you make a good point," Mr. Regret replied.

"See!" Mr. Porcupine crowed. "Coddling him doesn't get you results. Shame the man."

It wasn't my tactic, but it was clearly his. I rebelled against pressuring anyone to do anything—I hated when it was done to me. No way I'd inflict it on others; that was how Mom parented. I'd love to see a cage match between Mom and Mr. Porcupine.

"I'm confident he'll make the right decision."

"Thank you, Sophie." Mr. Regret stuck a defiant tongue at his friend. "I appreciate it."

Mr. Porcupine shook his head. "What are you? Six?"

The kettle whistled.

"Sophie, I've been told you're getting your accreditation. This is good. What do you have to do?" Mr. Porcupine asked.

"Gather enough testimonials from matched clients to get a hearing and reassessment before my deadline."

"And this deadline is when?"

"A little under four months."

"Now I know why you two are friends." Mr. Porcupine frowned. "You're enabling each other to procrastinate."

We opened our mouths to protest, but Mr. Porcupine cut us off.

"You need to choose a woman." He pointed at his friend. "And you need to get that accreditation. It's not a matter of getting a piece of paper to hang on the wall—it's about self-respect and the satisfaction that you've completed something. It's all about the pride of your career, of being a matchmaker."

He was right, it was a matter of personal honor and self-respect.

"Now that I know your deadline, you can be sure that I'll be nagging you to get it done." Mr. Porcupine accepted the cup of steaming tea. "And I'll enjoy every second."

"He's serious. His heart is in the right place though."

Before I left the condo, Mr. Regret had narrowed down, with help from me and Mr. Porcupine, the bakes to three. Mr. Porcupine continued his argument that hastening the lady selection would help me with my accreditation. The added pressure left Mr. Regret sweating.

In the lobby on my way to meet with another prospect for Mr. Moon, I ran into Mabel and Flora.

Mabel clutched a paper bag from a nearby bakery while Flora handled a tote full of books.

"Has he made a decision yet?" Mabel asked.

At his mention the women's threads reacted with hopeful sparks.

"He hasn't." I withdrew two flyers from my purse and handed them to the women. "This has the details for the open house."

"Ah yes, we've seen it pinned on the community board." Flora tucked her copy carefully into her tote. "I'll give this one to my cousin to put up at her building."

"Thank you, that would be great."

"If you have extras, I have a few other places I can think of to put them up—like the library, the grocery store." Flora opened her tote wide. "I think five will do."

I gave her four more flyers. "Wow, thank you!"

"He is going to make the decision next week then?" Mabel's thin penciled brows creased. "I don't think I can wait any longer."

Her anxiety made her snowy perm crackle.

"I understand. It'll be soon. He's well aware and is making his decision with care."

Mabel couldn't conceal the hint of displeasure across her face. On the other hand, Flora remained calm without saying a word.

"Are you coming to the open house?"

"Of course." Flora patted Mabel's arm and smiled. "We're both going. We can't wait."

They walked away with sharp whispers, Mabel's irritation rising above the din.

I hoped for Mr. Regret's sake that he would make the right choice—the sooner, the better.

Chapter Forty-Two

⋈

I awoke on the day of the dinner with my short hair standing up in quills.

Mom had called again last night to ask about the reservation and to nag me about my wardrobe and shoes. I'd half expected my phone to wake me up, yet nothing—no texts, no emails, no voice mails, no missed calls.

The quiet unsettled me. It wasn't that I expected a brass orchestra to jolt me out of bed; it was that silence was like the calm before the storm. I didn't check in with my mother as I feared it would set off a barrage of demands.

Mr. Regret sent me a quick note of encouragement and also passed on Mr. Porcupine's seal of approval for the dinner. The latter's enthusiastic endorsement for my act of filial piety had won me points I knew I didn't deserve.

If this didn't make Mom happy, I didn't know what would.

She was my mother: I had no other.

I spent the day catching up with my clients and coordinating the two dates I had lined up for Mr. Moon. The balances on my bank accounts made my lips pucker. This was unsustainable. Tonight had to be the last major expense—heck, the last minor expense too—from my parents. They had taken everything, there was nothing more to give. All that remained was my apartment.

The thought of moving back home put my mood on edge as the possibility—or was it inevitability—increased with every passing day.

PAPILLON WAS LOCATED IN THE financial district in downtown Toronto. Taking transit in fancy dress wasn't ideal; neither was driving with the limited paid parking lots. I booked a taxi.

Mom still hadn't responded to my messages.

Dad had, confirming that they were coming and giving updates. The latest being: Your mother is trying to figure out which pointy shoes to wear with her dress. All of them are black and I can't tell the difference.

Me: Don't say anything!

Dad: Okay. You'd think that having the day off, she would be relaxed. She's not.

Me: Try and be supportive. She's under a lot of pressure. She wants everything to be perfect.

Dad: I know. She tried to tighten my belt two extra notches and it broke.

The sad face panda emoji he sent made me laugh.

Me: You better get going or you'll be late.

Dad: We'll see you at the restaurant.

I arrived half an hour early. The oval sign hanging on the side of the building bore the silhouette of a black swallowtail with the restaurant's name in fine cursive. Inside, bell jars with fluttering monarch and swallowtail butterflies lined one wall; the opposite was adorned with bleached planks of driftwood stamped with golden butterfly silhouettes. A chandelier sculpted from birch wood with dahlia blossom lights hung overhead.

Papillon was smaller than I had expected. No wonder reservations were so difficult to obtain.

Anya had requested we chat before the party was seated. She was an attractive brunette in her early sixties with sharp, assessing gray eyes. I met her at the front desk, where she had another host relieve her post, allowing us to talk in the adjacent room.

The waiting room merged with the lounge, with its tall, narrow tables and high chairs. Guests without reservations enjoyed tapas and elaborate cocktails. Their signature drink was a white rosebud served in an elegant martini glass that resembled the galaxy with its swirling purples and blues.

"You approach matchmaking in a different way, don't you?" Anya asked.

Her red thread dangled from her chest, listless.

"Yes."

"Good. I need something new." She drummed her fingers along the upholstered lavender arm of her chair. "When I saw that you specialized in older clients, I was relieved."

"I want to do what's in your best interest. It's a fun process. In fact, if you can come to the open house, you can talk to my successes yourself." I handed her a flyer.

She scanned the information before folding the paper in half. "I should be able to trade my shift with Michel. I might also bring two friends, if that's okay."

"That'd be wonderful."

Anya checked her watch. "We better get you seated. The kitchen is already prepping, so you won't have to wait long for your courses."

We moved back to the lobby.

No one was here.

I checked my phone. No messages.

"It's normal for a group to be a little late because of traffic and such. Don't worry." Anya introduced a handsome South Asian twentysomething with golden-brown eyes. "Khalil will be your server and escort you to your table. When your family arrives, we'll take care of them."

Khalil smiled and gestured toward the dining room. "Please follow me."

He led me to a table for five. The gold-accented cutlery, jeweled napkin ring, and purple-and-cream camellia centerpiece reflected the high-end price tag of this meal.

"Normally, I'd do the introduction now, but given that everyone hasn't arrived yet, we can wait." He pulled out a chair for me.

I sat down and thanked him.

"I'll notify the kitchen that your party is a little late. In the meantime, would you like anything to drink while you wait?"

"Tap water," I requested with a straight face. I didn't want to be charged far more for any kind of fancy water from some supposed virgin European spring.

He nodded and left to fulfill my order.

I fired off texts to Dad.

No answer.

As the minutes ticked by, my irritation rose. My apologies to Khalil came at ten-minute intervals until thirty minutes passed, then it became every five. The death grip on my phone kept me from smearing my face into the beautiful art nouveau patterned plate.

Still no messages.

She wouldn't have stood me up.

There's no way she'd have missed this—I'd already paid for the meal. My credit card steamed from the charge.

Then I heard it—the unmistakable loud laugh, the kind reserved for her friends. Mom.

Khalil escorted the party to my table as I scraped away any signs of negativity from my being. Relief helped sweep it all away.

After everyone was seated, Khalil performed his introductory speech and took everyone's drink order. Mom ordered champagne for the table. Rosalind and Talia exchanged amused glances. Our server left to fetch the champagne and talk to the kitchen about their late arrival.

Once the bubbly was served, my mother sipped from her glass. "Oh, Sophie, you should have told us the right time. I can't believe we're late."

"Yes, establishments like these run on a tight schedule." Rosalind leaned forward in a paltry effort to conceal her mortification. "It's embarrassing to come in late. They're unlikely to take any future reservation."

Talia clucked. "Yes, it's a definite faux pas."

Mom shook her head. "You've embarrassed us. You need to be more careful with details—especially in your line of work."

Dad stared at his lap.

"Umm . . . I told you the right time on several occasions." I lifted my phone up. "I can show you the texts."

Mom's face hardened. A blast of cold air hit my skin. No one noticed the temperature change but me—the target of her wrath. Her expression shifted, sweetening as her attention returned to her friends. "Ladies, how's the champagne?"

Talia lifted her almost-empty glass. "Quite good, as you can see."

Dad moved to refill her flute.

"Our server mentioned the king crab gyozas." Mom rubbed her hands together. "I can't wait."

Rosalind placed her hand on her chin. "I wonder if they'll be similar to the ones I had at the Tokyo location."

"You get to eat at the best places. Please tell us more about how Aaron is doing in his studies."

"Well, I am so happy you asked." Rosalind beamed, folded her fingers into a steeple, and launched into a master class of humble-bragging.

Mom watched as the entire table focused on Rosalind. She studied her friend's face with a mixture of admiration and resentment. This woman epitomized everything Mom wanted—prestige, respect, finesse, wealth, influence.

Dad squeezed Mom's hand.

I didn't listen while the others took in Rosalind's words as if every syllable granted their wishes. There wasn't anything I wanted from Rosalind—least of all, her approval. I'd already survived a trial by fire from those like her.

Khalil and two other servers emerged from the kitchen with our appetizers.

The three crispy-bottomed gyozas lay in a clear lake of broth with miniature floating edible flowers. The complex aroma prompted a series of rumbles from my empty stomach. I turned the plate and examined it from every angle. This was art.

An art only I had appreciated. The others had swallowed their portions without so much as chewing, washing them down with more alcohol.

I stabbed a dumpling when my mother cleared her throat.

"Sophie, I need you to help me with my dress. I think there's a snag in the zipper." Mom stood up over her empty plate.

I held my gyoza-loaded fork for a moment before following her out.

Chapter Forty-Three

The color of Mom's wrath had always been blue—the hue of anti-freeze that I poured into the radiator of my car. The instant we stepped out of the dining room and into the lobby, the air chilled. The source wasn't an open door or poor insulation. I rubbed my hands against my bare arms.

"Why did you contradict me?" Mom hissed.

"You mean about the time? I told you it was seven. I kept reminding you every time you asked about the reservation."

"All you had to do was agree with me." She pressed her fingertip against my collarbone. "Rosalind now suspects that I lied. This is all your fault. Everything was fine until you had to open your big mouth. It only takes one single grain of doubt for them to shun me or kick me out."

She'd been so obsessed with every single detail—taking the entire day off, picking out my dress, her outfit, her perfume, her shoes, her jewelry, her manicure, Dad's belt, even the sparkling tennis bracelet that I'd paid for hanging from her wrist—that there was no way she hadn't known the reservation time.

She had known and yet they'd arrived late.

For all the instances she had accused me of lying, she did it herself. She had lied and blamed me for it.

"Mom, you did lie—"

I stepped back and grabbed my burning cheek.

She'd slapped me.

"I allowed you to go to Shanghai—against my better judgment—because I thought you'd come back humbled. But you always screw things up. You make me the villain of your story despite being the one at fault." She continued to press into my chest.

"You humiliated me in front of the Su-Winstons and their friends."

Poke.

"You returned home a failure. Couldn't even graduate from matchmaking school."

Poke.

I winced in pain. Tears streamed down my face. Mom kept advancing, pushing, pushing, shaming, pointing out my every failure. With every stab of her finger, my vision blurred.

"Are you listening?" Mom shook my shoulders. "You think you can run away from everything. You have no accountability. I'm tired of fixing you."

The last of her words registered, leaving me confused. "What?"

"You are broken. You've always been broken. I knew the moment you were born." Mom let go of me.

I sobbed. "Mom . . . ?"

"I had hoped to get a son, instead I had you—a burden I've been carrying for far too long." She made a gesture of wiping her hands. "Tonight was it. I'm done. You're worthless."

She composed herself before returning to the dining room.

I stood alone in the lobby.

The weight of my mother's words rushed into me, leaving me swaying.

Broken.

Worthless.

My father came from the dining room, holding my purse.

Dad!

I threw my arms around him and sobbed, soaking his pressed dress shirt. My muffled cries vanished into his shoulder as he patted my back. The soothing gesture combined with Irish Spring soap made me cry even more.

"I'm sorry, Sophie. You know what she's like."

"She doesn't love me."

"She does. She just doesn't say it. You know how much pressure this dinner is for her."

"It doesn't give her the right to treat me this way."

He tipped my chin up. "She's your mother. She knows what's best."

"Dad, she called me worthless and broken."

"She's . . . She didn't mean that. She's under so much stress. Everything at work isn't going as well as she likes. She got into a tiff with some of her office mates. It's her birthday. She wants to feel special . . ."

He was defending her.

"Dad, she hit me."

"She's not like this normally. It's the stress. The opinion of these women is important to her. Impressing them will help her stay in the book club and open up other social events."

Why was he defending her? He was always defending her.

He was defending her after Mom laid the fault for their tardiness at my feet.

He defended her even when he *knew* she was lying. Like when she went off and accused me of lying for what she had done—the broken vase she had struck in anger, which she claimed was my fault when I was seven. Dad walked in to broken pieces of ceramic on the floor. It had been a gift from his mother. I had been upstairs reading in my bedroom, yet somehow it had been my fault. He accepted her word and grounded me.

I should have known.

He would always choose her.

It was easier for him.

"Sophie, I'm sorry, but your mother doesn't want you to come back to the party. I tried to talk to her, but she's adamant. I'm really sorry." He handed me my purse. "Just give her what she wants. We want to make her happy."

"But Dad—"

He patted me on my stinging cheek. "Go home and don't make a fuss. If you won't do it for her, do it for me. Be a good girl. In time, this will all blow over."

He returned to the party.

How much did my parents love me? Measuring little to not at all. It was lose-lose. I retrieved my jacket from the coatroom and left.

Red threads flashed in and out around me. No, not now, not now.

Two couples walked past, threads joined yet fluctuating—oscillating between existence and oblivion.

I needed more time.

The threads were fading, disappearing. Once they were gone, they were gone forever.

If I had only graduated like my classmates, this wouldn't be happening.

I was losing me.

Hanging my head low, I tugged the collar of my coat closed.

Get home, get home, get home, get home.

Hide my despair away.

Home.

While it was mine to return to.

I slammed into someone, but didn't stop.

"Sophie?"

Fragile snowflakes drifted down from the cold, dark sky like falling stars. The overhead flood of streetlights illuminated each sparkling crystal, and in the middle of it all was Mr. Particular, in a thick wool coat with a soft red scarf wound around his neck. "Are you all right?"

"I'm fine." I rubbed my eyes. "What are you doing here?"

"I'm on my way to dinner with my mother and sister."

"I won't keep you."

"Wait." He walked beside me. "You don't seem fine. Can I help?"

I stopped walking. His red thread pointed at me, winking in and out. I tried to touch it, but it vanished. "You trust my ability as a matchmaker, right?"

"Of course."

My tears came again. I needed to save him from himself. To spend the rest of his life with a broken, worthless person wasn't fair. He deserved far more than me.

"This isn't going to work between us. We're not compatible. You should find someone else."

His eyes darkened. "Are you sure?"

"Yes. You need someone to give you what you want. I'm not that person."

"Then allow me to do one last thing for you." Mr. Particular unwound his scarf and wrapped it around my neck. "It's cold out. Keep it, Sophie."

His lingering body warmth and the scent of cocoa and Irish cream coffee enveloped me.

Hold it together.

If I fell apart, there'd be nothing left.

I sprinted toward the nearest subway entrance.

Chapter Forty-Four

⊁|⊰

"She's Leaving Home" was stuck on repeat.

The haunting melody and lyrics spoke to me.

It had been my song of freedom when I'd left for Shanghai.

And now, my recrimination.

I had refused to look at anyone. The beautiful red threads I'd seen most of my life were being taken away from me. Yanmei and the others had had their gifts renewed and affirmed upon graduation, while a failure like me would lose my gift.

Who was I without my ability?

All I envisioned was a dark, depressing future without any color, joy, or purpose.

Just like Fanny.

She'd been so in love with Jin. So desperate to have him. The warning signs were all there—the obsession, the mood swings, the neediness, the constant texts and emails. I wanted to help, but it was to the wrong person and the wrong cause.

Helping others was the only way to help myself—to prove to the world that I existed and I mattered. It was why being a matchmaker was so important, why I'd wrapped myself in my work until there was nothing of me left without it.

Nothing.

Whatever remained was broken and worthless.

I laid on my bed and stared into space.

My phone buzzed, jostling me from my stupor. It had been so quiet since yesterday.

The Matchmaking Society!

I sat up, reading the contents of the email. An in-person reassessment in two weeks—the first step in the accreditation process. But I wasn't ready! My client reports and testimonials weren't enough. Passing and qualifying for the next step would be impossible, and I couldn't afford to go back to Shanghai for the final ceremony even if all went well.

Everything was crashing around me. I covered my face and sobbed.

This future I'd dreamed of was slipping away.

Perhaps it had been foolish to think I could have all this. There must be some defect in me to think that I could . . .

All I heard was Mom's voice.

All of those lectures I thought I'd forgotten or never paid attention to or drowned out with music or crunchy candies thundered in my head with the same tone one used when dealing with a nuisance. Not angry, just profoundly disappointed.

My phone rang with an instrumental version of Tom Jones's "It's Not Unusual."

"Dad?"

"Have you called your mother yet?"

I snapped my eyes shut. "Why?"

"She's waiting for you to say sorry."

A hysterical laugh escaped my lips. In the pits of despair, comedy was a welcome companion. Issuing apologies was how I historically resolved any conflict with my mother, but today, I'd run out.

"I don't really want to."

"I'll apologize for you. I don't want you two fighting." He lowered his voice to a whisper. "We want you to move back home."

"Dad, I don't want to—"

"It's important to think about your future. What if this matchmaking thing doesn't work out?"

I rolled over to my side on the bed and made a sound—the kind that indicated I was listening but not ready to respond.

"You can't afford to keep that place. It'll be too hard. Your mother and I are barely keeping up with our mortgage payments and you have a bigger one. You're leasing though, right? Then it's easier for you to move back."

"Mmm."

"It'll be nice to be under one roof again. I miss you. I can think of many good reasons why you should come back, and the biggest is your mother's cooking. I bet you're not eating well on your own. Candy and ramen aren't very nutritious. You might get scurvy . . ."

Dad droned on and on with his pitch to win me over. It wasn't that he was wearing me down; I'd already stripped myself bare of my defenses. A matchmaker without an ability to see the red threads was no matchmaker. My clients would abandon me, and with them went my income. There was no way to stay in this apartment.

I didn't have much. Whatever was left I'd sell.

She'd want a grand apology. The one I refused to give. It would be the price of reentry into my old house. Holding on to my anger would do nothing but leave me homeless. Like the rest of me, my pride was damaged goods.

Why delay the inevitable?

"I'll think about it. That's all I can promise for now." I pulled my knees to my chest. "And Mom's okay with this?"

"Of course she is. She wants you home. I don't think she ever wanted you to leave."

"Right."

"Oh, and Sophie, you know you do need to apologize before we can take you back."

"Yeah."

"I'll see if I can ask your mother if she can make you something special for dinner. I hope that we'll see you soon."

THE SUM OF MY POSSESSIONS fit into two small boxes and one suitcase. Two trips to the car and it should all fit into the trunk. My minimalist aesthetic, the polite term for cheap and broke, made moving easier.

When we were vacating our shared apartment in Shanghai, Yanmei cried as she stared into her closet. She'd needed three suitcases to accommodate its contents—not counting her shoes, which had required another big box.

In contrast, I had one stuffed suitcase.

"Your possessions are how you know that you exist," she muttered while throwing her entire weight on one suitcase in order to get it closed for zipping. "It's important for the world to know you exist, Soph. Remember this when you're living your life."

Yanmei would be disappointed if she had seen my small pile in the hallway.

Like a patch of dust, all I had would blow away by breathing.

I reached into one of the candy jars in the boxes and yanked out a packet of Ovaltine candy. I ripped it open and popped three

254 ‡ ROSELLE LIM

brown round tablets into my mouth. The chocolaty malt disintegrated on my tongue.

I had wanted a fancy candy vault complete with a steel door and turning lock. Shelves upon shelves of pristine jars full of every color, flavor, and shape. So many rainbows captured in glass. A saccharine sanctuary where I found instant happiness—not only from partaking, but from the simple pleasure of being present and surrounded by what I loved.

The small-scale version from my kitchen fit into this box. A small measure of happiness crammed into cardboard that once housed the microwave on the counter. After I listed all the appliances on Kijiji, there'd be no trace of Sophie Go in 2E.

This dream of mine was dying, sputtering out into embers.

The Old Ducks would find out after I canceled the open house. Why bother hosting an event for a career I'd no longer have? Saying goodbye to them would be the hardest. They were my friends. They invited me into their private group chat. Keeping in touch through the intangible stroke of keys or a phone call didn't compare to seeing them in person, but visiting the building without living here would cause too much pain.

I grabbed my suitcase and keys and left behind the life I'd always wanted.

Channeling my inner Yanmei, I pushed down against the trunk. The Honda creaked in protest. Either the trunk was too small or what I'd tried to shove into it was too much. I stopped and laughed. Even what little I owned was too much to cram into my crappy car.

I adjusted the red scarf around my neck and tried again.

The Honda groaned; the trunk remained open and ajar.

If I only had some rope.

A group of three people appeared in my periphery. I closed my eyes. I didn't want to not see their red threads. It had been too much; the way they flickered was how the flame of a candle danced in the wind before being extinguished.

"Sophie!"

Mr. Regret emerged from the north end of the parking garage.

"Hi!" I hoped the smile on my face masked the turmoil simmering underneath, at least from a distance.

He made his way to me, and as he approached, a quizzical expression formed on his face. "What's going on? Are you going on a road trip?"

"No, actually, my parents want me to move back home."

"Why?"

"I can't afford to stay here anymore."

"Wait, wait." He held up a hand. "Why?"

"Everything is a mess. My parents . . . I . . ."

"What happened with the dinner?"

I laid bare every painful detail.

"She shouldn't have blamed you. How she acted isn't right." Mr. Regret leaned against the side of the car. "You're still a matchmaker. You still have time. You said it wasn't permanent unless you miss your deadline."

"It's too late. There's not enough time and once they disappear, I can't get them back. I'm a failure, like I always knew I would be."

He smacked the trunk. "No, you're not! I'm not going to stand here and listen to you disparage yourself."

I lowered my head. He shouldn't have to defend me, but I would not defend myself.

Mr. Regret clasped my shoulders. "Look at me. Please, look at me, Sophie."

I met his eyes.

"I'm an old man, yet I'm about to start an exciting part of my life—this grand romance that you—you!—helped arrange. Love! You're giving me a chance at something I never thought I'd have again. At the open house, I'll tell Flora that I want to be with her."

Flora.

He'd made his choice.

His red thread sparked.

I wept, brushing the tears from my cheeks. My last act as a matchmaker.

"Yes. I am going to tell her. I'll bring flowers and a signed copy of her favorite novel. It's the one about this old man with cats by a Swedish author." He lifted his grocery bag. "And this is almond flour. I'm hoping to make three macaron towers for your open house in shades of reds and pinks. I came down here to ask you what flavors you'd like. I'm thinking strawberry, raspberry, and pomegranate. What do you think?"

"What's the point? The open house was to help with my career. That's over."

"You're going to have it! You've worked so hard for this. The rest of the Old Ducks are looking forward to it—I'm looking forward to it. Don't you dare disappoint us and yourself."

Chapter Forty-Five

Arguing with old people, same as it ever was. I'd never win.

"How else are you going to get enough clients in time for your deadline?" Mr. Regret lectured.

"What if I lose my gift before that happens?"

"The point is that you haven't lost it yet." He placed a hand on his hip. "I'm seventy-one years old. Have I given up on life? No. Because giving up is too easy . . ." The longer his reprimand, the more he sounded like Mr. Porcupine—underneath the marshmallow exterior lay a foundation of Le Creuset stoneware. "This is your celebration as a matchmaker. You can find more clients there and build your case for reassessment."

"All right, all right. I'll have the open house."

One last celebration before I moved back in with my parents and applied for the same soul-sucking position I'd had at the bank. Back to the long commute, and peanut-butter-sandwich lunches; the symphony of soulless typing, and groans of elevators. At least the food would be amazing at this farewell party.

He patted my shoulder. "Keep working on the positive attitude."

"I'll try."

"I better go. I need to get the colors right before I start the test baking." He patted his bag. "I'll set up the food before the open house starts. Then I'm off to submit my baking contest application in person."

"You've figured out what you're making?"

"Yes. After I made my decision about Flora, everything else was simple in comparison." He touched my cheek. "Stay your course. You know who you are—the best matchmaker I've ever met."

"Thank you."

He headed to the elevators with a lightness in his step. His visible ray of happiness had poked a hole in my bag of sadness and resignation. The tear in the fabric made it hard to hold on to the negativity.

The man had twisted himself up into knots with his indecision. But was it as simple as choosing to fight despite knowing what the outcome would be? In every scenario I envisioned, the result was misery.

I jumped onto my trunk, bringing my whole weight down, hoping it would close. Instead, paper exploded everywhere—as if my car had decided it had had enough of my weak attempts at bullying. Swirling sheets of color arranged themselves into an unbroken ribbon, one after the other, moving in parallel.

I caught one of the papers in flight.

Photographs.

The shoebox had busted open.

My first job working at the movie theater—Dad had taken this one. The unshakable smile of my younger self effused an unbridled sense of joy in life's possibilities and the heady initial taste of independence.

A picture of me and Madam Chieng when we'd first met. We were so much younger. She had asked me to sit up and straighten my shoulders. She'd instilled a sense of pride and reinforced the belief that I was special.

A blurry photo caught my attention. I climbed onto the bumper, plucking it down like an apple from a tree. A selfie with Yanmei at our apartment. Two earnest young matchmakers ready for a night on the town. I snapped this heading out the door and had forgotten to clean the lens. A fuzzy moment of friendship.

Yanmei.

The pictures fell down with a shake.

I gathered the pile and deposited them back into the misshapen shoebox. Without thinking, I grabbed the biggest box and pulled it out. The trunk slammed closed.

Moving would wait until after I spoke to my best friend, and the only way to start the conversation was with an apology I now had no problem giving.

Pick up, pick up, pick up.

Come on, Yanmei.

Pick up, pick up, pick . . .

"Soph?" Yanmei yawned. "You look like shit. Are you okay?"

"I'm so sorry. You're right about me and my parents."

"Oh God, what happened?"

And just like that, it was as if our silence had never existed. Our friendship had survived, more secure. No matter what, I always had her—and she had me.

"I'm so bitter. You didn't even eat anything. You paid for it all!" Yanmei shook her fist. "Your parents are the worst. Yes, I said it: parents. Your dad is a coward."

"He did say I can move back home."

"I can only imagine how scary this is. I don't know what I

would do. But you have time. You'll ace your accreditation. Soph, you're the best matchmaker I've seen."

"I'm so afraid. What if I lose it all?"

"Okay, can I be real? It would suck. A lot. You'll be back at the bank in some dank basement, but that doesn't mean you have to move back with your parents. There are other options for apartments. Maybe not as swanky as where you are now, but decent. I know you think your world is burning . . ."

"It is. I feel like it is, and that postponing the inevitable is going to make it more painful."

"It's not inevitable. Hell, you can apply to one of those crappy matchmaking agencies and try your luck that way income-wise. Might end up being richer than all of us. I guess all I'm saying is that you'll be okay, you'll find a way. You always do."

I started crying. Water pooled around me, washing away my despair.

"Being a matchmaker is who you are—it's not about the threads."

All this time I'd been so terrified of losing myself.

"Oh, Soph, if you only saw yourself how everyone else sees you. Your clients adore you. It takes a lot of patience and heart to deal with old folks."

Yanmei never lied. Her easy compliments had startled me at first. My honed instinct was to deflect and dismiss, but she wouldn't accept that. Her honesty broke down my walls, filling my malnourished soul.

"Good, take it in. You deserve all the happiness." She sat up in bed and turned on her nightstand lamp. "Now, tell me everything else I missed."

We talked about the open house, my wonderful clients, and my waitlist. She gave me a rousing applause at the last bit of news.

"Your list is longer than mine!" Then she launched into updating me on her life.

I had missed her so much. For someone who blanketed themselves in loneliness, having Yanmei and the Old Ducks in my life was a new experience—people who cared about my welfare, my dreams, and my life beyond familial obligation.

"By the way, what is that around your neck? You don't wear red."

"Oh." I held Mr. Particular's red scarf against my cheek. "A gift."

"It looks like cashmere, and it's not a woman's scarf."

"I think I care about him."

"Oh?"

I still remembered the way he'd looked when he gave it to me. This man represented a future I didn't deserve—one where I was happily in love. Dates at the zoo, evenings full of starry nights and soft music.

I'd made what I'd thought was the right decision at the time, but with this new perspective on the world and my place in it, was I wrong? Easy to deprive yourself of something you didn't think you needed.

Love, this great immovable force, finally confronted me. For a person involved in the business of love, I sure had done a terrible job with my own life.

"He gave me this when I said goodbye. I told him that I didn't think it would have worked out. My life and career are a mess." I twined my fingers around the scarf. "He told me that he likes me."

"He did what? It's close to one in the morning and you buried that lede. You're killing me here."

"Is it wrong for me to want to see if this could work between us?"

"Are you dead? If not, then go get the man."

Chapter Forty-Six

∗|∗

Having the courage to correct your mistakes was harder when it involved someone you cared about. The difficulty lay in navigating the landmine of their feelings without thinking about your own. Despite Yanmei's enthusiastic encouragement, I hadn't contacted Mr. Particular. I feared the outcome. It was a Schrödinger's cat situation.

The open house was far easier to tackle.

I'd spent yesterday cold-calling contacts to ensure a healthy turnout for the event. Patty, Lindsay, Anya, and the others confirmed their attendance, including eager parents who wanted their children married off like Alfred and Yvonne Huang. The interest surprised me—Yanmei was smug. She demanded updates and pictures of the event.

Last night, Mr. Durian and Mr. Dolphin had helped me set up the venue. The arguments over balloon placement and table settings lasted long into the evening, but it had been all in good fun. Mr. Dolphin had insisted on paying for the decorations—shimmery latex heart balloons of every size, gold tinsel fringe backdrops, fresh rose centerpieces to be delivered half an hour before the event, and tablecloths with a chair cover rental. He offered to hire a live band, but I declined. Mr. Durian convinced him to rent a sound system from the building instead.

The three of us met outside of the party room an hour before the open house.

I hugged them. "Thank you for all your help."

"It'll be a success." Mr. Dolphin patted my shoulder. "I still think you should have used my face on your website. I can be your spokesperson."

Mr. Durian jabbed him in the ribs. "The only modeling you should be doing is in private."

Mr. Dolphin waggled his eyebrows. Mr. Durian groaned and hid his face.

I laughed. I loved these two so much.

Mr. Dolphin led us inside the party room. We were all surprised to see Mr. Porcupine busy at work setting up the macaron towers. Three huge plastic carriers full of the beautiful treats were perched on the table. Two empty stands flanked one completed tower. Mr. Regret must have set it up before he left.

"He's heading downtown to drop off his form. He'll be late," Mr. Porcupine informed us while consulting a chart. He arranged the pastries in an ombre formation on the tiered white-painted stand. "He told me to tell you that he changed his plans." He began reading the handwritten scribbles on the paper: "'I decided to make the buttercream filling the flavored component. The color palette of the cookies themselves should be the showstopper.'"

Mr. Dolphin reached for one as Mr. Porcupine smacked him away. "If you mess this up, I'll kill you with my bare hands. You can wait like the rest of us."

Mr. Dolphin stepped away, playing up the faux injury.

"We should go and set up the sound system," Mr. Durian said

to his partner. "What you're doing is labor-intensive. We'll get out of your way."

The couple moved to the other end of the room. Arguments about technology and switches soon occupied them. I laughed. Their connected red thread was muted in its color and clarity. My initial alarm had faded—not from the acceptance of the inevitable loss, but from the acceptance that it was no longer within my control.

"The amount of arguing hasn't gone down. Are you sure they're together?" Mr. Porcupine asked.

"They are indeed."

He pointed to the full plastic containers. "Be useful and help me with this."

I studied the sheet he had been following, put on nearby plastic gloves, and began handing him the macarons at a steady rate. "Did he tell you who he chose?"

"He did. It's the right one. She's better suited for him."

"I agree. He was happy when he told me."

"He should be." Mr. Porcupine completed a row, then pointed to the corresponding alignment in the plastic trays. "He deserves love. All of them do."

"What about you?"

"Still too late for me."

"In the words of my wise friend Yanmei, 'Are you dead? If not, do something about it.' I can ask her to take you on as a client, though she is based in Singapore."

Mr. Porcupine adjusted his glasses as he reread the instructions. "I wouldn't want her. Too far away."

"What about someone in the province? There's a matchmaker in Hamilton who has a few older clients."

"Not interested. I don't want someone dabbling who's not well acquainted with what seniors need."

"What about—"

His pointed look stopped me in my tracks. "Are you always this dense?"

"Excuse me?"

"You. If I'm going to hire anyone, it'd be you." He rolled his eyes. "You do tiptoe the line between brilliance and—"

"I'll move you to the top of my waitlist!" I interrupted him with a giddy hug. "You're not going to regret this."

Realizing my impulsiveness, I jumped back and apologized. He didn't seem offended by what I'd done. My smug smile didn't seem to faze him either. The best part—I came away with no quills.

"We can deal with the details later." I handed the next set of macarons over. "This is so exciting."

"I won't compromise."

"I wouldn't expect you to. Besides, you can't be as bad as him." I gestured toward Mr. Dolphin. "He gave me a hard time."

Mr. Porcupine snorted. "And he thought I'd be worse."

"I guess we'll see."

Tom Jones emanated from my pocket.

"Go ahead and take it." Mr. Porcupine waved me off. "But make sure you come right back when you're done."

I squeezed into an unoccupied corner of the room. "Hi, Dad."

"Why didn't you come yesterday? Your mother and I were expecting you back home."

His irritated tone made me pause. Late yesterday afternoon, I'd sent him a message that I wasn't coming home. He kept sending texts, and his repeated calls went to voice mail. "I've been busy. I'm preparing for the open house right now."

"And your apology to your mother? The least you could do was call her. She is not happy with you."

"Please, Dad . . ."

"Sophie, be a good girl and do what I'm asking."

A good girl.

When had I ever been one in their eyes? Only when I acquiesced to their demands and then it was forgotten until the next request.

"I promise to call her." As soon as those words escaped my lips, I regretted them. "Okay?"

"I will hold you to that."

He hung up.

I returned to Mr. Porcupine's side with a different mood. He held out his hand for the next batch as I fell back into our routine, filling rows and rows of beautiful pastries going from raspberry to the softest of baby pinks. Mr. Regret had outdone himself. Pushing to new heights of mastery.

"I hate apologizing for something I shouldn't be sorry for."

"It's clear your parents feel differently."

"He wants me to ask for Mom's forgiveness when I'm the one who was wronged."

"If you feel this strongly about it, have you considered forgoing the apology?"

Not what I'd expected from him. Mr. Porcupine had advocated filial piety in our conversations. "Are you saying I don't have to?"

"I'm saying you have a choice. Why bother if it isn't genuine? I'm sure your mother will know there is nothing behind it."

I chewed on his words as if they were Kasugai lychee gummy candies. "Aren't parents always right?"

"Ask our baker friend that. Losing Annie cost him decades of happiness. I don't know what the situation is with your parents. What I do know is that there are always options if you're willing to see them."

I hummed "Here Comes the Sun" as I finished unloading the last container. To my delight, Mr. Porcupine joined in, surprising me with his flair for holding a melody. We hummed five more songs. By the time we finished, the rest of the Old Ducks had streamed into the hall to help add the last touches.

My open house was ready.

Chapter Forty-Seven

When a matchmaker announced their presence to their home cities, there was always a party. The size of the celebration correlated with the personality of the guest of honor. Yanmei's was a gigantic glittering bash that filled the rooftop of Singapore's most prominent hotel. Two thousand guests! Some flying in from as far as Luxembourg and Johannesburg. She had invited me out of courtesy, but told me not to come—knowing a party that big would lead to a panic attack. The event was covered by every gossip blog and the entertainment columns in the newspapers. She was thrilled by all the buzz and attention.

I, however, didn't want a huge, fussy affair. I cared more about the company and emerging with new potential clients. But I wouldn't have objected to something ridiculous and frivolous like a chocolate fountain or a candy service bar—animal related, like a puppy or kitten corner, or jewel-feathered birds, or mischievous monkeys.

Mr. Sorrow and Clara entered the room with the refreshments.

Their red threads, like the others, were faint, almost ghostly. Still, the hazy sight warmed me from the inside.

"We made this lovely sparkling raspberry basil lemonade." Mr. Sorrow brought a full ceramic drink dispenser. Dark pink raspberries, lemon slices, and basil leaves floated in an effervescent liquid full of bubbles. "It's Clara's signature recipe. If you love it as much as I do, you can ask her for it. She likes you."

Clara carried a box full of elegant plastic cups. She unloaded it on the table and began lining them up in neat rows. "We volunteer to handle the refreshments. It'll be fun to be able to talk to everyone this way."

"You mean charm." Mr. Sorrow placed his arm around Clara's waist. "She means charm everyone because she's so good at it."

Clara blushed and laughed. "Oh, you."

"I mean it."

She leaned over to kiss him on the cheek, but he turned at the last moment, capturing her lips with his. The connection was there.

I teared up, wiping the corners of my eyes.

Mr. Dolphin clapped from across the room and whooped.

Mr. Sorrow and Clara blushed, stepping apart with sheepish smiles tugging at the corners of their lips. They held hands, whispering to each other. Occasional giggles sprinkled their covert conversation.

"Teenagers," Mr. Porcupine heckled from the macaron stands.

We all laughed at the good-natured ribbing.

Mr. Wolf and Beatrice arrived. He was holding a tray of pink cat-faced cake pops. Beatrice carried a companion basket containing milk chocolate ones with caramel noses and whiskers.

"He insisted we visit his favorite bakery." She leaned in, whispering. "The place is marvelous and, of course, doubles as a rescue cat café."

Mr. Wolf dropped off his tray by Mr. Porcupine. They soon began figuring out the best place for the cake pops. Soft laughter punctuated their hushed conversation. Mr. Wolf's thread stretched across the room, joined with Beatrice's.

I took the tray from her. "What have you two been up to?"

"We're planning a cruise. A pet-friendly one so the girls can come with." She grinned. "Can you believe such a thing exists? He told me that he's been going for years. It's transatlantic."

Mr. Wolf had shown me the brochures soon after his victory at the cat show. Departing from Florida and landing in Southampton, the cruise had cabins that were fitted with everything cats might need—play area, bathing pool, litter boxes. The unique itinerary had activities tailored to cats and their owners. It was the perfect way for them to spend time at sea.

"Sounds exciting! When are you planning on going?"

"Next spring or fall." Her peonies and gardenias perfume suited her like a comfortable knitted sweater. She wore her joy well.

I left the tray with Mr. Porcupine and Mr. Wolf. Beatrice settled between her brother and her boyfriend.

Mr. Durian called me over. He had been adjusting the playlist while Mr. Dolphin wandered off to weigh in on the arrangement of the cake pops.

"Beatles instrumentals. Something unobtrusive and soothing." Mr. Durian clicked the music app of his laptop. "I sent him away. He's hovering over me like an obnoxious fly without helping."

I stifled a laugh. "He's not a techie. He hires people to do it for him, right?"

"Sure. He solves his problems with money. He's lucky that he happened to be born into it. Although, I should give him credit for his management skills. He's quite adept."

"One of his many talents, I'm sure."

"Somebody told me you were planning on moving back home."

Mr. Regret.

"It's complicated. My parents want me to move back, but I don't want to."

"Have you told them?"

Procrastination, when paired with avoidance, was the perfect tool for cowards.

"No."

Mr. Durian patted my arm. "You'll need to. My life changed when I allowed my heart to speak. Yours will, too, when you find the courage to do so."

"If only your belief in me was what I felt for myself."

"Look around you." He gestured toward the rest of the Old Ducks. "You made this happen. Power comes from action."

I pressed my hand against my heart. The red threads around me had faded nearly into nothingness, yet I clung to hope. My friends believed in me, and it was overwhelming.

"Are you ready for your open house?"

"Yes."

"Good. You've been hiding your talents with the Old Ducks. I have a feeling that the rest of the world is ready for you. You'll be so busy you'll forget about us."

I patted his hand and squeezed it. "No, I'll never forget the Old Ducks. You all changed my life."

"As you have changed ours."

Mr. Moon strolled in and closed the door behind him.

I left Mr. Durian's side to greet him. "I'm glad you could make it."

"I wouldn't miss this!" Mr. Moon appraised his surroundings. "You do know that I preapproved and consulted with everyone so it wouldn't look like a complete mishmash. Establishing the overall color palette and decor is important. To be honest, I wasn't sure about the tinsel until I saw it in person. It looks pretty good."

"You approve?"

"Yes. We want the best for you on this special occasion."

I drew him close and lowered my voice. "How was your date with the lovely radiologist?"

"I think it went well. Adeline is nice. We'll need another date to decide; she had to deal with a family emergency. Other than that, it was a promising start."

Adeline had mentioned that her brother had ended up in the emergency room from slipping on ice in his driveway. The timing was unfortunate. She, too, expressed a desire to have another date.

"I can do that. I'll check her availability and arrange something."

Mr. Moon perked up. "This whole dating process is more fun than I thought it would be."

"It's supposed to be enjoyable."

"Had I known, I would have tried it years ago." He rubbed his clean-shaven chin. "I like the idea of dating around, though, before settling down for the right woman. If I'm going to do this, I want to do it right."

"We have time. We're still early in the process."

Mr. Porcupine waved from across the room and tapped his watch.

"It's getting close."

I straightened my shoulders and headed for my purse, which contained fistfuls of business cards.

Mr. Porcupine left the pristine food station to man the doors with Mr. Moon. Through the small window, I could see a crowd growing outside. Lindsay and Patty jostled to be first in line. Once the doors opened, the buzz filled the hall.

So many familiar faces greeted me as they took in the decorations, food, and refreshments. The hungry locust swarm moved from Clara and Mr. Sorrow to Mr. Porcupine's macarons stand.

Round tables with cream tablecloths and matching chairs encouraged mingling and conversations between the smaller groups that traveled together.

Anya walked in with two of her friends. She leaned in to give me a set of air-kisses on the cheek. "Everything looks beautiful. I'm so happy for you, Sophie."

"Thank you so much for coming."

"These are Irina and Alexa, my two best friends. And yes, they are single."

The two women laughed at their introduction.

Mr. Moon sidled up to my side. "Sophie, who are these lovely ladies?"

I introduced the three eligible women. Mr. Moon offered to escort them to the drinks table. The women smiled and exchanged interested glances. The man oozed charisma, and when directed at the right targets, he devastated the female population.

Adeline might have competition with Mr. Moon's dance card filling up.

I turned toward the door and my smile froze.

Standing there were my parents, disapproval and disappointment painted on their faces.

Chapter Forty-Eight

⋇

The moment my parents walked into the party, I wanted to hide—
to blend and sink into the curtains of golden tinsel decorating the
walls so no trace of my presence existed. I hid my shaking hands
behind my back. My internal temperature spiked inside my simple
black sweater dress.

Why were they here?

No matter how much my flight instinct screamed at me to
run, I remained. Fighting was the last thing I wanted, but I was
tired of running.

They moved toward me in unison, each step matched by the
other in a pace calculated for confrontation. I was the prey with
two approaching predators.

A crow had once perched in the peach tree in my backyard. It
was a shadow until a chickadee landed in the grass. The explosion
of feathers created a snowfall of white against the chlorophyll green.

I was the chickadee.

Mom and Dad were dressed as if attending a parent-teacher

interview—casual enough to indicate it was a low-priority function, yet formal enough to express their status and capacity as parents.

They had attended one interview in elementary school, and after my grade three teacher sang my praises, they'd deemed their attendance unnecessary for future conferences. One less obligation from their busy social schedules.

"What is all this?" Mom made a sweeping gesture.

"The open house for my matchmaking service."

"It's a little ostentatious. With all your grumbling about having so little money, I guess we now know where it all went."

I swallowed my retort—everything was from the generosity of my friends. What did the truth matter to her when preconceived notions ruled? According to Mom, the truth was anything she deemed and defined as fact.

"This is my debut party. It's tradition for a matchmaker to have one when they start their career."

Mom turned to Dad. "Don't you think this is a bit much? Garish even."

"Sophie, how can you afford all this?"

I wanted to throw my head back and laugh. It was a question I'd yearned to ask them ever since I'd realized that they had always lived beyond their means. The hypocrisy encapsulated in that single query was astounding.

"I had help."

"Who? You don't have friends." Mom raised her index finger and pressed it against my left collarbone. "More lies."

Her elevated voice rose above the ambient instrumental of "Misery." My eyes were fixed on my parents. I didn't need to check around to see that we had an audience. Family drama on television drew in ratings, live events equated to car crashes, which this scenario was approaching. Nothing I did would prevent my mother's need to make me a spectacle. She'd already ruined my first debut . . .

"Mom, we can talk about this in private."

"So you can cower behind your lies?" She raised her voice even higher. "How many of these people have you deceived, Sophie?"

Her finger dug deeper into my sweater, hitting the bone. The applied pressure stung, and I knew it would leave another bruise.

"I'm not tricking anyone. Mom, please."

"Have you stolen their money to fund this party of yours?" She strolled toward the macaron stands, heels clicking against the hardwood. "How much does all this cost? Using a pastry chef for catering is expensive. We both know that you don't have enough clients."

Everyone watched my feeble protest die in my throat.

"You can't steal from people just to trick everyone into thinking you're successful when you've failed. Did you tell them that or did you lie about that to these good people too?"

Repressed sobs wracked my body. I swayed, my vision clouded with tears.

Humiliation on display for everyone to see.

Mom had achieved her goal: showing the world how worthless she thought I was.

Worthless and broken.

"They need to know. I can't in my good conscience allow you to defraud them. I'm your mother, and it's my duty to inform them of how I failed and who you really are—a lying, unfaithful, manipulative wretch. You shame your family with your actions."

She stood before me. "Apologize to these people."

Chapter Forty-Nine

Apologies solved all problems.

That's what I'd always believed, because they mended all the rifts and arguments with my mother. It didn't matter what the circumstances were, who was right, or whether one was even warranted. The end result remained the same—I was wrong, apologizing.

Years of saying sorry had left me without a shred of pride or self-dignity. Anyone who had a healthy sense of each would question whether an apology was necessary.

Yanmei was stingy with her apologies. It wasn't from a deep-seated idea that she was infallible; it was because she valued them far too much. She never understood why I gave in to my mother. At first, she'd assumed it was laziness or lip service on my part. The more it happened, the more she recognized it as a symptom of a greater problem. She never told me anything beyond that.

I stood before Mom with an apology assembling like jigsaw puzzle pieces in the factory of my brain. Premade for every occasion, marked according to usage, and rotated to avoid monotony.

Apologize and make this better.

Give her what she wants.

Make it go away.

Fix it the only way you know how.

Except the ready-made apology lodged in my throat.

Mom tapped her foot, the rapid thumps marking her impatience at the delay of what she expected.

"I . . ." I opened my mouth. "I'm s—"

A hand clamped over my shoulder, squeezing tight.

Mr. Porcupine.

Another hand grabbed for mine, holding tight.

Mr. Regret.

The rest of the Old Ducks stood behind me—Mr. Dolphin, Mr. Durian, Mr. Sorrow, Mr. Wolf, and Mr. Moon. All stone-faced, staring down my parents.

They cared more than my own parents.

I wasn't alone. Not anymore.

Another squeeze of my hand from Mr. Regret. I hadn't seen him come in.

I let their support fuel my words and build my courage.

"I'm not going to apologize." My wobbly voice steadied and grew louder with each successive word. "You're the liar. This party was made possible by my friends. You didn't ask me before throwing unfounded accusations around. You don't care about the truth unless it serves you."

"I'm not lying. You are, like you always do."

"Oh, you mean like at your birthday dinner? I reminded you of the reservation numerous times, yet you lied to your friends that I hadn't." I straightened my shoulders and took a step forward. "You've done everything to undermine me my whole life. I won't let you do that anymore."

She recoiled, taking a step back.

"I love you and Dad, you're family, but I can't do this any longer. I can't have a relationship with you unless you respect who I am and what I do. I am a matchmaker, and a damn good one!"

"Repeating a lie doesn't make it true."

"Why lie when the truth is so much easier? My clients will testify about how I helped them. Ask them. Go on. They have no reason to lie, they don't know you. They accepted me, but if you can't accept me for who I am and support me, I won't have you in my life."

I stood firm, rooted by the strength offered by the men behind me.

Mom yanked Dad's arm and turned to leave. The curses she hissed under her breath were clear for everyone to hear, including me.

"I hope that one day, you can love me as much as I've loved you." They paused for a brief moment before storming out. "I'll be here if you change your mind."

The instant they were gone, the Old Ducks swarmed me with hugs and words of encouragement, of pride, and of love. I cried, but this time, the emotion behind the tears was different.

"I thought you were going to be late," I said to Mr. Regret.

He patted my cheek. "It seems like I came back in time. I'm so proud of you."

"We all are," Mr. Durian added. "That must have been difficult."

Mr. Dolphin frowned. "With parents like that, it's a wonder you turned out as good as you did."

Mr. Porcupine grunted in agreement.

"We will always be here for you," Mr. Moon declared. "I don't think you can get rid of us even if you wanted."

Mr. Wolf moved to my side and gave me a tight hug. "You did good," he whispered in my ear.

The gap between the need to please my parents and doing what I wanted had always seemed insurmountable. For the first time in my life, I was at peace with a situation, and I hadn't needed to compromise.

If my parents wanted a relationship with me, I had left the door open, but it would be up to them to make it healthy.

A familiar face emerged from across the room, sandwiched between Lindsay and Patty.

Mr. Particular.

He raised his hand to catch my eye as he separated away from the two women.

I excused myself from the Old Ducks.

We met in the middle of the room and stood enough apart to maintain the appearance of respectability.

"You didn't see all that, did you?"

"Parents aren't always right nor do they always have our best intentions in mind. For what it's worth, I'm proud that you stood up to them."

"Why are you here?"

"I came to support you."

"Thank you. I appreciate it." I mustered a smile. "I know that I . . ."

Mr. Dolphin gave me a thumbs-up from across the room while Mr. Moon grinned.

Nosy uncles had taken the place of my absent and unsupportive parents.

"We can talk about that later."

"It would be better without an audience." The Old Ducks were waiting for an introduction.

I acquiesced and presented Mr. Particular to the rest of them. Everyone was welcoming except for Mr. Porcupine, who tried to stare him down, using his two-inch height advantage to its fullest.

Mr. Particular didn't flinch.

"Have you told her yet?" I asked Mr. Regret.

"Not yet. I suppose now is as good a time as any." He winked at me and began walking toward Mabel and Flora, who gave me a shy smile.

Mr. Porcupine flashed a rare smile. "This is his big moment."

"Flora is the luckiest woman alive right now." I positioned myself for a prime view of what was to come. "They are both going to be so happy."

A spectacle of a different kind unfolded in the room, cleansing the last of the unpleasantness that lingered. Mr. Regret spoke to Mabel first. A wistful expression crossed her face. Flora blushed when he took her hands in his.

Their threads lit up with the brilliance of the shimmering tinsel behind them. Such was the power of new love that it couldn't be tempered in its force.

"You picked me?" Her voice broke as she whispered.

"Yes. Is that so hard to believe?"

She lowered her eyes. "No one ever picks me."

"Why not? You're beautiful and intelligent. You make me see the world in such a wonderful way." The tenderness in his voice prompted feminine sighs all across the room. "I wish you saw yourself as I see you. It is I who feels lucky that you like me!"

"I care about you. If I know I'm seeing you soon, I consider it to be a great day."

"Oh, Flora, you make me so happy."

"You do too. I just . . ." She sniffed. "I still can't believe you chose me."

"Flora, you make me so happy. I hope we can cont . . . in . . . uee . . ." His last word was slurred as if stuck in slow motion.

Mr. Regret faltered, swaying—left, then right—like a top twirling in slow motion before it tipped over.

Mr. Porcupine ran, catching Mr. Regret as he collapsed.

Chapter Fifty

The instant Mr. Regret collapsed, every thread vanished and the room went dark. My dear friend lay on the floor unresponsive as I held his hand. The left side of his face had drooped. I grabbed my coat, rolled it up, and placed it under his head.

Please be okay.

Please, please be okay.

Don't you leave me.

My chest heaved from the sobs and hiccups.

A firm hand pried my hand free. "Sophie, you must let go."

"What?"

Mr. Porcupine held my hand. "You have to let go. The paramedics are here."

The party room was empty save for the Old Ducks and Mr. Particular. Paramedics lifted Mr. Regret onto a gurney and wheeled him away with Mr. Porcupine following in close pursuit.

"Is he going to be okay?"

"It's likely a stroke," Mr. Sorrow replied. "If they catch it in time, which we have, he should be okay."

Mr. Moon pulled out his phone. "He's being taken to Markham Stouffville Hospital. Let's go."

The Old Ducks filed out, giving me an affectionate pat on the arm as they passed by. Mr. Moon and Mr. Dolphin would each drive half the group. I collected my coat from the floor and ran to find my purse, searching for my car keys.

Mr. Dolphin waited by the doorway. "Sophie, do you want me to drive you?"

"It's okay. I can do it myself." I waved him off.

Mr. Particular said to him, "I'll drive her."

Mr. Dolphin nodded and left.

"You're in no shape to drive." Mr. Particular held my coat open for me—I had no idea when he'd taken it. "Please, let me."

I slipped my arms into the sleeves and buttoned my jacket.

Mr. Particular's black Lexus was parked in the visitor section of the underground parking garage. He opened the passenger side door and I hopped inside. I pulled on my seat belt, yanked a few sheets of tissue from the pack, and blew my nose.

Flora.

I sat up and fumbled for my phone. "I have to call Flora. She must be worried sick."

"Why don't you wait until we get to the hospital and get more information?"

"Right, that might be better."

The hospital was ten minutes away. I tried to control my runaway worries about Mr. Regret.

"He's more than just your client?"

"He is. I consider him family. He baked the macarons. He's such a fantastic baker. He used to be a cook and took up baking after he retired. Before the open house, he'd been preparing to enter this contest. I'm his taste tester so I get to try every wonderful pastry." The words tumbled from me, rushing to keep up with my beating heart. I broke down crying again.

"I didn't mean to upset you."

"I'm already upset. The sweetest man I've ever known is at a hospital, and I want him to be better."

He reached across the console and held my hand. "You'll see him soon."

My phone buzzed. Incoming video call from Yanmei.

"Oh geez, you look like hell. What happened?"

I told her through my tears.

"I'm so sorry. Who's driving you?"

I tilted the phone to show Mr. Particular behind the wheel.

Yanmei's wolf whistle caused him to blush. I laughed between my tears.

"Aren't you supposed to be in bed?" I asked. "You have work tomorrow."

"I am self-employed. I took the day off to be awake for your open house. Believe me, I'm awake now." Her dark eyes darted in the direction of the driver. "Have you told *him* yet?"

"Told him what?"

If Mr. Particular had any interest in the turn of the conversation, he didn't show it. He kept his eyes on the road and remained silent.

"That, you know . . ." Yanmei mouthed, "You like him."

"Now isn't the best time."

"There is no best time, but you have the opportunity."

"We're here. I'll text you when I get an update."

"Okay. Can you . . . ?" She gestured to the left of the screen. I rotated the phone to face Mr. Particular. "Hey. Thank you for being there for her. I'm glad she's not alone during this. Take good care of my girl."

"I will."

I ended the call in time to catch a glimpse of Yanmei dramatically fanning herself.

The brief levity wore off as we arrived at the massive hospital. Mr. Particular found parking, and we made our way to the front lobby.

The Old Ducks, including Mr. Porcupine, gathered in a group near the information desk.

I ran to them.

"He's being treated now," Mr. Porcupine explained. "It was a stroke. We caught it in time. Now we wait while they assess him."

"He's going to be okay then?"

The Old Ducks looked at one another with somber expressions.

"It's too early to tell. We won't know until they examine him," Mr. Durian replied. "This is something we've all experienced at one point or another."

I needed them to tell me not to worry so that this horrible, terrible knot in my stomach would subside. "I want him to get through this. This isn't fair. He and Flora . . . He wanted . . ." Again, I broke down.

Sadness suffocated me. I thought and felt nothing else.

My memories of Mr. Regret—his unfailing kindness, his sweetness, his sincerity, and the way he offered his friendship— looped over and over and over. He must recover. We had to have our afternoon tea.

"Why don't you go for a quick walk?" Mr. Moon asked. "We're all waiting here. We'll call you when the doctor comes back."

Mr. Particular placed his arm around me and escorted me outside.

"I'm sorry I'm a mess." I gulped and leaned into him.

The cold air stung my tearstained cheeks. He adjusted the red scarf that fell across my shoulders to cover my neck before holding me tight. "You love him. Of course this hurts. I felt the same way about my grandparents."

"Do you think of them often?"

"I do. At first, it hurt too much, but with time, I remembered the happier times and the funny things they did. I still talk to them sometimes." He rested his chin on my head. "When we love someone so much, we're connected to them—in their joys, and especially when they're suffering. It's the price of opening yourself up to love."

I let Mr. Regret into my life with ease; I couldn't picture him not in it. He wasn't the only one—the rest of the Old Ducks. They were more than my clients. They were a found family where we chose one another.

Life was short and unexpected. Why wait any longer when you never knew when it might all be over?

"The last time we saw each other, I wasn't in the right state of mind. I had left a disastrous dinner with my family. I didn't mean what I'd said—that I wanted you to be with someone else. Although, if you've already found another, I can—"

"Sophie, you're in my arms. I'm right here. What are the odds that I've moved on?"

I hid my embarrassment by burying my face against his coat.

"I know what I want, and I had no problem waiting for you."

I didn't need a thread to confirm what my heart knew to be true. After I received my accreditation, I would petition to restore my thread. I needed love like my clients. Loneliness wasn't my only option anymore, nor should it be.

"Good, because I . . ."

Mr. Sorrow emerged by the entrance. "The doctor's here."

Chapter Fifty-One

⋈

We gathered in a circle around the doctor, the Old Ducks, Mr. Particular, and me.

The young physician was South Asian with kind eyes and a gentle voice. "I'm afraid I have bad news. Even though we administered treatment to dissolve the clot, the stroke was massive. The hemorrhage in his brain created too much damage. There is nothing more we can do."

Mr. Durian sobbed, pressing his face against Mr. Dolphin's neck.

Mr. Wolf cried without a sound with Mr. Sorrow, holding his friend's shoulder, and Mr. Moon stood on the other side to hold him steady. All three were openly weeping.

Mr. Porcupine's spectacles fogged up, resembling windows during a cool rain shower with raindrops clinging to the glass.

It wasn't fair.

Mr. Regret was supposed to be fine. They'd caught the stroke in time.

He should be sitting up in his hospital bed, talking about

dates with Flora and his baking contest entry. He'd tell me his schedule and when I needed to drop by to help.

Instead, he was dying.

He couldn't be gone.

I wailed, my fists against Mr. Particular's chest. My heart's grief welled up in violent whimpers that shook me from head to toe. If it wasn't for the man holding me steady and stable, I would be a helpless heap on the floor.

Mr. Porcupine addressed everyone. "There will be time to say goodbye. We can only go in two at a time to see him. I'm going to talk to the doctor and handle the arrangements. He told me what he wanted done upon his death."

"We want to go first," Mr. Sorrow declared with Mr. Wolf. They walked toward the doctor to get the details.

"The rest of you . . ."

"I'll handle the scheduling. You go and do what you need to do." Mr. Moon patted Mr. Porcupine on the back. "I got this."

The taller man uttered his thanks and joined Mr. Sorrow and Mr. Wolf with the doctor.

"You two want to go next?" Mr. Moon addressed Mr. Dolphin and Mr. Durian.

They nodded.

"It'll be a good idea to go out and get something to eat," Mr. Moon said. "I'll call you when it's your turn."

"Okay, call me." Lingering hiccups littered my words.

Mr. Particular steered me out of the hospital lobby. I broke the silence between us on the way out of the parking lot.

"Did I do this?"

"No." His dark brows creased together. "Why would you think that?"

"Because he's old and . . . I pushed him too much. He worked so hard making all those macarons. I keep forgetting how old the

Old Ducks are and that they are fragile. I should have told him to take it easy! Before this, I pushed him, I pushed him to enter the contest. He baked every day, trying new things, and . . . All of this was too much."

I cupped my hands over my face. More tears.

"From what you told me, he loves to bake. He volunteered to make the macarons because he enjoys making them and because he cares about you. As for the contest, it was something he wanted to accomplish on his own. He was the one who brought it up, yes?"

"Yes."

"He sounds like a generous soul—the kind that derives happiness from giving it to others."

"How do I tell Flora? How do I tell her that he's gone? Because I should be the one to tell her. It's my responsibility."

"You can tell her when we're at the congee shop. Call your friends at the hospital and ask if she can come say goodbye."

"That's a good plan."

The congee shop he picked was three blocks away at an Asian plaza. The small establishment was popular judging by the crowded line waiting outside in the snow. Large storefront windows with rolled-up blinds showed packed booths and tables.

"My godmother runs the restaurant. She always told me that there was a table anytime I wanted," he said, holding the door open. "You'll like the braised beef tendon. Those were my Gung-gung's favorite."

We slipped inside. I kept my head low to avoid any unwanted attention for the grief reddening my face. He talked to the hostess, who recognized him, and then grabbed two laminated menus before leading me to one of two empty booths. We sat opposite each other.

The emptiness in my heart throbbed from the rawness of the

scraped, torn edges where something valuable had once resided. I'd never lost anyone I cared about before, with the exception of Madam Chieng. Mr. Regret was more my friend than he was a client. This loss and pain felt insurmountable.

Mr. Particular poured jasmine tea into my handleless white ceramic cup. "You haven't eaten since breakfast, I take it?"

"No. I didn't even have a chance to taste the food at the party." I didn't bother to look at the menu. Instead, I set it aside and trusted him to make the small decisions I couldn't.

"The macarons were perfection. I managed to taste three different buttercream fillings. The cookies were precise, so uniform that I thought they were machine-made. Believe me, I checked and stacked them."

The impromptu review caused me to smile. "Go on."

And he did, explaining in his unique way of seeing the world.

When the server returned to take his order, he ordered six times more food than I'd expected.

"Are you that hungry?"

"I am, but that's not the reason. I figured the rest of the Old Ducks would appreciate it if we brought them back dinner."

I wanted to reach across the table and hug this considerate, wonderful man. "Thank you."

"You don't need to. It's the least I can do."

Before the bowls of beef noodle soup and roasted duck congee and a plate of braised beef tendon arrived, I texted Mr. Moon to ask if Flora was able to visit. I waited for his approval and then called Flora.

"Do you know how he's doing?" The voice on the other end sounded frantic.

I swallowed hard. "I'm so, so sorry Flora. He's—"

"No . . ." She sobbed. "No, no, not him. We just . . . I never told him how much I love him, about how happy he makes me. I bought him a stack of books to read. He told me he was interested and I . . . How can I . . . I can't look at them now without . . ."

The melancholy of those words and the soft weeping that followed broke my already damaged heart.

"If you want to, you can see him at the hospital, to say good-bye."

"Okay, yes, please give me the information."

"She is coming to the hospital then?" Mr. Particular asked.

"Yes. I feel so responsible."

He filled my bowl with the congee and made sure there were choice pieces of duck in the portion. "It's normal. I think it's easier to blame yourself than to feel powerless."

"It's thinking about all the 'I should haves.'"

I should have been more careful with Mr. Regret, watched over him more closely, paired him with Flora from the beginning instead of prolonging the process, or insisted that he shouldn't have to work so hard for the open house. I would have done anything to have Mr. Regret be alive and well right now.

"It will be this way until enough time passes. The pain will also fade until it pricks you when you remember that they're gone."

I took a spoonful of the congee, blowing on it before taking a bite.

"Do you want to try some?" Mr. Particular asked, using his chopsticks to pluck a beef tendon from the plate.

"Yes, please."

He transferred the piece to my bowl.

"Thank you for being here for me. I appreciate the gesture—and you."

"You're welcome."

Our eyes met over our bowls. His free hand was on the table

near the condiments. My fingers slipped in between his. If he was surprised, his dark brown eyes never betrayed it. His thumb caressed mine as if he had done so a hundred times before.

"Can you tell me more about your grandparents?"

"There was this time Poh-poh had it in her head that going to the water park with five grandchildren was a great idea. Gung-gung told her over and over that it would be a disaster. It was me, my sister, and three of my boisterous cousins . . ."

He told me four more stories like it.

By the time we finished the meal, I understood why this man had such a capacity for love and empathy. Like Flora had said earlier before this all fell apart: "I still can't believe you chose me." This encapsulated my feelings about Mr. Particular.

I owed it to Mr. Regret to not ignore what I felt.

Not anymore.

My phone buzzed with a text from Mr. Moon.

It's your turn to say goodbye, Sophie.

Chapter Fifty-Two

The Old Ducks minus Mr. Porcupine were gathered where we had left them. We arrived with armloads of takeout containers.

"I hope you all are hungry. There's congee, fried rice, and various goodies."

The older men perked up with subdued smiles. Mr. Dolphin and Mr. Durian accepted the plastic bags. "This is so sweet of you, Sophie."

"Oh no . . . this wasn't—"

Mr. Particular finished my sentence. "It's from both of us."

"It's much appreciated," Mr. Sorrow remarked.

Mr. Moon sniffed the air. "Is this from Happy Wok Congee Shop down the street?"

"Yes, my godmother owns it."

"Ahh. Mary is such a fantastic cook." Mr. Moon tried to peek into one of the containers Mr. Dolphin was holding. "I know she doesn't cook anymore, though. More of the management."

"She still sneaks into the kitchen at least one day a week. It's a matter of Addie and Mike trying to keep her out most days."

"Kids. They're inheriting the business?" Mr. Moon asked.

Mr. Dolphin gestured in the direction of the cafeteria. "You can talk later. This food is going to get cold. If I'm not mistaken, I swear I smell beef tendon."

Mr. Particular smiled. "I made sure there are three orders in there."

"This is a good one." Mr. Dolphin winked at me. "Don't let him get away."

Mr. Durian hissed at him. "Leave them alone."

I blushed. I loved my new nosy uncles.

Mr. Moon waved the rest of the Old Ducks off. "Go ahead. I'll join you after I take Sophie up."

I squeezed Mr. Particular's hand. "I'll be right back."

"I'll be waiting for you."

Mr. Dolphin called him over to join them. The group headed toward the cafeteria. I heard the inquisition starting. Mr. Sorrow and Mr. Durian tried their best to corral Mr. Dolphin's unrelenting mouth.

"They feel like they're doing their due diligence," Mr. Moon commented as he noted the look of alarm in my eyes. "Though I have to say, one particular Old Duck seems to be deriving too much pleasure from it."

We made our way to the elevators. I didn't know what to expect. My form of saying goodbye would be a string of heartfelt apologies. A confessional would not be what Mr. Regret would have wanted.

"Flora is with him now. She came in a few minutes after your call. Mabel is upstairs with her." He pressed the number two button. "I'm going to help with the funeral arrangements."

"You mean your dear leader will let you?"

Mr. Moon shrugged. "He's going to have to accept it. He's stubborn, but he needs the help. He can't do this all himself."

The Old Ducks moved as a unit. It was true the first time I'd observed them. They took care of their own because they were family.

"Let me know what I can do."

"Don't worry, we will. You're one of us. An honorary duckling." He chuckled. "That's what he called you."

Duckling.

I was a part of their family.

I held back my tears. I didn't want to cry before I entered the room.

The elevator doors opened and we headed east. Mr. Porcupine stood in the hallway near an open door. Exhaustion emanated from bleary eyes behind his glasses and the slight slump of his shoulders. He had always been formidable. Today, he wasn't—as mortal and human as the rest of us.

"Flora is finishing up." He leaned against the wall and lowered his head. "They'll be out soon."

Mr. Moon addressed him. "You should go downstairs and grab something to eat."

"I'm not eating that cardboard garbage."

"Sophie and her boyfriend brought food for us from Happy Wok. The rest are in the cafeteria now, eating."

"That sounds good." Mr. Porcupine perked up. "Thank you, Sophie, and thank him for me."

I responded with a sheepish smile, choosing to forgo correcting them about Mr. Particular's status and his relationship with me.

"I'll stay with Sophie. Go eat." Mr. Porcupine patted Mr. Moon's arm. "We'll be down soon. Save some food for us."

Mr. Moon gripped the other man's shoulders before heading back to the elevators.

"How are you doing?" I asked.

"About as well as you. The only difference between us is that you have fewer wrinkles."

"I feel like we were robbed—that he wasn't supposed to go now. He just made his decision, and he didn't live to reap the benefits of it." Bitterness and anger saturated my words.

"You can't hold on to anger. It's not a good way to live."

"But this is so unfair."

My heart constricted from Mr. Regret's losses and every one of us grieving from losing him.

"No, it isn't fair." He rubbed his left temple. "You can fight against the inevitable or you can accept it and be at peace with it. All of us have limited time."

I leaned against the wall and slid down until I sat on my heels, knees folded. "I'm trying to understand where you are, and I can't get there."

"Think of it this way; right before he died, he did everything he wanted to do—choosing Flora, entering his contest, and helping out our duckling with her open house. It's a happier way to look at it, isn't it?"

It was. The picture Mr. Porcupine painted was far happier and joyous than the darkness and woe of my thoughts. I wanted Mr. Regret to remain a part of my life.

"He was the happiest of men. I want to honor his memory."

Flora exited the room with Mabel holding her steady. Flora kept her head lowered and avoided all eye contact. Mabel met our eyes, wet with tears, before heading out.

"Are you ready?" He held the door open.

No. I took a deep breath, trying to inhale as much oxygen as possible.

I wanted to be brave for Mr. Regret, to be the person he saw as his friend.

The best version of myself should walk through this door.

"Yes."

The room was filled with blinking machines and the lone sound of the vent blasting in the warm air. The monitors had been silenced, soundlessly displaying his heart rate and oxygen level. Mr. Regret lay on the hospital bed with a neutral expression, as if he were asleep. His clothes were folded and placed on a nearby table. I moved to his right side, sitting in the chair that was already there. Mr. Porcupine pulled a rolling stool up toward the bed.

I placed my hand over Mr. Regret's. "I had intended to apologize, but instead, I'm going to tell you about my wishes for you. I wanted to see you with Flora and to see you introduce her to the rest of the Old Ducks as your girlfriend. I also hoped to see you win the grand prize for the baking contest. Of all people, you deserve everything."

The tears flowed again, heavier, as I let my heart speak. "You've given me so much kindness and love. You saw something in me, and to this day . . . I still am trying to live up to that. You showed me how important it is to see the best in everyone.

"Is it okay for me to play music and sing to him?" I asked.

"Yes, of course. You sing?"

Wednesday nights were karaoke nights in Shanghai. Yanmei and I frequented a trendy one a short walk from the apartment. She chose the latest K-pop hits, while I stuck to the classic oldies. My best friend was an exceptional human being, but her enthusiasm for singing didn't make up for her off-key warbling.

"Maybe not as well as someone who has taken lessons, but decent."

I pulled out my phone and picked the instrumental version of Mr. Regret's favorite Beatles song, "The Long and Winding Road."

The music built up, and I sang the opening verse. The aromas of Mr. Regret's apartment wafted in: the sugar in the air, the underlying scents of brewing tea, the fruity undertones from home-made jams and fillings, the browning butter in a saucepan, and the ever-present clean cologne he wore.

The last line of the first verse tripped me up. The words hit me hard.

Where the next verse should have started, my voice shattered into pieces. The words were too heavy.

Yet the song continued. Mr. Porcupine sang in my place. His strong baritone voice carried the emotional depth of Paul's lyrics. He gazed into my eyes, coaxing me to finish.

Courage, Sophie.

I joined him. His baritone complemented my soprano. When the last notes faded, so did the last of the comforting scents I'd grown to associate with Mr. Regret.

"Do you want me to add serenading talent to your match-making profile?"

He reacted with a dry laugh. "I volunteer at local hospitals for music therapy. That's what I'd been doing when I met up with you at Scarborough Grace."

"Did the Old Ducks ever go to karaoke?"

"Why don't we sing him my favorite Beatles song, and you'll find out."

Chapter Fifty-Three

Mr. Regret's funeral was an intimate affair, as he had requested, in East Markham. Later his urn would be interred in the family mausoleum alongside his mother's. The bounty of floral arrangements by his coffin were courtesy of the small gathering of attendees—the Old Ducks, Beatrice, Clara, Flora and Mabel, Mr. Particular, and me.

Mr. Porcupine brought his guitar and played an old Teresa Teng song. The Old Ducks and I took turns saying a few words about our dear friend. Flora tried to speak, but cried in Mabel's arms. The mourning at the hospital allowed us all to come to terms with our collective loss. Everyone seemed to be adjusting better than me, even Flora. They had experienced loss before, and had learned to go on, but it was too new, too raw.

Mr. Particular held my hand during the ceremony and stayed by my side. I'd been spoiled by having him with me these past few days. When the funeral was over, he drove me back to my building.

"Thank you for coming with me."

"Of course."

Right before we left, he had a long discussion with Mr. Sorrow. He'd been conversing more with the group, being at ease with them despite being a relative stranger.

"Did one of my Old Ducks give you a hard time again?"

"They're a wonderful bunch. It's like I'm hanging around with a bunch of grandpas."

"You speak the geriatric language."

"So do you," he countered with a grin. "One of them wanted to know which bakery downtown had the best char siu buns. I told them my opinion, and we ended up debating the merits of the perfect bao and filling."

"Who won the argument?"

"It's ongoing."

His infectious smile lifted my spirits.

Would I be content with the recent time we'd spent together, or would I want more?

The answer was obvious. I didn't want to waste any more time.

I wanted this man in my life, and I was taking the first step.

"Will you go on a date with me?" I asked.

"Yes." He glowed. It was a diffused warm, golden light spreading across the interior of the car.

I wish there was a light to confirm that our threads had reacted with a spark. I'd studied all of the telltale signs of separate threads joining into one. Nothing confirmed the intangible when it came to a love connection better than the eyes of a matchmaker.

Yet I didn't care.

I didn't want to know.

It wouldn't change how I felt about him.

"Where do you want to go?"

I told him the time and where to meet four days from now.

SETTLING MR. REGRET'S AFFAIRS LASTED long after the funeral. Mr. Porcupine and the others had been streaming in and out of the vacant condo for days. I offered to clean or do anything else that was needed, and after a few days, I received the message from Mr. Porcupine inviting me to help.

Before I knocked on the door, a tremble shook my fingers. The person I wanted to be waiting for me inside was no longer there. The ache, a hollowness, settled in my chest as I rapped my knuckles against the wood.

Mr. Porcupine answered and let me in.

The bareness of the walls and the rooms jarred me. The air was too sterile—missing the delicious aroma of baked goods. I passed by the empty bedroom, bathroom, and living room. Only the kitchen remained untouched—the heart of this place. Stacks of unassembled cardboard boxes, along with ones ready to be used lined the far wall.

"I wanted you to be here when the last of his things go." He picked an empty box from the floor and placed it on the counter. "I've hired movers. We packed everything up and decided where it would go. He kept all of it immaculate despite the fact he collected too much. A lot has gone to donation."

I walked to one of the many crammed cupboards. The little black pie bird caught my eye on the second shelf. I cradled it against my chest.

"You can keep that if you want. After all these years, I still don't know what that thing does other than sit in his cupboards as decoration."

I explained the function of a pie bird.

"Hmm. I guess it is useful." He directed my attention to a packed box in front of the fridge. "Take a look in that box. I thought it might be something you wanted to keep so I set it aside for you."

I crouched down and opened it. Inside was Mr. Regret's tea set, complete with matching cups and all of his tea tins. All the conversations we'd shared over tea were committed to memory. I would have asked for it if it wasn't offered.

"Can I have the kettle too?"

Mr. Porcupine opened the lower cupboard door where the red teakettle sat.

I packed it with the tea set and moved the box aside. As for the more fragile pie bird, I wrapped it in Bubble Wrap and stuffed it into my purse. I pushed up my sleeves and dived into the task of emptying my departed friend's life into boxes. Mr. Porcupine and I moved in tandem, clearing each cupboard from left to right, top to bottom. The sound of stretching packing tape and the violent rips to sever it filled the empty condo. Seven boxes in total.

"Don't bother repositioning them. The movers will clear everything out this afternoon." Mr. Porcupine leaned against the counter and wiped his brow.

"Do you need something to drink? We should have taken more breaks."

"I'm fine. Don't start with that." His curt tone reminded me of the cantankerous old man I knew well.

I checked him over. Other than the slight flush of exertion, he seemed fine. He was the eldest, but also the fittest of all the Old Ducks.

"I know that you're concerned and a bit overzealous right

now. I'm fine. You don't need to fuss." He took off his glasses and cleaned them with the hem of his shirt. "When I asked you to come here, it wasn't only to help me with the kitchen."

"Oh?"

"I finished dealing with his estate yesterday. He set aside a part of it for the Old Ducks."

Of course he had. Mr. Regret loved his friends. They were his family and his life. He wanted to take care of them.

"We took a vote. It was unanimous." He withdrew a folded piece of paper from his pants pocket and gave it to me. "We decided that it should go to you."

It was a banker's check for twenty-five thousand dollars. I thrust it back in his hands. "I can't take this."

His large left hand placed it in mine, and his right sandwiched the check in place. The firm and gentle action left me speechless.

The rule of obeying your elders had been ingrained in me since birth. Saying no to this would be to reject every single one of the Old Ducks.

"We all believe that this was what he wanted as well."

I cried.

Mr. Porcupine, after placing the check into my purse, held me and rubbed my back. The awkwardness of the gesture made me cry even more.

"I thought you would have dried out by now," he muttered. "I've never seen anyone cry as much as you do, Duckling."

Duckling.

This one word transformed me.

The prickliness was still a part of him. I'd feared this man, yet he was nothing but the gentlest of giants.

The Old Ducks loved me as much as I loved them.

I chose them and they chose me.

Chapter Fifty-Four

⊰⊱

The next day

Yanmei barraged me with thousands of dating tips. She only stopped when I threatened to mute and block her. I channeled her need to help by having her choose what I was wearing instead.

"You're hamstringing me. How the hell am I supposed to dress you for a Canadian winter when all he's going to see is your winter coat and boots? There is nothing sexy about wool."

"Outerwear is a big thing." I laid out my coat and began using the lint roller. "And even you can't find fault with this."

"Your coat is nice. It cinches in the right place. I'll give you that." She threw her hands up in the air. "At least wear quality underwear in case you need to show that off later."

I dropped the lint roller. "Yanmei! You're not helping."

"Fine." She changed the subject. "Have you heard from your parents?"

"No. Is it terrible that I don't expect to but I still wish for them to call me?"

Dad was the one I thought would call first, yet there was

nothing. Even though they'd cut off all contact, I hoped they'd found a way to continue his acupuncture sessions.

Mom held on to grudges, and I wouldn't be the exception to the rule.

"I'm sorry, Soph."

I returned to the task of brushing. "While I finish this up, tell me about the lady boss client of yours. You haven't given me an update."

"I didn't think you'd want hear about it."

With every passing day that I didn't see the threads, I'd grown to accept that they were gone. Even with the accreditation, I wouldn't get my ability back, but I refused to allow it to change who I was—a matchmaker. I was determined to complete my recertification. It was only a piece of paper, but like Mr. Porcupine had said, it was the principle that counted. "No, tell me. I want to know, and I don't want you holding anything back. I love hearing about your clients."

She caught me up while I finished my task.

"Your makeup is perfect. You better get going. This is a very, very big deal. I'm so happy for you." Yanmei lowered her voice. "Try and give me most of the details. You can leave out whatever you want, but I need to know about kisses. I want all the kisses."

"Fine. I will tell you about the kisses. If they happen."

"Make them happen!" Yanmei blew me an exaggerated duck lips kiss before hanging up.

NATHAN PHILLIPS SQUARE, THE LOCATION for our first date. Summer's farmers market had given way to winter's skating rink. Mr. Particular and I met at Osgoode subway station and walked toward the outdoor skating rink near Toronto's City Hall. I hadn't seen him since the funeral. I missed him.

He was coming from work while I finished up signing another client before getting ready for the date.

"Have you skated before? I realized I should have asked you this before I suggested it."

He wrinkled his nose. "I guess you'll find out soon."

I fell in love with skating watching the Olympics and national competitions on TV. There was something rebellious and beautiful about being able to glide on such a smooth surface balanced on sharpened blades. I had asked for lessons, but my parents declined—as always, it was too expensive, and what good was it anyway. Instead, I learned during school trips, and when I was older, I practiced at the free outdoor rinks in the city, including this one. My worn figure skates were slung over my right shoulder with the laces tied and glittery purple skate guards in place.

He didn't bring a pair, which worried me. I'd never intended to organize something that would stress him out or make him uncomfortable.

As if he sensed my thoughts, he squeezed my hand in my fuzzy, dark mittens. "This will be fun."

The skate rentals were beside the rink. At seven thirty in the evening, the late February sky was black. Tall, empty office buildings with their lights on illuminated the skyline. The brisk chill in the air had thinned out the crowd. The giant letters spelling T-O-R-O-N-T-O glowed in rainbow colors. Over the rink were arches decorated in golden light complete with dangling blue star snowflakes.

After he got his rental skates, he joined me on a bench where I was lacing up. He pulled the laces tight around his ankles. Scuffs marked the sides of his borrowed hockey skates.

This rink had no guardrails for novices to cling to. We made our way toward the ice. Speakers blared the latest top ten chart-toppers. I got on with a little wobble and waited for him six feet away. The distance was to preserve his dignity in case he couldn't skate. I didn't want to hover or presume he needed help without being asked.

Mr. Particular stepped on the ice. He laid out his arms like a flailing flamingo. I moved toward him only to have him skate away with ease. An unapologetic smile stretched wider as he blew past me, skating backward.

He must have played defense. The sneak.

After showing off another burst of speed, he returned.

"You played hockey!" I pursed my lips. "You never told me."

"Gung-gung said that the secret to a great and enduring marriage is to continue to surprise your partner." The moment he finished saying this, he blushed and cleared his throat. "I mean, I'm not assuming that we . . . The context applies to any relationship."

I giggled. "But of course."

We navigated past a slew of helmeted toddlers in snowsuits. They tottered and toppled to land in helpless heaps. Parents nearby swooped in, pulling them back up again. With snow-covered butts, the little ones tried again only to repeat the cycle.

"I still get to pick dinner right?" he asked.

"Yes, that's your duty. I'm responsible for this part of the date."

He took my hand in his and matched my pace. "Good, because I can't wait to show you this little place nearby. They have the best—"

"Don't give me any hints. As you said earlier, it's important to be surprised." I tugged his arm to get him to slow down.

We stopped in the middle of the rink. The crowd, the lights, and even the music faded away. A large snowflake landed in his hair, prompting more to descend from the dark sky. Soon two were caught in the sweep of his long, dark lashes.

The man was beautiful in every possible way.

I drew closer and clung to the lapels of his coat.

I did what Yanmei had advised and grabbed what I wanted. I pulled him down for a kiss. His warm lips were soft. While my initiative started it, he finished it—tugging and nibbling on my lips until he stole my breath.

Heat rose from our bodies like sparks off a log in the fireplace. He continued to kiss me until my lips reached a level of hypersensitivity that spread across my body, exciting every particle of my being.

This moment wasn't anything like I'd ever imagined.

Nothing like smashing my dolls together.

Now, I knew what the joining of the threads felt like. It had to be this—the sensation of drowning so willingly and deeply into another person. With each passing moment, I craved more, building this insatiability for another being.

When he pulled away, I already missed the parts of us that fit together so well.

"That was my first kiss. I'm glad I waited."

He kissed me again; this time soft and brief, yet it left me breathless. He held me tight against him, his chin resting on top of my head. "I have to stop. I know I won't be able to control myself if all we're doing is making out in the middle of a public ice rink."

I laughed and pressed my hand against his chest.

The twinkling lights hushed into a low glow, and the city grew quiet. The speakers began playing "Across the Universe."

I sang along, and with the darkness growing around us, I craned my neck to watch the sky. A lone falling star streaked across, followed by another, and another. Everyone around us watched the impromptu meteor shower.

I continued to sing as he held me tight.

Time unwound in slow measure, every second precious. I no longer allowed my life to pass me by. The future, though uncertain, was my own.

And, for the first time in my life, I was happy and loved.

Epilogue

✦

The ceremonial hall was a round three-story red pagoda with polished brass roofs. A long banner hung from the north side displaying "The Matchmaking Society" in Chinese characters. Sandalwood joss sticks burned in ornate pots by the entrance, with its massive double wooden doors. Carvings of flying dragons dancing among the high mountains decorated the lacquered hardwood. The hall was one of many buildings within the extensive school grounds. Yanmei, my fellow classmates, and I met here during orientation.

Madam Yeung, my wise and no-nonsense mentor, walked by my side as we crossed the stone footbridge. Her ink-black hair was swept up in a severe bun above her heart-shaped face. Fine wrinkles surrounded the corners of her mouth and sparkling eyes. She had thick, painted-on brows that matched the red of her lips. In her late sixties, she had boundless energy.

Beautiful gardens and ponds that stretched out beyond the hall bloomed with rows and rows of blossoming magnolia trees. Pink flowers ruffled in the breeze, sending loose petals floating and dancing in the air. I caught one and tucked it into my pocket. A souvenir.

"I'm proud of you. Your final marks were excellent," she said in Mandarin.

I responded in kind. "Thank you. I had a wonderful teacher."

Getting my accreditation didn't guarantee my ability would be restored. I had undergone meditation, a precursor ritual for today's thread restoration ceremony. It was beautiful, with woody incense and sonorous chanting. All of this I did, not to bring back what I'd lost, but to finish what I'd started.

"I'm surprised your parents aren't here. Today is a significant occasion."

I wasn't surprised. I had sent two messages—one to Mom and one to Dad, informing them of my graduation. Neither had responded.

"I'm not blaming you. This is on your worthless parents. They should know better—to miss such an important event in your life." She added a few choice curses for good measure.

She opened the door to the hall and held it open.

Inside the circular main chamber were all the senior matchmakers, and my three guests of honor. Yanmei ran up to greet us. She had arrived from Singapore two days prior, and we'd spent every moment since together. She addressed Madam Yeung, then broke down into enthusiastic squealing while embracing me. I held her close.

"We'll call you when it's time," Madam Yeung instructed before joining the Society at the far end of the room.

"I missed you so much." I pulled back and touched a strand

of her purple and blond hair. "This is a change. It looks fantastic. Did you do this before your flight?"

"Yes." She fluffed the wavy asymmetrical bob that hung an inch below her jawline. "Short hair looks good on you, so I decided to try it. I mean, if it attracted someone like him . . ."

Mr. Particular stepped into view. He had taken two weeks off from work to be here and celebrate with me. It was his first time in Shanghai, and I was more than happy to be his tour guide: the apartment building Yanmei and I had called home, the restaurants we adored, and the karaoke bar down the street. He sang well after a few drinks. Beaming, he enveloped me in an embrace. "I'm so proud of you," he whispered into my ear.

"Thank you." I kissed him on the cheek.

Mr. Porcupine walked toward us and shook his phone. "This damned thing isn't doing what it's supposed to do. They can't see me, for some reason."

The rest of the Old Ducks were supposed to be connected to us via video call for the ceremony.

"Turn on the damned camera," Mr. Durian yelled from the phone. "I taught you this at least ten times. You'd think you'd have paid attention."

"Can I help?" my boyfriend asked.

Mr. Porcupine handed him the phone. "Take it."

Mr. Particular pressed a few buttons before handing the phone back to the older man. The instant he did so, part of the screen went black again. Mr. Porcupine cursed until my boyfriend gently removed his thumb from covering the front-facing camera.

"Touch this if you want the camera to switch outward so they can see what the hall looks like," Mr. Particular added.

Mr. Porcupine continued his argument with Mr. Durian through the screen. Madam Yeung from across the room tracked my tall friend. Even without the ability to see threads, the dynamics between her and my older guest from their mutual introduction this morning was electric. She smiled and, like him, never gave those out easily.

"I invited her to our celebratory dinner," Yanmei sang in my ear.

I gasped. "Oh no, you didn't."

"She specifically asked if he was attending. She said yes after I confirmed it."

We giggled.

Mr. Particular placed his arm around my waist. "What are you two plotting?"

"Nothing," we replied in unison, eliciting more laughter.

Madam Yeung raised her index finger, signaling that it was time to start.

Mr. Porcupine returned to our group. I had enough time to say hello to all of the Old Ducks—Mr. Wolf, who grinned and waved; Mr. Durian, who bragged about my accomplishments; Mr. Dolphin, who asked about my future wedding; Mr. Sorrow, who dabbed his eyes from tears of joy; and Mr. Moon, who sent his love.

Madam Yeung walked over to us, asking everyone to turn off their phones out of respect. Mr. Porcupine handed his phone to Mr. Particular.

"It's time, Sophie."

She guided me up the stairs to a spot on the second floor: an inlaid mosaic of interwoven red and gold threads with an interlocking teal border. I peeked over the balcony railing before me, leaning into the rail. My found family was below while the rest of the matchmakers lined the floors above, standing equidistant from one another along the corresponding railings.

Somewhere a gong was struck. The reverberating sound filled

the building. Once it dissipated, it was replaced by a low chanting in an ancient language I didn't recognize. The chant crested into this undulating wall of continuous sound.

My skin and my hair hummed.

Overhead, a huge translucent jade medallion accented with gold shimmered. Two strands, one red and one gold, like dragon whiskers emerged, snaking downward.

They formed a thick, spinning spiral as they passed through the matchmakers standing at the top floor. One by one, this mighty ethereal coil moved through them until it descended downward toward me.

The threads wrapped around my fingertips, then traveled up my arm and onto my torso until they encircled my eyes, bands of red and gold obscuring everything. With one final flash, they flooded my vision.

When the light faded, I wept.

A red thread sprouted from my chest. A beautiful, thick braided strand that connected with Mr. Particular's.

It had been there all along—the connection.

I met Yanmei's brown eyes. She sniffled, a smile filling her face.

The man whom I was connected to looked up and mouthed the words, "I love you."

I replied in a clear, unwavering voice. "I love you too, James."

Acknowledgments

※

This book is a love letter to my grandparents: Kong Kong, Amah Nene, Angkong, and Amah Juanita. Every moment together was a joy. My life is forever poorer with them gone. I wish we had more time: to eat, to laugh, and to tell stories.

My father-in-law, Jim, was the inspiration for one Old Duck in particular. It still hurts that he wasn't able to hold a finished copy before he passed, but I know he would have smiled his wry smile, recognizing himself on the page. His unwavering faith in my abilities uplifted me more than he could know.

Robert and Natalie: I love you! Thank you for your patience and support as I breathed this book into being. Your encouragement and love—and the Popeyes runs we took to commemorate writing milestones—were very motivating. Robert, my love, an extra special thank-you for your tireless dedication in helping me craft the words. It wouldn't have been the same without your skill.

A big thank-you goes to my amazing agent, Jenny Bent, along with Victoria Capello, at TBA. Jenny, you're always encouraging me, and I'm so thankful to have you in my corner. I am in awe. You are amazing.

Thank you to Mary Pender and Orly Greenberg at UTA. I can't wait to meet up again in NYC. I'll bring more Coffee Crisps!

I can't thank my editor, Cindy Hwang, enough, including the whole Berkley team: Angela Kim, Tara O'Connor, Dache' Rogers, Fareeda Bullert, Megan Elmore, Marianne Aguiar, Rita Frangie, and Vikki Chu.

For my sister, Racquel; my parents, Elizabeth and Romeo; Matt; and my niece Paige: COVID kept us apart, but you were always in my heart.

To Lorraine, Rosemarie, and Brennan: it was a stressful and sad year, but I'm so grateful to have you all in my life. I can't imagine how I would have coped otherwise.

To my critique partners and friends (It's a long list. Buckle up!):

Helen Hoang and Suzanne Park: my West Coast besties. Despite the time difference, we still manage to have the best text convos. We're still on for that sushi and wine writing retreat.

Annette Christie: you are a bright ball of Uma Thurman sunshine. I adore you and appreciate how you always encourage me to persevere. I hope to be as resilient as you are one day.

Sonia Hartl and Kellye Garrett: you two are so wise and you both center me. Our tarot card. We really should get shirts or jewelry made.

Farah Heron: I'm so grateful to have you close by. We need to meet up more often. You're such a grounding force, and any time I need a balancing perspective, you're my go-to. You push me, by example, to strive for more.

Karen Strong: you and I always share cackles. Your wisdom and wit sustain me, and I'm so grateful for our friendship.

Jenn Dugan: thank you for falling in love with the Old Ducks and being a friend in times of need. I'm in awe of how you manage to control a whirlwind of productivity.

R. M. Romero: my talented, wonderful friend who writes such beautiful books. You are the cat whisperer and a close confidante.

Samantha Bohrman: you are my ride or die, my fellow Aries. You always make me laugh and I'm so grateful to have you in my life.

Laura Weymouth: thank you for meeting the Old Ducks. Your cottagecore lifestyle leaves me wishing for an even more quiet and idyllic life.

Tamara Mataya: thank you for your edits and your friendship. I love that our senses of quirky humor jibe well.

Mike Lasagna: Milo baby pics sustained me. You're a positive ray of sunshine, and I'm thankful to have you as a friend.

A special thanks to Andria Bancheri-Lewis, Rina Tjoa-Liang, and Dr. Joe Chan. Andria, you are always there for brilliant insight. Rina, thank you for your help. Dr. Joe, thank you so much for your time and your wisdom.

Another special thanks to Ruby Barrett. Thank you for your generosity and time when I was researching this book.

To readers, bloggers, booksellers (a special shout-out to my local indie, Firefly & Fox Books, run by Catherine), and librarians: thank you for continuing to support my books by reading and recommending them. Without you, there would be no magic.

Sophie Go's Lonely Hearts Club

ROSELLE LIM

Questions for Discussion

1. Sophie is a matchmaker who is passionate about her vocation. Do you believe in love and matchmakers? What do you think about the idea of having only one soul mate?

2. Sophie is addicted to candy and its comforts. What is your favorite candy from childhood? Do you eat it to remember moments from your past or to cope with life's rocky bumps?

3. What is the significance of Sophie's unique nickname system for her clients? What nickname do you think Sophie would choose for you?

4. When signing up new clients, Sophie uses a simple questionnaire to help her to gain insight into the person. In what ways do her four questions help a matchmaker make a better match?

5. Seniors are not the conventional demographic when one thinks about matchmaking, yet the Old Ducks all chose to become Sophie's clients. What are some challenges to finding love later in life?

6. Parental relationships are often complicated; sadly, they're not all supportive and loving. Discuss Sophie's relationship with her mother and father and how Irene and Raymond's own marriage contributes to this dynamic.

7. The music of the Beatles is featured prominently as they are Sophie's favorite band. Did you find all the references, and can you list the titles of all the songs? Which is your favorite song, and why?

8. The exploration of love and all of its forms—familial, romantic, platonic—is a central focus of the novel. How do you think Sophie handles all of these relationships? Is she successful?

9. What is the difference between biological and found families, and how many families can you identify in the book? Which are stronger, and why?

10. Mr. Porcupine and Sophie had a rocky start to their friendship. What was the cause of the initial antagonism, and how did they manage to develop a lasting friendship by the end of the novel?

Author photo by Shelley Smith

Roselle Lim is a Filipino Chinese writer living on the north shore of Lake Erie. She loves to write about food and magic. When she isn't writing, she is sewing, sketching, or pursuing the next craft project.

CONNECT ONLINE

RoselleLim.com
🐦 RoselleWriter

Ready to find
your next great read?

Let us help.

Visit prh.com/nextread

Penguin
Random
House